THE LOST GOSPEL

PATRICK J. MCHUGH

Table of Contents

CHAPTER 1

Ethiopia, October 1936

Lt. Angelo Colavari felt, more than heard, the engine of his Breda Ba 65 level off as he completed his banking turn and headed northwest towards the Simien Mountains some 425 miles north of Addis Ababa, the Ethiopian capital. His base was approximately 100 miles from the capital, which made the mountains their maximum northerly flight range.

Colavari looked back over his right shoulder and saw that 2nd Lt. Carlo Spinoza, his new wingman, had failed to match his turn and was now out of position to support Colavari had there been enemy fighters to contend with. The two-plane formation was the basic technique taught in flight school, but, since they feared no attack, the pilots had become lax in following formation strategy.

Colavari pushed the throttle forward and the engine roared in reply, catching Spinoza's attention. Colavari shook his fist and pointed his hand towards his right rear. Spinoza acknowledged his error and quickly maneuvered his Breda into position. The bright sun, warm air, and empty sky lulled the two young pilots into a series of lazy banks and turns as they approached the limit of their afternoon reconnaissance mission. They had been sent up to look for troop or supply movements and had been in the air for over an hour, traveling almost 160 miles northwest of their base.

They were part of a small air and mechanized infantry battalion, the 11th Fighter Squadron, that had been moved deeper into the wilderness and had established a forward base between the capital and the mountains from where the Italian high command believed Haile Selassie, Emperor of Ethiopia, was directing his army.

As Colavari was about to signal Spinoza to bank right for their trip back to the base, his attention was drawn to movement at the foot of the small mountain range just off to his left. He leaned out of the cockpit and cut his air speed so that he could better see what was moving below. He saw them; a line of pack animals led by several dozen men making their way towards the edge of the mountain tree line where they would disappear out of sight. He looked at Spinoza and repeatedly pointed down. Spinoza followed the direction, acknowledging that he had seen them as well.

Colavari lined up for his dive at the line of men and animals. The plane sported twin machine guns on each wing, making the Breda 65 an effective air-to-air fighter.

Colavari would make the first run and strafe the column from end to end while Spinoza would follow close behind and concentrate on hitting them as they moved left and right for cover. With a moving target of men and horses, what defense could they possibly mount against an attack from the air? As he began his dive, Colavari showed the exuberance of youth and became so fixed on his target that he violated several of the cardinal rules of air-to-ground assault, the first being: SPEED IS YOUR FRIEND. The greatest defense against ground fire for any aircraft is first speed, then altitude. Keep your plane above the range of ground fire, but, if necessary, fly low, come in fast and get out faster. Colavari forgot both.

He reduced speed thinking he could stay on his target longer and, thus, do more damage, and, furthermore, equally forgot about altitude and dove low towards the column. These errors alone would have been enough to place him in jeopardy, had they caught the enemy on some open road. However, this was not just a path into the mountains, but the beginning of a main supply road for the enemy, and well protected.

Although young and possessing no formal education, Mohammed Adiwa was an experienced combat veteran for a man not yet 20 years old. He had been given responsibility for this supply train and had chosen his path carefully. Always on the alert, he heard the engines of the approaching planes before he saw them. The supply train was just entering the cover of the trees when Colavari and Spinoza swung into sight and prepared for their strafing run. Had the Ethiopians been on the desert they would most certainly have been helpless targets and easily destroyed.

However, this wasn't the desert and they were more than prepared. Adiwa had taken great pains to be prepared for the unexpected appearance of enemy planes.

Hidden off to either side of the trail were two well-placed M1919 Browning machine guns. At first sighting, he ordered the gunners to hold their fire until the planes were well within range even allowing the Italians to take the first shots.

Colavari swung low and lined up on the end of the column before firing the first burst. He had barely fired a dozen rounds when both Browning's opened up with a withering interlocking fire that struck the Breda from both sides at once. The first burst sliced through the rudder, causing the plane to veer sharply to the left and out of the deadly trail of fire that raced skyward. Although severely damaged, it gave him some room away from the fight in which to maneuver as he fought to bring the plane level.

Spinoza wasn't as lucky. Surprised by the unexpected attack on his wingman, he froze and continued his dive straight through the rain of lead racing towards him. The first rounds splintered the propeller but he never saw it disappear as the rounds from the second Browning stitched up his chest and continued across his face. He was dead before the plane nose-dived towards the trees and slammed into the ground.

Bleeding from a bullet wound in the right shoulder, and blood running into his eyes from a head wound caused by flying bits of the plane's shattered cockpit windshield, Colavari fought the stick and worked the pedals as he tried to pull his plane level. The shoulder wound left him with just his non-dominant hand to try and fly the plane. He couldn't get the feel of the plane as it lurched from side to side, over-compensating in his fight to regain control.

Although damaged, the rudder was still partially working. He had some movement from port to starboard — or left to right — but the elevator appeared to have also been damaged. Without full use of the elevator, he was limited in his ability to raise or lower the nose of the plane, and, thus, couldn't effectively climb or descend. All he could do was to try and keep the plane level and in the air.

He knew the Breda was mortally wounded and his only thought now was to put as much distance as he could between himself and the men in the pass, hoping to find a flat piece of ground on which to land, or, more likely, to crash-land his aircraft. His shoulder was on fire and it was all he could do to try and keep the blood out of his eyes. He found himself having to shake his head from side to side to shake the running blood from his face while fighting to focus his vision ahead.

In confusion and pain, Colavari attempted to turn his aircraft east towards his home base and hope to put her down near one of the main roads where a scouting party, or another plane, might spot him. But with his vision impaired, unable to see the dash gauges, and struggling with the non-responsive controls, he inadvertently completed a 360 degree turn and had again pointed the nose of the plane north, continuing towards the mountains and further away from the safety of the Italian lines.

For what seemed like hours, he played with pedal and stick to keep the Breda barely in the air. The engine began to sputter and Colavari sensed her dying in his hands. He fought to raise his right arm high enough to wipe the blood from his eyes, hoping to find a place to put the plane down before she gave out entirely. When he could finally look out the side of the cockpit, he realized he had turned too far and was heading deeper into the mountain range, and that a level piece of ground to land upon was most likely out of the question.

He continued to lose speed, and, with that, altitude. There was no way he could turn the plane again. He was dropping quickly and there was nothing he could do to stop it. If he had had use of both arms he might have tried to bail out, although at this altitude he probably wouldn't have had enough time for the chute to completely open. Just when he was ready to accept his fate, his straining eyes saw what looked like an opening in the trees off to his left. The plane was fighting to stay airborne when he decided the opening might be a path or road, or, better yet, the entrance to a valley. Crashing on a road, however small, was far better than driving into the side of a mountain.

As he fought the controls he began to feel the plane slowly begin a shuttering bank towards the opening. It was a path, a wide path, and clear of any large trees. The ground was coming up fast, but the plane continued to fight forward. If he could just get the nose up and set the tail down, he might keep her from breaking apart and sending him skidding across the countryside in pieces. The Breda seemed to hear him as the engine gave one last loud rev and the nose rose just enough.

The tail section hit first with a bone jarring crash, which then sent the nose slamming onto the ground, causing the tail to rise again. At this point, all he could do was to try and brace himself for the ride and pray. If she started to cartwheel, there would be little hope of him surviving and he would most certainly die in the crash. His only chance was for the plane to skid along the ground and remain intact. He hoped there wasn't too much fuel left in the tank, as he did not wish to survive the crash long enough to end up burning alive in the cockpit.

The Breda didn't cartwheel, but she did begin a wild counterclockwise spin as pieces began to break off and the plane began to disintegrate. At the same time, the control panel collapsed and pinned his legs to the floor at the shins. The force of the plane's spin and the rise of the plane's tail section threw Colavari forward and he felt both legs snap just below the knees.

The pain was so intense it seemed to jolt him alert so that he watched in slow motion as his seat collapsed and his legs were freed from beneath the panel. The harness holding him in his seat broke free, sending him airborne as he was thrown clear of the cockpit. He seemed to float through the air as if in slow motion and saw the plane continue forward. After what seemed like minutes, the ground approached to meet him at alarming speed. He landed with an unusual bounce and rolled uncontrollably while feeling a sense of relief that, instead burning to death, he would probably just break his neck and die. His legs twisted beneath him as he rolled, and the pain overcame him.

CHAPTER 2

He didn't know how long he was out, but the intense pain that had sent him into unconsciousness was the same stinging sensation that forced him awake. He used his left hand to wipe the blood from his eyes. The Breda had broken apart and pieces could be seen from where he had first slammed into the ground, right up to where the plane finally came to a halt. Surprisingly, she had not burned. He was lying on his side amongst some tall grass and tried to focus on what parts of his body hurt the most. He fought to breathe and coughed a mouthful of blood onto the grass before him. His sides hurt and he was certain he had broken some ribs. His nose was bleeding badly and his jaw ached and felt swollen, so knew he'd probably broken that as well. He strained to look at his legs, discovering they both lay twisted in unnatural positions and that splintered bone stuck through the right leg of his fight suit.

"I'm going to bleed to death right here and no one will ever know what really happened to me. My parents will receive a telegram telling them I died bravely fighting for my country and that my sacrifice will always be remembered." As her first born, Colavari knew his death would be especially hard on his mother.

The pain was numbing now. Colavari knew he was dying and that it was nature's way of preparing for the end. The pain would slowly fade away and then so would he.

Colavari passed out again and awoke some time later only to find several men bending over him. They were Ethiopians, the enemy. He instinctively reached for the pistol in his shoulder holster, but it was gone. The leather flap that held the gun in place was torn. The gun must have broken loose as he tumbled on the ground. He tried desperately to look for it but one of the men touched his hand softly and shook his head as if to say, "don't be afraid, you don't need your gun."

The men talked quietly amongst themselves and, every so often, turned to look at him before returning to their discussion, but he couldn't understand what they were saying. A stretcher was brought in and placed next to him as the men continued to gesture and talk softly. Dazed and semi-conscious, Colavari watched and slowly realized that they weren't going to kill him, but, rather, were trying to decide how best to move him. For a time, the men moved in and out of his consciousness as they worked to treat the young pilot's wounds in an attempt to stabilize his injuries. He remembered one of the men looking down at him and smiling as he spoke softly to the rest. With nods of agreement, pairs of hands appeared around Colavari and took hold of, or supported, the various parts of his injured body. He felt the tribesmen lift him slightly above the ground and felt the stretcher slide beneath him. He was then softly laid on the stretcher, but the hands did not move. They held him against the stretcher so that he could not move while they made the final transfer. The pain from his broken ribs and the bullet wound to his shoulder were like pin pricks compared to the agony he felt as they gently moved his shattered legs onto the stretcher. The pain and loss of blood was enough to cause him to again lose consciousness.

He vaguely remembered opening his eyes several times during a journey that could have been a few minutes or a few hours. The last time he remembered waking was just long enough to see that he was being carried further up into the mountains by his rescuers as the men moved slowly and quietly, as if trying to avoid causing him any more pain.

What must have been days passed, with Colavari regaining consciousness for a few moments and then falling into a calm sleep with the occasional nightmare reliving the crash. He remembered being bundled in heavy blankets pulled up close to his chin to keep the cold away and the warmth in. He began to wake more frequently and the pain appeared to become less and less intense. They must have given him medication for pain because his sleep became more peaceful and the nightmares slowly disappeared. The men moved in and out of his consciousness and he could recall voices speaking softly as they ministered to his injuries, but no one ever spoke to him directly.

His room was dark, except for several candles, which were always kept lit. There were no windows and the furniture was solid, but primitive. The only sounds he heard, other than the murmuring voices of his caregivers as they cared for his injuries, were the chanting of male voices in the morning or evening. He couldn't be sure which it was. He had lost track of time and the number of days he had been there, and, in fact, had even lost track of day or night. The only thing he knew for sure was that he had survived a crash that should have certainly killed him, and that, somehow, he felt he was getting better.

As the periods of consciousness became more regular, he tried to engage his nurses in conversation whenever they came to care for him. Through clenched teeth, like an amateur ventriloquist, so as not to hurt his damaged jaw, he tried to ask the basic questions: "where am I, who are you?" In response, they would only smile and nod, but no one ever spoke to him or answered any of his questions. It appeared that they spoke no Italian. They were men of varying ages, from late teens to men of advanced years looking to be in their 80s. All wore the same black robe with a braided rope sash.

Twice a day, an older man would come to see how he was progressing. He was tall and thin and appeared much older than the rest. He, too, wore the same black robe. He never spoke, but would smile, lay his hand gently on Colavari's head, as if checking to see if he had a temperature. His touch was warm and soothing and significantly calmed the young pilot. As Colavari appeared to relax beneath the hand, the old man would smile, nod, and then leave the room without uttering a word. The others always showed a certain degree of deference to the tall man and Colavari eventually realized he must be in a monastery and his benefactors were monks or priests. Several times each day they brought him a light broth and some bread and patiently fed him until they felt he was able to eat more solid foods.

The pain in his jaw gradually subsided and he realized the pain he endured after the crash must have just been caused by his bouncing along the ground. His jaw no longer hurt and he was able to chew the small meals they brought. His shoulder wound had been dressed and his right arm wrapped tightly across his chest so as to immobilize it. His legs were wrapped from ankle to thigh and splinted so he was unable to see the extent of his injuries, but he still had them both, which was amazing considering their condition after the crash. He was breathing easier and the pain in his ribs was gone. As he regained his strength the monk's visits became fewer. They brought his meals and placed them on a small table next to his bed but avoided looking directly at him, and now didn't even speak amongst themselves in his presence.

He felt stiff from his bandages but, remarkably, almost pain free, wondering what kind of miracle drug they could have given him to dull the pain, yet keep his mind alert. Although the heavy bandaging of his arm and legs kept him from moving much in bed, he could move his fingers, and, more surprisingly, move his toes without the excruciating pain he had felt before.

Finally, after what seemed like weeks, the day came when the elder monk, or Abbot, as Colavari had come to think of him, came to his room carrying a small cup in his hand. For the first time, he spoke, and in heavily accented Italian, stating, "I am Brother Samuel, how do you feel, Angelo?"

Colavari was taken aback by the familiar sound of his native tongue. "How do you know my name?" he asked. "We found your identification papers in the pocket of your uniform," the old man replied softly.

"There are so many questions I want to ask you, Brother Samuel," Colavari quickly spoke. "A million questions to be exact. The first being, where am I and who are you?"

The monk shook his head and smiled down at the young pilot. "That's not important right now." He lifted the cup he had brought in and held it to Colavari's lips. "Drink some of this tea, Angelo," he said. "It will help you on your journey." Colavari swallowed several mouthfuls of the sweet tea and thought to himself that he was already well on the journey to recovery. In Italian, he again asked the Abbot where he was and why they had saved him. The Abbot merely smiled and then began to fade from Colavari's vision. He felt his eye lids grow heavy. He tried to focus, but he was becoming sleepier with each second. "He drugged me," Colavari realized. After all they'd done for him, they had drugged him. Why?

When Colavari next opened his eyes, he was in the back of truck on a stretcher with an Italian soldier holding a canteen to his lips.

"Where am I," he asked quickly.

"Sir, I am Pvt. Scotti and we just picked you up from some nomads in the desert who were bringing you back to our lines." Colavari looked around and saw that he was lying amongst stacks of supplies and could hear the sound of other vehicles. He was in some sort of convoy, back with his own army. But how had he gotten there?

When they arrived back at the base, he was immediately taken to the hospital for examination where he learned that two weeks had passed since he and Spinoza had left on patrol and would be listed as missing in action, eventually to be presumed dead.

After being transferred to a hospital bed, he explained to the doctors the details of the crash and the extent of the injuries he had sustained. As he lay in the hospital bed, the doctors began to remove the old wrappings from his right shoulder. When his arm was finally free, he was surprised at how easily he could lift it without a trace of any pain in the shoulder. He looked at the shoulder and was amazed to see there were no sutures. In fact, there was no wound at all, just smooth, unmarked skin. Next, they began to remove the splints and leg bandages.

The doctors moved slowly, so as not to cause any unnecessary pain to the young pilot. Several nurses held and supported Colavari's left leg just above the mattress while the doctors removed the dressings. When all the dressings had been removed, the nurses placed the leg back on the bed. They looked at one another with a mixture of uncertainty and confusion and then repeated the procedure on his right leg. When that leg was also unwrapped, the doctors and nurses exchanged looks, raised eyebrows, and looked at the legs again. Colavari was surprised at the absence of pain and said he hoped he would someday be able to walk again, even if he had to use crutches.

"How do you know your legs were broken?" one of the doctors asked him. "It was easy", he said. "The bones were sticking out from one leg and they were both bent and twisted in ways they weren't meant to be. You can see by the wounds how bad they are."

The doctors continued to examine him and he felt their touch as each leg was gently moved from side to side as they looked from different angles. "When did you break your legs, Lieutenant? How old were you?" the chief surgeon finally asked. "How old was I?" Colavari answered, "I was two weeks younger than I am now!" he snapped.

"Lieutenant, we have no doubt that you were badly shaken up in the crash, but you are clearly confused about your legs." Colavari sat up in his bed and pointed to his legs, "What are you talking about? Look! Are you blind?"

Angelo Colavari propped himself up and pointed at his legs. But, before he could say another word, he looked at the unwrapped bare legs beneath the exam light. His legs were perfectly straight. There were no signs of injury and his legs were free of scars or marks from his thighs to his ankles. He moved each leg from side to side and there was no pain.

"Son," said the chief surgeon, "you're pretty shaken from your ordeal and may be a little confused as to the facts, but one thing is most certain. Your legs were never broken."

CHAPTER 3

Boston, 2006

The restaurant was crowded and the wait staff moved quickly between tables as they took orders and placed steaming plates before hungry patrons. Napolitano was BB McFadden's favorite dining spot, and he was a frequent and always-welcome guest.

Momma Rizzo rushed to give him a hug and a kiss on both cheeks as he approached the hostess desk. "Francis, I've missed you these past few weeks," she yelled as he returned her hug with a bear-like squeeze of his own. At six feet four inches tall and more than three hundred pounds, McFadden wasn't easy to miss wherever he went.

"I just got home on Wednesday, Momma," he said, "and this is the first chance I've had to get out and enjoy myself. My first thought was a plate of your Fettuccini Alfredo and three or four of those homemade cannoli. I didn't eat that well while I was in Turkey, and I'm determined to make up for it tonight."

As might be expected of someone owning an Italian restaurant and doing most of the cooking herself, including her "to-die-for" desserts, Momma Rizzo was a large woman. Although short and heavy, she moved quickly and with purpose. Her grey hair was pulled back in a bun and her dress, as always, was black, contrasted only by the white cloth apron she always wore. McFadden couldn't remember a time when he'd seen her without the apron. Momma smiled at him as if he were her own son.

Her son Michael had been childhood friends with McFadden, and she had fed both boys regularly at the restaurant throughout their high school years and first two years of college. Mickey was at Boston College and Francis was away at Princeton on a full scholarship. Momma Rizzo had been so proud of her Mickey, the first Rizzo to go to college. She wished her husband Carmine had lived long enough to see their only son move on to Boston College. She knew the boy would do well and make her proud at whatever he chose as a career.

But it wasn't meant to be.

Late in his sophomore year, Mickey started hanging with the wrong crowd outside school and started experimenting with drugs. He eventually dropped out of college and landed with both feet into the drug scene.

Momma Rizzo tried to talk to him, but Mickey refused to listen to anything she had to say. Then the stealing began. First a few dollars out of her purse, and then the register at the restaurant would turn up missing a few 10s and 20s after he'd stopped by for a quick visit. She finally called Mrs. McFadden and asked her to have Francis stop by and talk with Mickey the next weekend he was home. Maybe he could get Mickey to listen to some sense. But he never got that chance to talk with him – Mickey overdosed in a boarded-up tenement the Thursday before Francis came home; dead at 20 years old.

Francis stayed home for the next week; by her side throughout the wake and funeral, and had steadied her as she watched them lower poor Mickey into the ground.

Like any parent who loses a child unexpectedly to tragedy, Momma Rizzo kept asking herself if there was something she should have seen, something she could have done, should have done, to save him. She began to second-guess all the decisions she had ever made, every conversation she'd ever had with Mickey, trying to see if there was that one thing that could have made the difference. It was McFadden who had called regularly or sat with her through those early stages of the grieving process, and it was he that helped her accept that there was nothing any of them could have done to save Mickey unless he had wanted to be saved. From that point on, Francis became her son as well.

Momma Rizzo set a place for McFadden at the table reserved for family and ordered all the things she knew the big man enjoyed. They talked about his trip to Turkey and the expedition to the ruins at Gobekli Tepe where he had studied the inscriptions on the foundation stones and tried to determine if there was a mathematical progression to the figures, which could be used to shed greater light on what destroyed this ancient civilization.

"It was a great trip, Momma," he said, "and I had a chance to see a lot of the same folks I'd worked with the last time I went to the Valley of the Kings. I could spend my whole life digging in the ruins of every ancient society all over the world." Momma looked at his eyes as he spoke and saw the excitement that only the young can have when talking about the things that drive them. She wondered if Mickey would have enjoyed exploring the world.

"How are your mother and father doing, I haven't seen them since New Year's?"

He smiled at the mention of his parents. "Dad's semi-retired, although he likes to think he is. Between part-time teaching at the college and doing some consulting for the government, he's really working full-time. Mom is teaching a microbiology course to a graduate class on Tuesday and Thursday nights, and volunteering with the Iraqi and Afghanistan Veteran's Outreach Program during the day, so they're really pretty busy. We're going to come here for their anniversary in a few weeks," he added. "They always ask about you."

At a table nearby, three young men were talking loudly and using language that would be considered, as McFadden's father would have said, inappropriate in mixed company. The conversation was getting louder, and the language more embarrassing and uncomfortable to the couples and families sitting at the tables closest to them. McFadden leaned over and quietly asked them to consider their language, since there were ladies present at the restaurant. Two of them nodded, but the third man, a guy the others had called Nick, told him to "screw off!" and went back to describing his recent date with a woman named Mandy.

McFadden excused himself for a moment and walked to the table, smiling. Leaning down, he placed the palm of his left hand casually on Nick's right wrist, effectively pinning it to the table with his ample weight while he leaned forward, blocking the other two men's view. What Nick originally saw as a fat man butting into his business, suddenly became a moment of shock and confusion. He quickly realized he couldn't move his hand or free his wrist.

As McFadden spoke softly to the other two men and rest his hands flat on the table as he leaned down, the fingers of his left hand slowly closed around the fingers of Nick's pinned hand. While he explained how rude and offensive their behavior was, of course acknowledging that he was sure they were not behaving intentionally, McFadden's left hand continued to close tighter and tighter. Nick's eyes widened as the knuckles became compressed and began to grind against one another. Nick realized that he could do nothing to stop his hand from being crushed other than grabbing the huge hand and begging his assailant to let him go. For a guy as tough as Nick, and in front of his friends, that was not going to happen. But just before he thought he would hear bones breaking, the vise suddenly eased its grip and the pain immediately stopped. What followed was a rush of blood back to the bruised and numb tissue that was almost as painful as the crushing had been. Almost!

McFadden thanked the men for understanding and lightly placed his hand on Nick's shoulder in a gesture of congeniality. The hand began to close again, and Nick froze as the big fingers dug deeper and deeper into the muscles of his shoulder. This time, they released quickly and McFadden offered to buy the men a drink as a gesture of their newfound understanding. The other two men looked at Nick who appeared to be a little pale, but remained silent. When he finally spoke, he said they had other plans and would take him up on it the next time they saw him. Nick dropped a hand full of bills on the table, apologized to Mama Rizzo, and left without another word before their dinners had even been finished.

Francis Thomas "BB" McFadden! "Beach Ball" was a nickname he'd acquired in High School because of his size and he hadn't been able to kick it, so he embraced it and became "BB" to his friends. A Ph.D. theoretical physicist at 24, he was BB to most, Doc to many, Francis to a few, and always Frankie to his mother. McFadden was not an easy man to miss in a crowd – tall and heavy with a shaved head and goatee.

Francis had always been big. Not necessarily fat, but just big all over. Being exceptionally bright and having a genius IQ didn't help make him popular with the in-crowd. Too heavy for baseball, not tall enough for basketball, and definitely too delicate for football — at least as his mother saw it — McFadden wasn't exactly a jock in high school. Although she was a smart and progressive thinker, Margaret McFadden had very definite ideas when it came to the safety and well-being of her only child. Finally, with the support of his father, McFadden convinced his mother to allow him to take lessons in the martial art of Aikido. Since Aikido didn't involve "chopping" or "punching" your opponent, Margaret agreed to let him try, so long as he wasn't hurt.

Aikido is designed to use your opponent's weight and movements against him, along with your own counter moves and adjustments in stance. Large heavy men are not usually found studying this form of martial art. A man his size would normally be found in the Judo or Ju-jitsu schools.

He proved to be a natural for this form of self-defense. His time in the classes enabled McFadden to develop extremely quick reflexes and he found that, as his studies continued, he was able to move deceptively fast with just a few steps and shifts of his weight. His reflexes continued to improve as he moved steadily up the belt order.

By seventeen, he had become the youngest legitimate Aikido black belt in New England. He thrived on the competition and enjoyed a certain degree of satisfaction as he quickly defeated opponents who had discounted the skills of the fat kid. He had the weight to move opponents, but Aikido is an art of skill and grace and he didn't want to just overpower them. To improve his skills, he recognized the need to develop greater hand strength so that he could maneuver his opponent using their own weight.

To improve his grip, he purchased a pair of spring-loaded hand exercisers. He eventually was able to squeeze the handles together and place a dollar between the ends, hold the bill without it slipping out, and carry on a conversation. His hand strength became such that once he grabbed hold of someone or something, it could not be pried from his grip. Friends knew that if pushed to his limit, which was extreme, the big man's actions were quick and painful. Nick had experienced that up close and personal!

After an amazing dinner, Momma Rizzo told McFadden she had recently seen her nephew Tommy Marino. "I know you haven't seen him for a while," she said. "He was here last Friday asking for you and wanted to talk about some search he was going to make in Greece or Turkey or Africa; I can't remember where."

"I don't think I've seen Tom for a couple years now. Not since he accepted the teaching position at Brown University in Providence?" he asked.

McFadden thought about Tommy Marino. Tommy had spent his summers with the Rizzo's as the boys were growing up. His family lived in Brooklyn, NY and his mother was afraid to have him roaming the streets all summer when school was finished, so she sent him to stay with her sister in Boston. Tommy was a year younger than BB and Mickey, but the boys would be inseparable until he returned to New York at the end of August each year.

A little bit of McFadden and Mickey must have rubbed off on Tommy because he stayed out of trouble back in the city and wound up going to NYU where he earned a bachelor's degree in archeology. He volunteered to work a few digs in Egypt and eventually got his Masters in Middle Eastern Civilizations before accepting the teaching position at Brown.

Momma Rizzo took a blank receipt from her pad and wrote Tommy's phone number down. "I promised him you'd call when you got back," she said. "I hope you don't mind, but he sounded so excited I couldn't say no."

"Not at all!" he replied. "I'd like to hear what he's been up to. I'll call him tomorrow."

They talked for another hour and, finally, after 3 cannoli and several cups of Espresso, it was time for McFadden to head home. He kissed Momma goodnight and promised to see her again the following week.

CHAPTER 4

McFadden left the restaurant and began the short walk down the street to where he had parked his battered Ford Explorer. As he walked down the quiet sidewalk, he seemed to sense that something wasn't right, and, if he'd had any, the hair on his neck would have stood up. He heard a sound off to his left and looked across the street in time to see three figures come out of the darkened doorway of a closed butcher shop. He knew exactly what was happening before they began to cross to his side. It appeared Nick wanted to continue their conversation after all. McFadden decided that it would be useless to try and talk his way out of this confrontation, so he began to look for the best place to meet his would-be attackers. The last thing he wanted to do was to get his back against a wall. He stood a better chance of defending himself if he had more room to move.

"Hey, Fat Boy, I'm ready for that drink now," he heard one of them call after him. He knew it was Nick and he could hear the arrogance in his voice. Despite the three-to-one odds, McFadden was relaxed and ready. He knew the advantage initially would be his, since they already underestimated their opponent.

The art of Aikido is based more on defense than on the attack. That wasn't to say that a strong offense wasn't also part of this art form. But offense was reserved for close quarters when your opponent was less than an arm's length away. It was then that the force of your attack would be the more damaging. The student of this martial art would allow his opponent to make the first move and would then counter with speed and technique gathered over years of study and discipline. Let them come to you and make their move.

McFadden saw a small parking lot just ahead on the right and quickened his pace to arrive at it before the three reached him. Stepping between the two buildings that bordered the lot, he gave the area a quick look and saw that it was flat, with sufficient room to move. It was strewn with trash and a few empty wine bottles. He'd have to be aware of the bottles and anything else that could be used as a weapon against him.

He turned back towards the street just as the three men reached the entrance. They walked casually and looked confident as they spread apart, covering the entrance to the lot, effectively cutting off his only avenue of escape. He knew that his choice of the parking lot to face them was exactly what would give him that extra edge.

"Hey, Fat Boy, you wanna' try holding hands again?" he taunted. The other two laughed and stepped further apart as if to give themselves room to attack from both sides. The man that moved to his right was shorter than the other two but appeared more muscular than his buddies and had the look of a street fighter. He sidestepped and moved slowly but smoothly. He would be the one to watch. The other man didn't have the look of the fighter and seemed too casual, as if thinking that Nick would take care of this quickly and he'd just have to watch.

Nick slowly began to close the distance between himself and McFadden. "I'm gonna' kick the crap out of you, Fat Boy!" McFadden watched his face and read the over-confidence; he would be the quickest to deal with and provide the much-needed element of surprise.

Since the other two hadn't moved, McFadden had been able to draw Nick far enough into the lot and further away from them to reduce their reaction time. Time seemed to slow down as he felt himself relax and let the tension leave his body

He hadn't said a word since the three men cornered him. His silence would only further their belief that he was defenseless. McFadden stopped and allowed Nick to step closer. Nick was now just several feet away and closing in.

Nick reached out and pushed McFadden in the chest, forcing him to take several steps back.

"You still want to buy me that drink, Fat Boy?" Nick sneered and looked over his shoulder at the two men as they stood apart and closed off the exit to the street. "I don't think he's thirsty anymore, Artie," he laughed. "Are you thirsty, Fat Boy?" he said and again pushed McFadden in the chest. By now they had moved further into the lot and further away from the other two. They were now too far away to come to Nick's aid in time to make a difference.

McFadden decided that he had moved back far enough and it was time to get Nick's undivided attention.

As Nick thrust his hands at McFadden's chest as if to push him again, the big man quickly took a half-step to his left and turned to his right, so that he was now at a 90-degree angle. Nick's outstretched hands found nothing but air. He was thrown off balance and stepped forward, reaching for something to grab onto. McFadden's left hand was a blur as he reached out and locked onto Nick's right wrist in a vise-like grip. McFadden pulled Nick towards him and twisted the other man's wrist over his head so that Nick appeared to be chasing his own hand in a small circle. Nick tried to adjust his weight to relieve the tearing pain in his shoulder, but McFadden stepped back and swung the arm forward again and let Nick's own weight drive him back in the direction he had just been going. McFadden's agility caught Nick at the perfect angle as he followed the direction of his twisted arm. The momentum of his body and his immobilized wrist were just enough to cause him to flip forward in an attempt to avoid breaking his wrist.

It didn't help. Nick screamed as he felt the bone snap in his left forearm. Not only did the arm break, but the change in direction caused Nick to be lifted several feet in the air as he flipped before slamming down flat on the pavement. The fall had taken the wind out of him and there was no longer any fight left. The entire encounter had happened so quickly that the other two men didn't have a chance to move, let alone come to their friend's defense.

For a moment they just stared at McFadden as he turned back towards them and stopped. Artie reacted first and came at McFadden as he had expected he would. He came ready to fight a street fight with everything he had; fists, feet, and whatever he carried on him.

He closed the distance warily and started to circle as if trying to get McFadden to turn his back towards the third man who stood frozen in place and hadn't moved an inch since this all began. McFadden slowly sidestepped, not allowing Artie to turn him.

"Don't try any of that Judo crap on me, Fat Boy. I've kicked the hell out of a couple of you Kung Fu boys before," he threatened.

As he talked, he shuffled closer like a boxer trying to maneuver his opponent into the corner of the ring and cut off his movements. It wasn't working as McFadden continued to sidestep and keep the fighter in front of him. They were finally close enough for the man to begin to throw jabs with his big left hand. He was smart and avoided committing himself to a close quarter fight just yet. Jab and move, jab and move. Each jab was deflected as McFadden moved slowly to the right and then to the left; always to one side, never forward or back.

The other man's jabs weren't hitting anything, and all his skill was to no effect. He began to show a little frustration which led him to become impatient. He decided to throw the bomb and go for the knockout. He drew his right arm back ever so slightly and set his feet flat on the ground to get as much force as he could behind the punch.

McFadden easily blocked the man's left-hand jab, which was meant to distract him. The jab was followed by the crushing right cross that didn't quite reach its mark. McFadden block the punches and suddenly stepped in closer to his opponent. As Artie tried to compensate for the missed punch, he turned and unsteadily threw a looping left at McFadden's head.

McFadden caught the left hand as it came towards him and quickly raised it over his head and stepped forward and under the outstretched arm. As he continued raising the hand, he changed direction and moved in close behind the man. He continued moving to the right and Artie's body began to change direction and turn towards him. It was this position that allowed McFadden to use the full force of his 300 plus pounds to bring this to a close. He jerked the man's arm back toward him, and, as Artie seemed to be regaining his balance, McFadden stretched his own right arm out, away from his side and horizontal to the ground. It looked like the limb of a large tree.

As Artie straightened up, McFadden jerked him forward and then used his entire weight as he quickly stepped forward and brought the big arm across and under his opponent's upraised chin.

Artie's feet shot out past his body as the head and neck stopped dead. His body went horizontal to the ground and he landed flat on the pavement. The back of his head hit first and bounced several times with a sickening thud each time. Blood from the gash on the back of his head began to slowly spread out in a circle as he moaned and lay semi-conscious.

The third man finally regained his senses and reached down for a length of two-by-four that was lying near him. If he thought that McFadden had forgotten about him in the midst of the fight, he was gravely mistaken. Out of fear and desperation, he charged McFadden with the two-by-four held high over his head like a club. As he got close, he swung the club down, aiming at McFadden's head. Before the blow could gain momentum, McFadden positioned his hands in the shape of a big "V" and thrust them up to catch the man's arm and twist it quickly away until he was forced to drop the club. As the man regained his balance, he prepared to throw a right at McFadden's head.

Before the blow could develop, McFadden threw a short, but powerful, fist squarely on the man's nose. He could hear the sound of bone and cartilage breaking. It looked as if the man's nose had flattened against his face. He screamed and reached up as if to cover and protect it from further damage, but McFadden followed the punch with a short swinging elbow to the man's temple. His eyes rolled back in his head and began to flutter as his brain appeared to process what had just happened. He seemed to hang in the air, expressionless. His body leaned to the right and he slowly fell like a tree that had just been cut down. He was out cold before he ever touched the ground.

The one-sided fight with the three men was over so quickly that McFadden hadn't even broken a sweat. As he straightened his jacket and shirt, he heard the sound of sirens in the distance. Someone must have heard the shouts and called the police. He quickly left the parking lot and continued his walk to his car until he saw the first police car screech to a halt. As the driver got out of the car, he looked down the street and saw McFadden.

Before they had a chance to order him back and begin to ask questions, McFadden turned and casually walked back towards the cruiser as a second car arrived. The best way to avoid getting involved was to try and get involved.

"I think somebody was hurt in that alley!" he volunteered to the first officer. "There was some shouting and then I heard a car race away going real fast. Do you know what happened?" He began to pepper the officers with questions until one of them finally told him to leave and keep out of their way. Nobody wanted this pain-in-the-ass hanging around. Properly chastised, he turned and walked to his car and went home.

The next day, there was a small article in the paper detailing a gang-related fight in a Boston parking lot. Two men were admitted to Boston General and a third man was treated for a broken nose and released. No one was arrested, and none of the men assaulted could give any details on the five guys who jumped them in the dark.

CHAPTER 5

McFadden unlocked the door to his Cambridge apartment, went to the kitchen, and opened a bottle of beer. He settled in the big chair in his study and looked at the mess surrounding him. He had designated the smaller of the two bedrooms to be his study/office and enjoyed sitting amongst his books and papers. On the small table next to the chair sat the four books he was simultaneously reading. There were several reference books he was reviewing in preparation for the new semester; the latest report on the ongoing digs in Egypt, and, of course, the latest book by Ernest Dempsey, his favorite fiction author. McFadden felt comfortable sitting in the middle of this organized clutter and was able to shut out the occasional traffic noises and stay focused on his latest project.

He picked up the stack of folders and began to review his notes from the Turkey expedition for the hundredth time. It had been a great trip, but he had nothing substantial to show for it. The examination of the carved foundation stones had failed to shed any light on what had happened to an entire people so many generations ago.

The carvings and symbols appeared to chronicle a brief history of their civilization, wars, peace, growth, and expansion. Then it ended and there was no further word on them. He planned to draft a paper on the trip and try to convince the University for funding to continue the search. In the meantime, he hoped to enjoy his summer away from school and forget about the new crop of students he'd pick up in September.

At 32 years of age, McFadden had been a tenured professor for almost 2 years. Upon graduation from Princeton at 24 years old with a Ph.D. in theoretical physics, he presented his theory supporting the possibility of time travel in relation to black holes. This scholarly paper had come out a mere two months after his doctoral thesis was published in an edition of Scientific American magazine. His thesis had been widely read amongst the scientific community and there were many who likened him to a young Stephen Hawking, or Michio Kaku – some calling him the best new mind to enter the theoretical physics community in years.

But it was this theory on the time travel that brought him the most attention and recognition. With that notoriety came teaching offers from many of the most prestigious colleges and universities in the country. But McFadden was a Boston boy at heart, and he loved the city. The decision had been easy; Boston College got the young genius. Plus, he had been able to stay fairly close to his parents.

As a tenured professor and popular lecturer, McFadden acquired a certain amount of freedom to pursue the other disciplines that drove him: history and archeology.

That was what made Tom Marino's message so important. Over the past 5 years, Tom had been involved in several of the most important archeological finds in the last hundred years. He was a member of the expedition that discovered the mass graves at Machu Picchu in Peru, and had volunteered as a digger at the most recent burial vault uncovered in the Valley of the Kings. "If he's calling me," McFadden thought, "It has to be something involving a find or a lead." It was 10:45 pm, probably too late to call tonight, but he'd call first thing in the morning.

At 7:30 am the next day, McFadden was dialing Tom in Providence, Rhode Island. The husky voice that answered the phone told McFadden that he'd woken Tom. "Hey, kid, what are you doing sleeping this late." he asked jokingly. "It's almost noon."

Marino cleared his throat, "Noon, my ass," he replied. "Who the hell is this?"

"It's Slim McFadden,"

"Slim, my ass," Tom laughed. "What time is it, really?"

McFadden boomed into the receiver, "It's 7:30, my boy, and you're wasting a perfectly good day."

Suddenly awake, Tom said, "BB, I'm glad you called. I've got a real mystery on my hands and I think this is right up your alley. I've been thinking of you ever since I read the diary."

Now it was McFadden's turn to be serious, "What diary did you read?"

Tom lowered his voice as if trying to keep the conversation confidential. "The diary belonged to my Uncle Angelo, who was a pilot in the Italian Air Force before and during World War II. This is some serious shit, BB" he said. "If you have the time, I'd like to come up and talk to you about it."

McFadden could feel the excitement in Tom's voice and found himself getting wrapped in the suspense. "I'm home for the next few of weeks," he answered. "Come over whenever you want."

There was a pause before Tom replied, "Good, I'll be there before noon. See you then." The line went dead, and McFadden was left to wonder what the big secret was.

At a little after 11:00 Marino was ringing McFadden's doorbell. He looked a little different from the last time he had seen him several years ago. He still had those dark grey eyes; the hair was a little longer, but still coal black. His 5 ft. 11 in. frame was thinner, leaner, and more muscular. All those weeks and months in the field had treated him well. He looked tan and healthy. After an exchange of hugs and back slapping, they went to the kitchen and McFadden poured them each a cup of coffee, his coffee black, and Marino's with milk and endless spoons of sugar.

"Would you like some coffee with your sugar," McFadden teased.

"Look who's talking, Slim," came the reply. McFadden smiled wide, "Touché."

They spent a few minutes catching up on each other's lives before McFadden finally asked, "Okay, what's the mystery about your uncle's diary?" Marino opened the briefcase he'd brought with him and took out a large envelope from which he pulled a tattered, leather-bound book.

"When I was in Europe last year, I stopped in Italy for a few days to visit relatives and had a chance to spend time with my mother's oldest brother, Angelo. He was in his 90s, but was sharp as a tack," Tom added. "He was confined to bed, but his mind was alert and his voice strong and clear. We somehow began to talk about his time in the Air Force before World War II."

"Actually, as I look back, it was he who steered the conversation in that direction." Tom paused. "The whole family knows about the plane crash when he was in Ethiopia in the 1930s, although he never really talked about it. But the night before I left for Egypt, we spent a few hours drinking wine and eating cheese and peppers in his room. The conversation eventually turned again to Ethiopia and he just brushed over the crash he'd been in."

Marino became quiet and subdued. "He said some strange things had happened to him after he crashed, but he wouldn't be specific. "Someone needs to go there, Tomas, and find answers to the questions," he told me. "I remember trying to pin him down. Answers to what questions, Uncle Angelo?" but he continued to be vague." Tom looked McFadden in the eyes and told him, "Just before I left, he took my hand and said, 'Tomas, you go, you find the answers and you close the book.' With that, he closed his eyes. I kissed him on the check and left for the airport. I attributed the conversation to old age and way too much wine. A week later, he died in his sleep."

Marino took a long drink from his cup. "About a month after he died, I received a package: this envelope. This is what was inside; his diary beginning in 1936 with entries every so often after that, until the final one a few days before he died. I'll leave it with you. Take your time, read it and call me when you've finished it and we can go from there. I want you to read this without me giving you any background. After I finished reading this, I realized why he'd sent it to me. He knew I was an archeologist, a digger, and I think he felt I could dig up the answers to his questions."

Tom seemed a little drained after talking and declined McFadden's invitation to stay for lunch, leaving less than an hour after having arrived. McFadden looked at the envelope containing the book sitting in the middle of the kitchen table. It seemed to be pulling his hand towards it; a peculiar and compelling attraction like a magnet to metal. He made another pot and fixed himself a large ham and cheese sandwich with chips. When everything was ready, he took the sandwich, and the envelope and parked himself in the chair in his study and settled in for a little reading.

McFadden removed the diary from the envelope and saw it had been written in a strong, steady hand beginning in February, 1936. The handwriting became less steady as the years of entries passed. Unfortunately, it was also written in Italian. While McFadden was able to satisfactorily converse in multiple languages, he wasn't fluent enough in Italian to read such a lengthy document. He was about to call Marino when he saw there was also a stack of papers in the envelope. He pulled them out and found that Marino had translated the diary and included the typed pages. With the clear legible pages in hand, BB settled in and began his 70+ year retrospect journey through the old man's own words.

CHAPTER 6

The first page was dated almost a year ago and was a translation of the brief letter Angelo Colavari had written to his nephew several days before he died.

"Tomas, this book will tell you a story that you wouldn't have believed if I had shared it with you the night before you left. You would have thought it was the ramblings of a senile, old man. But if you read my diary, the one I began when I was a young man — younger than you are now — you may find proof of what I already know is the truth."

Intrigued, McFadden settled back and began reading the first series of entries. They began in early 1936 when the young Angelo Colavari entered flight school and dealt with the challenges of learning how to fly, and the equally important lessons on learning how to land. By his own admission, he was a quick study and seemed to take naturally to the air. There were quite a few candidates who washed out of the program, but Angelo absorbed everything he was taught and graduated number one in his flight class. The next few entries dealt with his assignment to the 1st Flight Wing of the 2nd Fighter Command, and several of his duty appointments before eventually being shipped to Ethiopia in July 1936. His entries after this became more personal as he wrote about his feelings and experiences in war until August.

August 23, 1936 – "Today, I flew my first patrol with Lt. Longo. I was his wing man, which meant I was always in position to defend him against attack by any enemy plane as he led us over the desert roads looking for enemy troop movements. At first, I was very nervous, and continually scanned from right to left, up and down, looking for any trace of enemy aircraft.

There were none, and there never would be. Ethiopia had no Air Force. The sky was ours!"

McFadden skimmed the next few days and finally settled on September 27th. Colavari had been promoted and would now lead the reconnaissance flight on the next morning. September 28th turned out to be the day he was shot down so there were no entries until October 15th.

More than two weeks after the crash.

October 15, 1936 – "I'm in the hospital, but I don't know why. There's nothing physically wrong with me, except that my legs should be broken, my jaw shattered, my shoulder should have a bullet wound, and my ribs should be cracked. I shouldn't be able to move, let alone walk in my room. I have no pain, but I think the doctors are keeping me here because they believe I may have battle fatigue, or I'm suffering from hallucinations. But they're not hallucinations. It really happened. When I close my eyes, I feel the blanket pulled up to my neck and the warmth it gave as I slowly made my recovery. I can see the monks changing my dressings and feeding me until I was able to sit up and eat with my left hand. And I can see the Abbot, smiling and feeling my head; his skin rough, but his touch gentle and reassuring. All of this I remember as clearly as I see the window in my room and feel the floor beneath my feet."

Colavari wrote about the patrol that led up to the crash. His memories were vivid and clear as he recounted as much detail as he could about his ordeal. Things were so clear that he attempted several sketches of the terrain and the trail he and Spinoza had attacked. The drawings weren't very good, but they provided a little detail of the area surrounding and leading up to the trail. He described a low, flat tree line covering the left side of his approach and what appeared to be an almost sheer climb on his right. It wasn't much, but at least there was something specific to look for. McFadden wondered how tall the trees could have grown in 70 years.

The entry went on, *"But I still don't know why they drugged me and released me back in the desert. I was finally feeling strong enough to talk with my rescuers and learn where I was and how they had cared for me so well with such primitive resources. I don't recall receiving any medication or injections. No surgery or anesthesia, yet my pain subsided and my injuries healed quickly. No, this was no dream."*

October 16, 1936 – "Major Solari, my Wing Commander, stopped to check on me and said a patrol had found Carlo Spinoza's plane. It had crashed and broken apart with Carlo's body still in the cockpit. They would be sending him home to his family on the next transport out. They haven't found the wreck of my plane yet. They searched the area where they found Carlo, thinking I must have crashed near him. But I know I was miles away from there when I finally went down."

October 18, 1936 – "I'm still waiting to be discharged and returned to my unit. The doctors question me every day about the crash and my claim of injuries. I think the only way to get out of here is to give them what they want; pretend to be confused about the crash and my injuries. I'm going to admit that I don't remember anything after the crash and that I'm not sure of anything and must have dreamed about being hurt. I must have dreamed it since I have no wounds to show for it."

October 23, 1936 – "I played my role for the doctors this morning and showed 'remarkable recovery' after finally being able to remember the crash and the fact that I had been lost until being rescued by some desert nomads. I had some aches and pains from the crash, so I think the natives tried to bandage what they thought I had injured."

"I must have been convincing because they discharged me to light duty and no flying for two weeks. During that time, I made certain I continued to show steady improvement until I was sure I had never been injured and had just been disoriented when I was returned. The doctors were very proud of their success and I was eventually cleared for flight duty."

As McFadden read the entries covering the next several months of the Ethiopian campaign, there were fewer mentions of the crash or his recovery. Colavari's time in WWII was documented in the diary as well, but nothing appeared again about the crash until May of 1947.

May 23, 1947 – "The war has been over for two years, and, like so many other survivors, I sometimes wonder why I lived while so many others died. But that's not what really keeps me awake at night. What haunts me constantly is not why I survived, but HOW! To keep my sanity, I have to find the answers. I have to go back to Ethiopia and find the monastery, the monks, the Abbot."

There were entries for the next several months as Colavari outlined his plans and attempted to organize his trip back to that day in 1936. Finally, in September 1947, eleven years after the crash, he arranged passage aboard a ship leaving from Solerno bound for Ethiopia's main seaport of Massawa. There he planned to retrace his steps, first to the old air base, and then northwest to the mountains in the hope of finding the valley entrance. If he could find the opening, he would have a point from which to begin the search.

On October 4th he arrived at Massawa and soon boarded a bus for the capital carrying just two bags containing the short list of personal items he chose to bring. In Addis Ababa, the people had not so quickly forgotten the Italian occupation. Colavari found himself truly alone; an unpopular man in a somewhat hostile environment. He knew from where his search must begin, a small abandoned air base almost 150 miles north of the capital. The diary recounted his daily search for a guide to lead him through the desert to the old base.

After almost a week, he wrote that he found a man, Josef, a small Ethiopian who claimed to have come to the capital from a small village in the desert hoping to find work. He spoke some broken Italian, with a mix of English. It seemed that between the man's limited Italian and Colavari's limited English, they were able to communicate on a very basic level. Josef said he hadn't eaten in several days and told Colavari that he would rather return home and eat goat in the desert than starve in the city. He said he knew of the old base and agreed to guide him at least that far. Once they were there, he would leave Colavari and continue on his way back to his own people.

Colavari agreed and he and his new guide went to one of the food stalls by the marketplace and Josef ordered food for both of them and made sure that the vendor charged him the Ethiopian price for their food, not the marked-up Westerner price that most foreigners paid. After their meal, Colavari brought Josef back to the room he occupied in the small dingy hotel a short walk from the marketplace. Josef was happy to sleep on the floor and was soon sound asleep with his first full stomach in days.

The following day, they went in search of transportation, and Colavari purchased a World War II survivor, an old, but apparently sound, American jeep. With extreme reservations, he gave Josef money to buy supplies and gas for their journey and watched as the little man walked off towards the bazaar, disappearing into the marketplace. Several hours later, he was relieved and somewhat surprised to see Josef return seated on a wagon pulled by an old donkey and driven by a wizened older man.

The wagon contained five 5-gallon cans of gas, water, and an assortment of supplies that would be sufficient to keep the both of them fed for the 2-3 day trip, and still leave enough for Colavari to travel at least a week further. Josef told him that if they stayed on the narrow, barely visible road leading from the city, they would most certainly come across merchants and travelers who would sell them additional supplies. With the purchase of an old army tent to protect them from the cold desert nights, they were finally ready to begin their journey.

Shortly after dawn the following morning, and after breakfast of strong black coffee and sweet bread, they were on the road leading out of the capital. Colavari wrote that he was heartened on that first day to pass small camel and donkey trains every 10 or 15 miles, loaded with goods and headed for the market. The ruts and bumps of the camel trail took its toll on both men, provoking them to stop for the day at about 4:00 pm after having traveled a little more than 100 miles. They set up the tent together and Josef went about preparing their small meal. Colavari wrote that he was almost too tired to eat but had forced the food down and made sure he drank a sufficient amount of water.

Dehydration could creep up on a man quickly in the desert. Dying of thirst was a slow and agonizing way to go, and Colavari wasn't interested in experiencing it. As they sat around the small fire, Colavari tried to quiz the Ethiopian about whether he knew of a monastery, a home for holy men in the mountains further west. Josef said he was from a desert tribe and knew little of the mountains. The cold of the desert night finally moved them into the tent and Colavari wrote that he quickly fell into a sound sleep.

He recalled waking just before dawn, and was enjoying the utter silence of the desert, before realizing he was alone in the tent. He went outside and called, but Josef was nowhere in sight. He'd been abandoned, was his first thought; left by Josef to find his own way in this oven. But before he could curse his guide's treachery, he heard a low voice coming from the far side of the parked jeep. He walked around and found Josef kneeling on a small rug, facing the East and reciting his morning prayers.

After a light breakfast, they were on the road again, now just hours from the base. How much would be left, he wondered? By mid-morning, they spotted the control tower in the distance. He wondered whether his barracks would still be standing. Better yet, would his hospital room still be there. The frames were there, but most of the buildings had been stripped clean. They looked like spiders with long skinny legs standing in the distance. The desert people had taken almost everything else: the siding, the sheet metal roofs. Anything that could be burned, reused, or bartered was gone. Now the base was a way station in the desert for small groups of entrepreneurs.

A thriving marketplace was open and active when they pulled in. Camels and donkeys roamed freely amid the hustle and bustle of the bazaar. There were merchants selling everything from food to clothing to firewood. The locals halted for fear that they were hostile, but once the people realized that they were no threat the haggling resumed.

To his surprise, Colavari wrote that they were able to refill their gas cans and add a variety of fresh fruit and bread. It was here that Josef was to leave Colavari and head home to his own people. Josef spoke with the merchants and shoppers for some time before telling the Italian that these were not his tribesmen and they had not seen anyone from his village for weeks. Colavari used this news as an opportunity to try and convince the Ethiopian to continuing west with him. He told Josef that if he stayed as his guide and traveled deeper into the desert with him, he would not only pay a handsome bonus, but would also drive the little man directly home to his people.

He needed help to find the right road to the beginning of the Simien Mountains. Josef knew that the extra money from the Italian would serve his people well and allow them to purchase additional supplies and much-needed tools for cultivating the harsh land. He told Colavari he would stay with him for as long as it took to reach the mountains. Once they would arrive, Colavari agreed to then take him home and return to the mountains on his own.

They spent the next day going over a map of the area and marking likely spots where the young Colavari might begin his search. Finally, after they had selected several places on the map, and with the setting of a new milestone, the two men drove from the old base at dawn and headed west toward the Simien Mountains.

McFadden looked at the clock, realizing he'd been reading for almost four hours. The diary intrigued him, even if he didn't know where Colavari's journey was leading him. He'd taken extensive notes as he read the Italian's journal. His mind was rereading the entries, sorting out the details of the trip, and assigning importance to those small bits of information he thought might prove useful. It was time for a short break to fill that void in his stomach, but he was now in full research mode.

CHAPTER 7

It was almost 7:00 pm when McFadden returned to the office with a fresh pot of coffee and a satisfied stomach filled with a 5-egg Spanish omelet, half a pound of bacon and a fistful of home fried potatoes. He was going to finish that off with a generous slice of cheesecake but decided to reward himself after he'd finished reading more of Angelo Colavari's diary.

October 17, 1947 – "My English has been getting better and Josef's Italian has greatly improved. We were now able to converse freely and with the comfort of easy speech came more personal and candid conversation. Josef told me he had left his family a month earlier to see if he could get a job and make enough money in the city for him and his 3 wives to buy more goats and make his clan wealthy and more independent. He had not found his fortune, but he admitted he was thankful for the chance to return home and be with them."

McFadden continued to read the daily entries and saw that Colavari appeared to talk more about Josef as a friend or colleague than just a guide. He wrote that one evening, following a particularly slow day of driving northwest across the desert, Josef had asked him why he was looking for a house of holy men.

Colavari was reluctant at first to share his experience with the young Ethiopian. But he finally realized that he would probably never achieve his goal without some help, and who better to know something about the vast desert and mountains than a man who had lived his entire life there? Besides, he no longer had to be concerned what people thought about his claims of incredible healing. So, he lit a cigarette and, with a cup of hot coffee to warm his hands, he stared at the stars overhead, recounting every detail of his crash and recovery to his new companion.

Josef listened quietly and asked no questions as Angelo described everything he so vividly remembered about his ordeal. When he was finished, he looked at Josef's face for a clue, some sign that his new friend understood what he had said or whether he thought he was crazy. The dark face reflected the light from the fire as he seemed to digest what he had just heard.

After what seemed like minutes, Josef's expression seemed to change, and he looked at Colavari as if seeing him for the very first time, a dauntless austerity to his gaze. "My friend," he began. "I will tell you a story in answer to yours."

"In my land, my people, my tribesmen are faithful followers of Allah and his prophet Mohammed. Further north, the Christian followers of the prophet Jesus also live and tend their camels and sheep. For generations we have lived in peace and accepted and respected each other's beliefs and traditions. Although we serve different gods, we share one thing in common that dates back a thousand years and more. We recognize our duty to serve and support the Tekelakayochi."

Josef waited for Colavari to absorb what he had just said, but the words were beyond the Italian's grasp of their limited common language, so he merely nodded and waited for Josef to continue. Josef smiled, stared ahead as if trying to remember something, and then it appeared to come to him.

"My friend, although I don't know what the translation would be in Italian, the Tekelakayochi would translate into English as the Protectors. For generations, longer than any man can remember, members of the Tekelakayochi have come from their home in the mountains every 10 years, alternating between my people and the Christian village to the north. Each time, they come to select the next boy who will leave his family and dedicate his life to prayer and service. It makes no difference whether the child is Muslim or Christian.

"The parents of each boy would not see their son again until he returned in 10 years for the next child to be selected. This would be the last opportunity for parents and child to see each other. This is when he would be offered the opportunity to remain with his family or return to his work with the monks. For more than a thousand years, no boy has ever chosen to return to his family. They have eagerly made their choice and left with a smile and a blessing on all those left behind."

"This common bond of selection and service has joined our two peoples together, Muslim and Christian alike for longer than any man can remember. There have never been hostilities between our two tribes, as we know we share something spiritual and holy.

Who are these holy men? They are of the old stories that pass from elder to elder. No one can remember that far back to know why or how this all began."

Josef's voice dropped to almost a whisper as he looked at Colavari. "I know this to be true since my older brother Ismael left with the monks while I was quite young. My family spoke of his leaving with great respect and pride. I had hoped to be the next from our village to go on the next 10-year anniversary, but war with your people prevented the monks from returning. When the war was finally over, I was too old and another was chosen in my place.

Colavari sat transfixed, listening to Josef's account of the traditional selection. If they were the same men who had cared for him — and in all likelihood they were — that would explain the varying ages of the men who had ministered to his injuries. Suddenly, Colavari was seized with question upon question. "Who were the men serving? Where did they take the boys? Had anyone ever been to the monastery?"

Josef raised his hand in response to the Italian's excitement. "My friend," he began, "I have no answers for any of your questions. But what I can tell you is that what happened to you after your crash, happened to a small girl in my village more than 20 years ago. It was a day before my brother returned with the holy man to choose a new boy to return with them. She was only 5 and was running with other children and tripped and fell into a cooking fire and her robe immediately caught fire. Before anyone could grab her and beat out the flames, she was burned over almost her whole body. There was nothing anyone could do to ease her pain. She would die soon from her burns."

Josef paused and looked off into the distant night as if trying to either remember or forget the experience. "The next morning Ismael and another man came to the village, and, when Ismael saw the dying child, he wrapped her in a blanket and said he was taking her for help. The older man ordered him to leave her and let Allah take her, but Ismael refused and they argued for a few minutes before the man realized he could not convince Ismael to obey him, nor would he physically try to stop him."

Colavari's journal went on - a week later, Ismael and a different holy man returned with the child. This time she was wearing a much too large dress fashioned of linen. It looked as if it had been sewn by someone without knowledge of how to fit children's clothing.

"But that was not the remarkable part," Josef said as he paused to gather his thoughts. "When she returned, there were no burns or scars on her body. She returned just as she had been before the fire. Ismael refused to talk about her recovery and stayed just long enough for young Mohammed, a boy of just 10 years, to gather what little he had and leave with my brother and his companion."

"My friend," said Josef, "Allah made her whole again. There is no mortal man on earth that could have cured her. It was a miracle that saved her. I can tell you no more, as I know no more. Ten years later, Mohammed returned and left with the next child chosen to serve God, and it has continued to this day." As if drained by his telling of the miracle, and before Colavari could ask anything further, Josef snubbed out his cigarette, turned on his side, said good night, and was quickly asleep.

Colavari wrote that the story finally confirmed what he had personally experienced 11 years prior. For all the years since his return to the Italian Air Force after his crash he had dreamt of his rescue, sometimes doubting whether or not it had actually happened; thinking that maybe the crash had indeed given him hallucinations and that he had just imagined being hurt. But this child was the proof that the miracle of his recovery was real.

"The next morning, after Josef had completed his prayers, I asked him whether the young girl was still with the tribe. He said that she was now a married woman with children of her own." At this point, Colavari wrote that although his desire to reach the mountains was still his primary goal just as before, he had to talk to this woman and learn of her experience firsthand. That would be his proof. That would confirm his search. That would lead him to the answers.

After their meager breakfast, Colavari told Josef that he wanted to take him home to his people and that he was not interested in the mountains just now. Josef appeared happy at the news that he would soon be home and agreed to still guide Colavari when he was ready to resume the search.

Carefully, Colavari brought the conversation back to the village girl who had been burned. Would he be able to talk with her about the experience? Josef tried to explain that strangers, non-believers, men who had no relation with the family were never allowed to talk with married or single women, except under strict rules and with special permission from the family elders. Although he was not optimistic about the possibility, in his gratitude for bringing him home, Josef agreed to try and arrange something.

CHAPTER 8

The following morning, they turned away from their journey towards the mountains and Josef led them deeper into the desert. After hours of driving in the sun they approached a small village set against the backdrop of the only oasis for miles. The village had been there for years and had suffered much during the war because of its location to the camel trails and the water. The Italians had made the village a radio and communications site, abusing the villagers, and using them as slave labor. The war was over and the Italians were gone, but the oasis remained the central point for camel caravans and travelers to refill their water casks and rest before resuming travel. It wouldn't be until the late 1950s before the trails would become roads and the camel caravans would be replaced by cars and trucks. But in 1947, the oasis was essential to anyone traveling to or from Addis Ababa.

When Colavari pulled the jeep into the oasis area they were low on gas and saw no chance to refill their tank and cans anytime soon. It looked as if they were stuck there until another caravan came through and hopefully had gasoline. Looking around, he found several small groups camped near the water. Camels drank their fill as women filled jars and men sat in the shade to talk and smoke. Josef left Colavari with the vehicle and approached one of the small groups. There was an exchange of greetings before Josef embraced several of the men and sat with them to smoke.

After about 20 minutes, he made his exit and returned to the Italian. "We are in luck, my friend," he said smiling and gesturing to the group of men he had just left. "These are the followers of the prophet, Jesus. They are friends and will loan us two camels to travel to my village. We will leave your Jeep and set off at dawn.

The next morning, as they mounted the camels, Josef told Colavari that it was a small journey, but after hours on the rocking, swaying camel the Italian was nauseous and ready to walk. But just when he thought he had reached his limit, Josef tapped his camel with the small stick used to direct and steer the huge beasts, and the animal took off at a fast trot. Colavari's camel quickly joined the race and he saw they were fast approaching a small gathering of tents standing alone amidst the mountains of sand in the distance.

As they approached, he could see there were a few trees, an area where crops were being tended to, and what appeared to be a well. The women in the fields stopped to watch the approaching riders, and soon a man yelled and waved to those around him. It was obvious that Josef had been recognized and word quickly spread. A small crowd quickly gathered as the camels slowed and eventually came to a stop. Josef tapped his camel on the neck with the switch and the animal slowly lowered itself to the ground where he could jump off. He was immediately surrounded and engulfed by the welcoming crowd.

Meanwhile, Colavari said his camel just stood and refused to lower itself to the ground no matter how many times he tapped it with the driving switch, like the camel begrudged him. He was stranded and unable to leave the beast without jumping. Finally, a young boy of 6 or

7 walked over and tapped the camel's front legs while speaking softly. The camel obediently knelt forward, almost throwing Colavari over its head, and then settled its rear legs into the sand. The Italian was then able to step off the beast onto solid but sandy ground and regain his equilibrium.

Josef looked back and pointed to Colavari and apparently told them that he was an Italian and on a journey. The atmosphere of the crowd suddenly changed, and conversation died off as all eyes focused on Colavari. Josef smiled and put his arm on Colavari's shoulder and spoke to the crowd. Slowly the tension seemed to leave the crowd and people began to smile and nod at Colavari. Josef turned to his companion and told him there were some among them that did not want any more Italians in their village.

"But I have told them that you are my friend and that you have brought me home. I also told them you are a friend of the Tekelakayochi and that you come to thank the holy men for saving your life," he explained. "We are an honest and forgiving people, Angelo. You are welcome here among us."

Josef's three wives arrived with what appeared to be almost a dozen screaming, laughing children. He greeted the women warmly and kissed and hugged each of the children as they looked at the Italian in silence. Josef again pointed at Colavari and smiled and gestured as he spoke to the new gathering. When he was finished, the children swarmed around him and reached out tentatively to touch his clothing, acting as if he were some sort of oddity.

A young boy took the reins of both camels and led them off and around the nearest dune to where the rest of the village's animals were kept. Josef placed his hand on his companion's shoulder as if to show that he was indeed a friend welcome in his home, and together they walked amongst the tents to his; a large tent with three smaller tents facing the opening of the larger one.

"You will stay here with me tonight, Angelo," he said. "Tonight, we will celebrate my coming home and you will share the feast as my friend."

As the sun began to slowly set, the village came alive with the sound of small children running and laughing as the women roasted the freshly-slaughtered goat over an open fire. There were olives and dates to eat and bread to dip into an unknown paste, the taste of which was at first bitter, but which he eventually began to find tasty. But it was the smell of the meat that demanded his attention. They had subsisted on coffee, bread, and fruit for the past four days and Colavari was ready to eat a real meal.

After endless cups of incredibly strong coffee and countless cigarettes, the meal was ready. The men sat around the communal fire as the woman brought the meat and set it before them along with bowls of vegetables, more bowls of heavy sauce, and loaves of hard, black bread. As quickly as they brought the food, the women were gone and into their tents with the children. It was quiet for some time as the men busied themselves cutting hunks of the juicy and sizzling meat onto plates and passing them amongst the gathered.

As their stomachs began to fill, the men resorted to loud talking and broad gestures, laughing and pointing to one another. Colavari continued to eat, and as he watched his host and the other men of the village, he realized that this was not unlike dinner in his own family. The women would prepare the meal, set the table, and then disappear into the kitchen for their own time.

Although he could not understand what was being said, he did notice that, every so often, Josef would gesture towards him and eyes would turn in his direction. Josef always smiled when he looked to his friend and the men began to smile as well, and he sensed that he was somehow being accepted on some level. As the coffee was poured and the cigarettes lit, Josef leaned back on a pillow and looked at Colavari.

"Angelo, I have told my people of your miracle in the mountains and your stay with the Tekelakayochi and how you search to find them. Your story is similar to others passed down over generations, and they agree that you must be a special man since you were saved. But the old men say that to look for the Tekelakayochi is very dangerous, and you will most likely be killed by the bandits who live in the mountains. No man has ever gone looking into the mountains and returned. Stories as old as the oldest men in the village tell of the bandits that raid any caravan traveling too close or killing anyone who ventured into the mountains. They say that you must thank Allah for his mercy in healing you and let your journey end here with us."

Angelo listened to the advice of his new friend before speaking. Conversation amongst the men stopped as they waited for the Italian to speak, even though not one of them understood a word he said.

"Josef, I thank God, be it Jesus or Allah, for bringing us together," he began. "I don't know where my journey would have led me if we had not come together. It is probably unlikely that I would have learned of the Tekelakayochi and certainly would not have learned of your generations of service to them." He paused as if trying to find the right words to explain what he was feeling.

"I cannot have been led here, this far, without reason. An answer to the question of why I still live, and to who or what healed me. I must go on until I know the answer or am convinced there isn't one."

Josef was silent and the faces around the fire turned questioningly towards him as if awaiting an answer to an unknown question. He looked at the faces illuminated by the fire for several moments as he studied first Colavari, and then the flames of the fire before speaking. He spoke softly and Colavari assumed he was telling them what he had said. Josef spoke for several moments and answered the occasional question from the gathered group. There were some nods of recognition and a few of uncertainty, but when they were finished Josef turned back to Colavari.

"Everyone is not in agreement as to what should be done; if we should help you or lead you back to the city." Josef turned to the gathering again and, this time, a younger man spoke a few words and nodded. Several older men around him appeared to nod in agreement as the crowd was quieted once more.

"There are a few among us who, even though you are my friend, have not forgotten the Italian Army's treatment of our people and wish you to leave. Fortunately, the rest see you as having experienced something special and holy, and they are willing to provide some assistance. It is especially important that the family of Micah have accepted you as a link to their family."

The young man who had recently spoken looked at Colavari and smiled. Josef pointed to the young man and said, "That man is Micah, the son of Jacob, who is an elder of our tribe. He, too, feels that you are here for a reason. The young girl of whom I spoke, the child who was burned and should have died, still lives amongst us and is seen as a special gift from Allah. She is Ayinabeba, and she is the wife of Micah and he has agreed to allow you to speak with her," he paused.

"It is not allowed for a married Muslim woman to speak with an adult male who is not from her family, and especially to a non-believer. Micah loves her greatly and is a good husband and father, but he believes you both have shared something holy and, because of that, there is a special bond between you two; two people from different worlds and of different beliefs. Tomorrow, you may speak with her in the presence of her husband and his family."

Although he was thrilled with the opportunity of speaking with Ayinabeba, Colavari quickly understood the gravity of this occasion and looked across the fire at Micah and slowly bowed. Micah smiled back and nodded. The rest of the men seemed satisfied and appeared to mumble their agreement. With this agreed, the conversations ended and everyone moved off to their own tents for the night. Colavari would spend a long and sleepless night waiting for his chance to meet the young woman who had been spared a painful death by strangers.

CHAPTER 9

At mid-morning on the following day, Micah and several older men arrived at Josef's tent. Angelo stood quietly while the men spoke amongst themselves. Finally, Josef turned and gestured for him to follow. The procession made its way through the sea of tents before finally stopping at a large grey and tan canvas tent; one apparently left over from the occupation years ago. Micah ushered the group inside where the smell of coffee and tobacco hung in the air. The men settled themselves on goatskin pillows as several older women entered, bringing cups of coffee and tea, placing them before the gathering. After several minutes of silence, Micah finally spoke to Josef. The quiet exchange went on for some time before Josef nodded and turned to Colavari.

"Angelo," he began, "this is a great gesture on the part of Micah and his family. The fact that he has welcomed a non-believer into his tent is unheard of for our people." He paused as if for dramatic effect.

"That he is allowing you to speak with his wife is a great act of trust towards a stranger. She wears the hijab, and, while you may look at her, I ask that you do not make direct eye contact or look upon her too long. I shall speak for you and ask whatever questions you may have."

Colavari began to sense that this acceptance by the husband and family of Ayinabeba was critical to his search, and that allowing him to ask her questions was being viewed as a great honor. It was now his time to address this occasion.

He looked at Josef, paused for a moment and began, "Josef, please tell Micah that I am greatly honored at this gift and have only the greatest respect for him and his family. I will long remember their gracious treatment of a stranger to their village and will speak of their kindness always." Josef translated Angelo's words and Micah smiled as the elders of the family nodded and gestured their approval.

With that, Micah softly called, "Ayinabeba?" A small child-like figure entered from the rear of the tent carrying a child of maybe a year old. All he could see were the bright, intelligent eyes that peered out above the veil that covered the rest of her face. She walked to her husband and he made room for her to sit beside him.

"Angelo, this is Ayinabeba, the girl of whom I spoke," Josef said. Colavari looked in the direction of the young woman, bowed his head, and greeted her in her native Ethiopian with the respectful welcome Josef had taught him earlier that morning. She returned the bow silently. Colavari turned his eyes back to his friend and asked him if Ayinabeba would recount her time with the Tekelakayochi holy men. Josef spoke to the young woman and slowly translated Colavari's question. She turned to her husband and he nodded his approval.

At first, her voice was so soft that Colavari could barely hear her. But, as she spoke, she appeared to gain more confidence and her voice grew steady and clear. Josef waited and then began to tell her story almost as quickly as she answered. Before long, he was speaking her words as if they were his own and the story flowed smoothly like a normal conversation.

"I remember that day very well," she began. "I was only a child, but I remember that my clothes were suddenly burning and I tried to run from the fire. Someone knocked me down and covered me with a blanket to stop the fire." She paused as if reliving the experience. Micah reached over and placed his hand upon hers in a reassuring manner, as if to show he was sharing the memory with her.

"The pain of the burns was so great that I could not cry. I just moaned and called for my mother to make the pain go away. I remember hearing people talking and saying that they prayed I would die soon so that I wouldn't suffer anymore."

She stared at the floor of the tent as if replaying the experience before she continued. "When I awoke, Josef's brother Ismael was there telling me that he would take the pain away. There was arguing between Ismael and another man who said that I should be allowed to die as it was the will of Allah. Ismael would not listen. He picked me up and carried me away from my family and no one tried to stop him."

Ayinabeba's voice grew stronger as she remembered the time more clearly. "Ismael carried me in his arms and spoke gently and said that the pain would soon be gone. The camel ride seemed very long and I slept for most of it, but, when I awoke, I saw that we had finally left the desert and were getting closer to the mountains. As we arrived in a clearing, other men came and one of them took me from Ismael, carrying me up the side of the mountain and under the trees."

Ayinabeba was speaking faster now and Josef struggled to keep up with her. She said that she could not sleep because the climb was making her burns hurt with each step they took. Finally, they reached the entrance to a cave on the side of a mountain and went in. More men appeared and another carried her further inside until they came to a room with a bed. She said they placed her on the bed and everyone left except for an old man with a long white beard. He spoke to her gently and told her not to be afraid because they were going to help her get better. There was a knock on the door and a tall, old man with sad eyes came in carrying a bundle.

"Hello, Ayinabeba. I am Brother Samuel, and, with God's grace, we are going to make you better." Brother Samuel reached down and touched my face and smiled then left without another word. Then the old monk with the beard began to carefully unwrap the bundle. When he finished, I saw that it was a big blanket. He opened the blanket and covered me with it. At first, it scratched my skin and the pain made me cry, but then it became cool and my skin didn't seem to burn as much."

Ayinabeba was silent for a moment as if carefully choosing her next words. "He laid it across me and slowly began to pull off the burned pieces of my dress that were left after the fire." She waited to see if Micah would react to this personal bit of information, but he smiled and nodded.

"I think I must have been asleep for a long time because, when I awoke, I did not hurt any longer. I looked at my hands and they were almost like they had been before the fire. When I lifted the blanket, I could see that my skin was red where it had been burned before, with parts of the skin falling off. I could not see any burns on my body and I no longer hurt at all. The old man came in every couple of hours and brought me milk, bread, and fruit and sat with me while I ate."

She stopped once again, lost in that moment so many years ago. "The old man had some cloth and began to sew a robe for me. We both laughed because he did not know how to make something so small and for a girl."

"Within several days, I was able to get out of bed, and, in my new robe, tried to get out of the room to look around, but my friend would not let me leave the room. Finally, Brother Samuel came back and again called me by my name. He brought milk and fruit, spoke softly and kindly, and asked how I felt. I told him I did not hurt anymore and wanted to go back to my family. He said that it was time for me to leave and told me to drink the milk before he left. After I drank the milk I became very tired and wanted to sleep."

Angelo knew where this part of the story was going since the same thing had happened to him 11 years earlier. Ayinabeba would be sedated as he was and then taken back to her own people. She said that when she woke up, she was again in the arms of Ismael and had left the mountain, heading back to her village. That was the last time she saw Ishmael or any of the Tekelakayochi men.

There wasn't really much more that Colavari wanted to know, and he doubted that a 5-year-old child would remember as much detail as he needed. But he asked about the old man who had given her the milk. "Was he Ethiopian? How did his voice sound?"

Ayinabeba thought for a moment and said that all the men she saw when she was going to the mountain and while she was there were Ethiopian. Brother Samuel did not look like he was from her people, but he spoke her language perfectly, even better than her father and mother.

With her story told and no more questions, Micah spoke softly to his wife and she left through the rear of the tent as the gathering of men quietly spoke and nodded. It was now Colavari's turn to talk.

He told Josef that Ayinabeba's experience was remarkably similar to his and only reaffirmed his desire to seek out the place of the holy men. Josef seemed to accept the determination in Colavari's voice and addressed the gathering again, this time his voice strong and confident. There were a few men who appeared to question Josef's statement, but most seemed to agree with whatever he had said. After a few minutes, it seemed as if everyone was finally in agreement.

Josef told Angelo that it was agreed that they would help him in his quest. "Micah has volunteered to lead you on your journey, and I will also accompany you. Tomorrow morning, we leave for the trip west."

Now Josef turned serious again and said, "Angelo, you must fully understand the danger that we will face. The mountains are home to a war lord who it is said will attack and rob and kill anyone who enters their homeland. No one goes there for fear of attack, but we will risk this to help a friend."

CHAPTER 10

Colavari spent another restless night. A series of questions played over and over in his mind as he lay on the blanket in Josef's tent. Would he finally find the men who had saved his life eleven years ago? Would he learn how they did it and what would he say to them? How do you thank someone who takes a broken and destroyed body and somehow makes it whole? He often asked himself if it really did happen, or if the doctors were right, and had he just dreamed it or hallucinated the entire experience? No, it had been real. He'd seen the blood and felt the agony of his broken bones.

When those thoughts left, he was haunted by the stories of bandits capturing and killing anyone they found on their mountain. Could they find the monks and avoid being taken prisoner? That was the only real concern he had as he tossed and turned. Finally, the night closed in and his thoughts slowed enough for him to finally fall asleep. He felt he had barely closed his eyes when Josef quietly called his name.

"Angelo, it is time for you to begin the search for your past. It is time for you to find the answers to the questions that have haunted you for all these years."

"I am a fortunate man to have you as a friend," Colavari said sincerely. "Regardless of what I find, or don't find, you made this possible." Josef smiled and bowed to his friend and silently slipped out the tent flap.

He wasn't sure what time it was, since the sun had not yet begun to rise, but there was much activity going on outside the tent. Josef's wives each had their job to do to prepare their husband for his day; for his journey. A fire burned and food was being prepared. He could smell the aroma of coffee and knew immediately that that was the most important thing he needed this morning to start him on his journey.

The small breakfast was good. He was surprised at how quickly he had adapted to fruit and bread for his morning meal. At home, it would have been eggs, peppers, and sausage followed by a piece of cake or pastry. This morning he ate less than half that much food and felt satisfied.

Micah arrived. He smiled and bowed to Colavari who responded in kind, greeting him with one of the few Ethiopian phrases Josef had taught him. "May Allah bless you and all who follow you."

Micah smiled broadly and repeated the greeting back to him. Then he spoke Angelo's name and appeared to be offering his own personal greeting, none of which Colavari understood. It really didn't matter at this point. There was a connection between Micah and his family and Colavari that crossed an obstacle as insignificant as language.

The three men sat and nursed their coffee while several of the elders silently gathered around the fire. There was no conversation, but they all appeared tense as they waited for the sun to rise and the men to begin their journey. Finally, the eastern horizon began to glow as if there was a great fire burning behind the dunes. Colavari continued to stare as the desert began to appear and come to life where, a moment before, there was only darkness; a total darkness unlike anything he had ever experienced before. As the sun continued to rise it made the sand in the distance appear to glimmer as if shimmering water. It was the most beautiful sunrise he could ever remember seeing. It may have been the desert, or being with the desert people, but he felt content and at peace.

Finally, it was time. Without speaking, the men began to stand as if by signal. Several women appeared with water skins and carried them to the camels that knelt quietly in the sand. A young boy fastened them to the saddles and then packed the small bundles of food and coffee in the packs on the camels' backs. After a thousand years surviving in the desert, they knew how much water and food would be needed for the journey and packed no more than was necessary.

When all was finally ready, the three men mounted the animals and were then signaled to rise. Colavari had to hold tight to the horn of the saddle out of fear of being thrown off as the beast lifted first the rear, and then the front of its enormous body. When he was finally standing, Colavari looked at the ground seven feet below him. As Micah and Josef signaled their animals to begin walking, Colavari's followed suit. They left to the sound of greetings and blessings shouted from the small group of villagers gathered to watch their departure.

The desert was as it should be, hot and dry. Colavari tried desperately to keep his head and face covered from the sun. He wasn't as dark-skinned as his companions, and it wouldn't take long for him to badly burn. They had started their journey early and stopped for the day as the sun reached its crest. They sat in the shade of their camels and slept as best they could.

Finally, after almost two full days in the desert, they reached the end of the sand and the terrain began to rise slowly, becoming hard and rocky. Here they dismounted and tethered the camels to several small trees. The animals slowly lowered themselves to the ground. They were used to being tied and wouldn't attempt to break free. Since the sun was beginning to set behind the mountains, they decided to camp there until morning before beginning their climb. They built a fire and, after a small meal, the long journey finally took its toll on the three men. One by one they settled on the hard ground and fell soundly asleep.

The fire burned out overnight and the morning cold of the desert awoke the men early. After coffee, some cheese, and hard bread, the men began their climb up the side of the mountain, disappearing beneath the green canopy of the trees. Each man carried a water skin and enough food to last them until the following morning, in case they were stranded on the mountain overnight. They had no idea in which direction they would walk, so they randomly chose an area that looked the least demanding.

As they slowly made their way around and over trees and fallen limbs, Colavari constantly looked for any sign that might tell him they were heading in the right direction. There was no opening amongst the trees as had been when he crashed. He kept hoping to spot a piece of his plane or something that would identify the area. After a few hours, he realized that this didn't have to be the exact spot where he had crashed. It could have been anywhere on this mountain. You couldn't expect to walk into the crash site right away.

As they climbed, Colavari studied each step they took, looking for anything that might remind him of the climb he had made with his rescuers years ago, but nothing looked familiar. He smiled at his own naivety. "Eleven years have passed. Did you really think that nature would stand still until you returned?" They were far into the tree line and slowly going uphill. They had already passed over any flat ground where his plane could have finally come to rest after the crash. He thought that if they climbed high enough he might be able to look back down and possibly see something worth exploring.

After about an hour of climbing, they stopped to rest. It was still and quiet as they drank water and looked about their surroundings. Colavari passed his pack of cigarettes amongst his companions and they smoked in silence. They'd seen nothing of interest so far; nothing to indicate there was anyone around. It seemed as if they were the first to walk through this section of the woods. Josef seemed to read his friend's mind.

"This does not look like a spot for the Tekelakayochi to live. After hundreds of years, the ground would have been worn down to at least show us a path."

Micah spoke to Josef and pointed around at the area. Josef waited until he stopped and then replied. Although Colavari was beginning to pick up a few words, they spoke too quickly for him to really understand what was being said.

When Josef was done speaking, he turned back to Colavari, "Micah thinks we should climb for a short while further and then descend and try another area to climb. I think he is right," Josef offered. "We may be on the correct side of the mountain, but we could be off by several miles or more. It will be best to climb in a few more areas, and if we don't find something, we can move to another."

"That makes sense. No point in climbing too far the wrong way," Colavari added. "If we don't find something within an hour's climb we can begin again in another location." The men agreed that they had climbed far enough and would descend and look for a more promising area. After another hour of climbing without seeing anything worth exploring, the men turned and slowly made their way back down to where they had first started. They moved further east for several hundred yards until they found another area that could be considered the beginning of a trail.

This path proved to be much more difficult than it first appeared, and it wasn't long before they realized there could be no trail here. No man could walk up from here. They again descended and returned to their starting point, stopping to eat a brief meal before they were to begin the next attempt. Traveling further east, they walked another hundred yards or so before finding anything that could be considered an opening or path leading up the mountain. Of the three areas they had chosen, this looked the most promising.

The climb was steady and fairly easy to navigate. It wasn't as steep as the other two and appeared to widen the higher they climbed. After almost an hour, they came upon a clearing that appeared to have been used in the not-too-distant past. The ground showed signs of someone having walked through there recently. The only question on Colavari's mind was whether it was the path leading to the holy men, or a path leading to the bandits and their capture, or to something far worse yet. They decided to take a break there, and with the afternoon sun already passing over them, they would probably make camp and continue in the morning.

As they rested, they were completely unaware of the movements taking place around them. A group of men hidden amongst the trees began to spread out and encircle Colavari and his companions, without the slightest noise.

CHAPTER 11

Suddenly, and without warning, six men appeared, each one carrying a World War II Italian infantry rifle. They approached from three sides and stood staring at their captives. Colavari and his companions froze, making certain to make no threatening moves.

"So, the bandits do exist," he thought, "and we have found them, or, more accurately, they have found us. Now what?" One of the men spoke to Josef. He seemed to be in charge of the group. Josef and Micah nodded as they sat back on the ground. Josef motioned for Colavari to sit as well and quietly told him not to attempt anything. He said the men were going to take them to their leader who would decide their fate.

That said, two of the men laid down their rifles and approached the seated men. They pulled out strips of leather and began to tie the wrists of Colavari and his companions. After they were through, the one in charge spoke and another nodded, stepping away from the group. Josef leaned towards Colavari to speak. The leader yelled at Josef who replied with several words before the leader nodded and turned back to the man who stood away from the group.

"Angelo, the leader wanted to know what I was saying to you. He does not understand English or Italian. I told him that I wanted you to know everything that was happening so that you would do nothing to make them suspicious or angry. He agreed and said to tell you he was leaving one man to guard us, while the others returned to advise their leader of our capture. The guard has been told to shoot any of us who attempt to escape." Colavari looked at the leader and nodded his understanding.

The men were of varying ages, from what appeared to be early 20s to the leader who looked to be in his mid-40s. They were lean and appeared hard from having lived in the mountains. Each man was dressed in the clothing for this particular region: robes, vests, and sandals. The leader was the only one who spoke, and when he did, the others quickly nodded their understanding and then returned their gaze to their captives.

Colavari looked from man to man, trying to read in their faces what they planned for him and his companions.

"Josef, I'm sorry that I got you and Micah into this. I should have gone on alone and taken the risks myself without placing you both in such danger." His mind raced as he searched for a way out of this, at least for Josef and Micah.

"Tell them, if they will let you two go, I will pay them a ransom. More money than they would get from the three of us now."

Josef smiled at his friend. "We are beyond that point, Angelo. They have no use for money here. All they are interested in are our camels and whatever we have brought with us."

The leader quickly approached Josef and raised the butt of his rifle as if to strike him, but then stopped. He spoke to the two men and they both nodded their understanding. He turned his attention to Colavari and then to his companions. This time his voice was soft yet threatening. When he finished, Josef told Colavari that the man had said he wanted to kill them right now, but their leader would have to make that decision. He was going back to see if he should bring us to their camp or kill us right here."

After some additional conversation between the leader and the guard, he left with the remaining four men and disappeared into the trees. They left as quietly as they had first arrived, not a sound was heard. Colavari was resigned to his fate. He knew what he faced when he started this journey and had been willing to take the risks. But now he felt guilty at having brought his two companions along on a trip they had only accepted as a sign of friendship. He'd been in the war and had seen death. For whatever reason, he had been given an eleven-year extension on his life and was prepared to face his destiny. But Josef and Micah were innocent and should be back with their families.

The man left to guard them was relaxed, knowing that his prisoners were bound and couldn't move without great effort. He could afford a little down time until the leader came back, and a decision had been made. He pulled a bottle from his pack, removed the cork, and took a long drink. The expression on his face as he swallowed told the three men that what he drank was not water. After a short time, he began to show signs of sleepiness, resting his head against a tree and closed his eyes. Every so often, he would awake with a start and look quickly around as if looking to see if the others had returned. Each time he closed his eyes he remained motionless for longer periods of time.

During one of these naps, Micah leaned close to Josef and softly spoke while keeping his eyes on the guard. Josef leaned towards Colavari and whispered that Micah's bindings were beginning to loosen.

"Just sit quietly so we don't wake the guard while Micah tries to free his hands." After a few minutes, Micah again leaned into Josef and spoke. This time, Josef turned himself ever so slightly towards Micah as he moved closer to him. Although there was barely any movement at all, Colavari realized that Micah had freed his hands and was attempting to untie Josef's. Suddenly, Josef sat up straight and smiled at Colavari. His hands were free!

Now it was Colavari's turn. Just before they turned their backs to one another, the guard suddenly woke and looked around. All three thought they had been discovered and that the guard must have seen them get free, but, after a few moments, they realized that he had just woken on his own. He glanced at his prisoners and then settled back against his tree.

They waited a few moments until they felt the guard had again fallen asleep, and then Colavari and Josef repositioned themselves so that Josef could reach the other man's bonds. His fingers worked quickly and, in less than a minute, Colavari was also free. Now what could they do? The guard slept with the rifle across his lap, and, although it was an old bolt action gun that fired one round at a time, it was likely that one of them would be shot if they tried to overpower him.

It was Colavari who came up with the escape plan. He leaned into Josef and whispered his idea. "Tell the guard that you will give him the gold you have if he will let us go free. If he comes to take the gold from you, we will have a chance to grab him." Josef smiled and nodded. In turn he leaned over to Micah and shared the idea. Micah nodded his understanding. After a few minutes Josef called to the guard who appeared startled until he realized the voice was from one of his prisoners.

Josef looked pleadingly at the guard and offered him the gold he carried in exchange for their freedom. The guard was immediately interested and rose from his spot next to the tree.

Smiling broadly, the guard laughed. "You fool! I can take the gold without having to let you go," he told Josef. With that, he approached the men and knelt down in front of Josef to search for the treasure. In order to get close enough, he had to straighten the rifle and rest the butt on the ground with the barrel pointed carelessly skyward. As the guard reached towards him, Josef leaned back a little as if afraid of the man. The guard leaned closer and was a little off balance as Josef reached out and grabbed the front of his robe and pulled the man towards him with Colavari and Micah attacking from both sides. The guard had no chance to defend himself and was quickly pinned to the ground while Colavari grabbed his rifle. The man looked terrified as he was held tightly by his former prisoners. Josef spoke to the man who eventually nodded and relaxed in their grasp.

"I told him we didn't want to hurt him and if he didn't try to fight or yell out we would just tie him and leave him for his friends to find when they returned. He wants to live so I think he will do as we say," Josef volunteered. With that, Josef removed his hand from the guard's mouth and, true to their agreement, the man didn't make a sound. The three men quickly bound the guard's hands and feet with their former restraints and Colavari tied his handkerchief tightly around the man's mouth as an added precaution in the event the man should change his mind and yell for help before they could make good their escape.

Without any discussion, the three men prepared to make their descent down the mountain. What had taken them almost an hour to climb and reach would take them much less going down. Their motivation now was one of self-preservation and no longer exploration. Running down the side of the mountain took concentration and, more importantly, agility. There was no point in running blindly and risk a fall that could leave one of them injured and easy prey. They stumbled and bumped into trees as they tried to negotiate their way to the bottom. Every few minutes, they would stop and listen for anyone that might be coming down behind them.

So far, the woods were quiet. Colavari thought they might have a slight edge over their captors since their hands were free and could help guide them past the endless obstacles while their pursuers would be carrying rifles and would have use of only one hand. They worked their way down, and, after what seemed like hours, the woods began to get brighter and they realized that they were fast approaching the bottom. There was still a little further to go when they heard the shouts of men far behind them. The bandits had returned and learned of their escape and were most likely in quick pursuit to capture or kill them before they could get away.

But they had a good head start on their captors and were almost out of the trees. They just needed to stay focused and move as quickly and safely as possible. Suddenly, the bright sun momentarily blinded them as they finally reached the clear ground. Their haste in descending had caused them to drift off course so that they were still some distance from their camels. Despite having run steadily downhill, the adrenaline still gave them the added energy necessary to cover the distance to the tethered animals.

"Having to run this far west may buy us a few extra seconds if they followed our exact path down," Josef called. "They will have to wait until they are all down and then organize and try to locate us."

Running as fast as they could from the point where they cleared the trees, they reached the camels and quickly untied the beasts, and, within seconds, the two Ethiopians were on their animals and signaling them to stand. As the Ethiopian's camels began to stand, so did Colavari's before he could climb on its back. A similar, but reversed occurrence to the one in the village several days before when his camel refused to kneel for him to dismount. They could hear the voices getting closer, and, after several failed attempts at getting the camel to kneel, Angelo turned to his friends, "Leave! Go without me. I'll hide in the trees further down. With all three camels gone, they won't be looking for anyone and I'll wait for night and then head into the desert." Without a word, Josef rode next to Colavari and as his camel came abreast of the stubborn beast, he reached down with surprising strength lifting Colavari by the collar of his shirt and swung him onto the camel's back. There was no time for a thank you.

Just then, the bandits broke from the trees and stood for a few moments as their vision adjusted to the bright sunlight. Finally, they began looking around trying to determine which way their ex-prisoners had gone. This bought the three men just the time they needed to turn their animals back towards the desert and were quickly at full gallop. They could hear shouts and gunshots and realized the bandits had spotted them and were firing at them, but they were on foot and unable to chase after them.

Colavari looked back and saw the men gathering in the area they had just left. Instinctively, he and his two companions leaned forward across the necks of their camels so as to make as small a target as possible. Good luck was with them as none of the bullets found them or the animals. Within a few moments, the firing stopped and Colavari realized they must now be out of range of the old rifles.

This time there was no casual, easy ride back. They pushed the animals and themselves and arrived at the village in a little over a day, exhausted and hungry, but, more importantly, alive and unhurt.

CHAPTER 12

McFadden paused from his reading and realized it was time to break and eat something. He took the diary with him into the kitchen and continued to read as he heated some Chinese leftovers from earlier that week. While the food warmed in the pan McFadden read the final entries which covered the old man's last few weeks in Ethiopia.

After their return to the village there was much discussion amongst the men after hearing the details of the capture and subsequent escape by the three men. It was agreed that Allah had been watching over them and confirmed that the mountains were a place where no innocent man should venture. Colavari couldn't argue with their conclusions, and, while disappointed that he did not find what he was looking for, he was also happy that neither of his companions had been injured.

The search for the Tekelakayochi was over for Colavari; at least for now. He would return home and plan for his next attempt to search for his rescuers. The next day, Josef led him back to the oasis and returned the two camels to the friends who had loaned them. Colavari was surprised and pleased to find his jeep still there and under the watchful eye of Josef's Christian friends. In his absence, a large trading caravan had stopped at the oasis and one of the Christians had bargained for some of the gasoline they carried. In exchange for access to the water and some goat's milk and cheese, the traders not only filled the 5 5-

gallon gas cans, but also the vehicle's gas tank. When Colavari returned his jeep, he was fully prepared for the journey back to the capital.

He and Josef took a few minutes and walked off from the crowd around the oasis. It was time to say goodbye and each man appeared to be searching for the right words. Colavari reached for his wallet and attempted to give Josef the money they had agreed upon what seemed like years ago. Josef held up his hands and refused the wad of bills.

"When we made that agreement, you were just a man who needed a guide. Now you are my friend and friends are not paid for their loyalty. Go in peace, Angelo, and may Allah show his mercy on you. Remember, you are always welcome among us." Angelo thanked his new friend for all his generous help and promised to return the following year.

With that, Colavari started the old vehicle and turned south, headed for the seaport and the first step of his journey home. But Colavari did not return the next year, or any year thereafter. The entries became fewer in number, separated sometimes by months. There were the odd entries about his post-war life and the beginning of a family. It wasn't until he was a sick, old man, left with just his memories that his diary entries began to increase and look back on his life with greater detail. One of the final entries dealt with his conversation with Tom just prior to his nephew's departure to the United States. After talking with Tom, he felt rejuvenated and decided to send the diary to his nephew in the hope that the young man would be willing to continue the journey and find answers to the questions that had haunted him for all these years. McFadden finally closed the book and stared out the window as the sun slowly disappeared and night began its return.

"So much for some light reading."

The following morning McFadden called Marino and told him he had finished the diary. Tom said he would rather discuss McFadden's thoughts on the diary in person and set 2:00 pm as the time he would be back in Boston.

After Marino arrived and finished his first of many cups of coffee for that afternoon, the two men settled in McFadden's study. "Well, what do you think?" was the first question Marino asked. McFadden seemed to ponder the question before finally answering,

"I honestly don't know what to think. This is the most confusing and challenging experience I have ever heard of a man being involved in." He continued, "There is something mysterious going on behind all this. We have a story of two different people from two different worlds experiencing a similar and almost miraculous recovery from injuries that should have killed them. If I had read of only one of these episodes, I would have chalked it up to an imaginative storyteller or someone's day dreams. But this is too coincidental not to have some basis of fact."

Marino nodded and said, "The common denominator in both accounts are these men they call the Tekelakayochi. They appear to be a religious order of some sort, although I haven't been able to find anything on either of these names or groups. You would think we should be able to find some information on a monastery that existed as recently as World War II, yet I can't find anything written about them anywhere."

McFadden agreed, "They played such a significant part in the healing of two separate people and no one seems to have any idea who they are."

"How do you begin a search for a group of people with amazing healing powers that no one has seen for over 70 years?" Marino added. McFadden smiled and looked at his friend. "I don't know who they are, but I do know one very important thing."

"What's that?" Tom asked, as if already knowing the answer. McFadden didn't delay, "I know that you want to go and try to find the answer, and I know that I want to go with you."

Marino's face was suddenly covered with a grin that stretched from ear to ear, "I knew that would be your answer after you read the diary. We're going to go to Ethiopia and search for some magic medicine men regardless of how vague this whole story sounds, aren't we?"

McFadden casually replied, "Was there ever any doubt?"

It was settled. They would go to Ethiopia and search for Uncle Angelo and the young Ayinabeba's guardian angels. Suddenly, McFadden had that Cheshire cat grin on his face and looked at Tom and said, "There is one source for information I hadn't considered until just now."

The phone rang twice before Margaret McFadden answered. "Hello?" said a woman's strong voice. "Hi, Mom," McFadden's voice boomed in the receiver. "Frankie, how are you, sweetheart? What a nice surprise."

McFadden could almost hear his mother smile as she spoke to her only child. "How are you?" he asked. "How's Dad?"

"We're both fine. Are you coming for dinner on Sunday? I'm making a pot roast." His mother always knew how to get his attention — through his stomach.

"I don't know whether I can make it yet. Give me a day or two to work out a few things. In the meantime, Mom, I need your help. Tommy Marino and I are researching an incident that took place in Ethiopia in the mid-1930s and I need to talk to the most knowledgeable theologian or biblical scholar you know." He could feel his mother's confusion. McFadden wasn't a particularly religious man, and to ask her for the name of a theologian must really have started her wheels spinning.

"Well, I'm sure you'll tell me what this is all about when you think the time is right, even though I am your mother and you can tell me anything in confidence." McFadden laughed to himself. As bright and progressive a woman as Margaret McFadden was, he was still her son and she would always treat him as a child.

"Mom, I promise to tell you the whole story when I see you, but right now time is working against me and I need some information. Is there someone you can recommend?"

Margaret McFadden could hear the sense of urgency in her son's voice, hesitating only a moment before saying, "Father James Cleary.

He was the resident theology scholar at Salve Regina when I was working on my Master's. He's retired now and living somewhere near Springfield the last I knew. He must be over 90 years old by now, but he has the greatest mind I'd ever dealt with. He would be the man you want to talk with."

McFadden thought for a moment. "Mom, would you please try to locate him and make the introduction for Tom and me. We'd like to talk with him. This is kind of important." Margaret knew that he wouldn't be pushing this hard unless it was something really big.

"Let me try to reach him," she said, "and I'll call you right back." With that, his mother hung up and BB went back to his own research. Twenty minutes later, she called back. "Francis, I reached Father Cleary and asked him if he would be able to talk with you. He's such a sweet man, he said that he would make time to talk with the son of his best student," she announced with a little sense of pride.

McFadden smiled and said, "You always were the teacher's pet, weren't you?" She laughed back, "And it's still paying off!"

She gave her son Father Cleary's phone number and suggested he call right away in case the old priest should forget about the call. He thanked her and hung up after promising to call her about dinner on Sunday. McFadden hoped that the old priest would be able to provide them with some of the information they needed, despite his advanced years.

The phone was answered on the first ring and a strong, young-sounding male voice could be heard on the other end. McFadden assumed that the younger man must be the caretaker of the old theologian and asked if Father Cleary was available. "Is this Francis McFadden?"

"Yes, it is," he answered. "Is Father Cleary there?" The clear voice responded, "Yes, I'm Cleary." McFadden thought he must have the wrong Cleary. This was not the voice of a retired 93-year-old college professor.

"So, you're Margaret McCaffrey's son?" he said, using her maiden name. "Margaret said that you were researching a topic that required a religious perspective and that you were in a hurry."

"Well, yes, Father. I'm doing some research and my colleague and I would very much like to pick your brain on a few things we need clarified. Would you have time to meet with us?" There was a chuckle on the other end and the priest said, "Son, I'm 93 years old, retired, and live by myself. If there's anything that I do have plenty of, it's time. When can you be here?" he asked.

"We'll be there in about an hour and a half if it's alright with you," he replied. The priest then gave McFadden his address in Springfield. He and Marino were out of the house in less than 5 minutes.

CHAPTER 13

As they cruised across the Massachusetts Turnpike towards Springfield, they talked about just how much they should tell the priest. McFadden thought that it would actually depend on how much Father Cleary really knew. In a little under two hours McFadden pulled up in front of a classic white colonial house on a quiet street lined with enormous oak trees. The two men walked up the driveway and followed the path to the front door. Before they could press the bell, the door opened quickly and a tall man with thick, grey hair extended his hand. "James Cleary, and you must be Francis."

It took McFadden a few seconds to process what he was seeing. The man who opened the door stood as tall as McFadden but had the build of a football player. His broad shoulders and trim waist showed a man who looked 63, not 93 years old. He was agile and moved with the quick grace of an athlete. McFadden introduced Tom and they all shook hands. Father Cleary's grasp was strong and he looked McFadden directly in the eyes.

"I'm glad you boys could make it down today," he said. "I was going to play golf this afternoon, but I lost $20 yesterday when I played my neighbor and I think he cheats." He smiled and added, "I can't prove it but, if I ever catch him. I'll probably crack him in the mouth and that would get me kicked out of the country club. Since I'm the oldest man in the neighborhood, and the only retired priest, they gave me a free membership. It doesn't hurt that the club president and the treasurer were former students. Anyway, you didn't come here to discuss my golf game."

Father Cleary offered them chairs in the living room. "I have a fresh pot of coffee on. Will you both join me?" He went into the kitchen before either of them could answer.

The two men looked at one another and Tom whispered, "I don't know about this. I was expecting an old wrinkled priest in a monk's robe sitting in a room surrounded by books with candles burning for light." Before McFadden could answer, Father Cleary returned with a tray with three steaming mugs and set them on the coffee table separating him from his guests.

"Before we begin, how is your mother doing?" he asked. McFadden answered that she was in great health and keeps herself quite busy with volunteer work outside the house. Father Cleary nodded, "She was one of the best students I had, although she could be a pain in the ass at times with her never-ending questions." McFadden laughed at the candor of the priest, but agreed that she hadn't changed that much over the years.

Finally, the priest became serious. "Alright, Francis, what is it that's brought you boys to see an old college professor on a beautiful Saturday afternoon?"

"Father, please call me BB. All my friends do," McFadden offered. Marino quickly added, "And you can call me Tom."

"Okay then, BB and Tom, what are you looking for?"

"Father, we're doing some research on Tom's uncle who was shot down in 1936 during Italy's war with Ethiopia. Tom is an archeologist and a few questions have come up for which we can't find any answers. McFadden watched the priest's face for any reaction to the vague beginning of their story. "Father, in our research we have come across the name of what we believe is a religious group, the Protectors. There have been stories of the healing powers this group apparently possessed and we'd like to know if you've ever heard of them."

Father Cleary was quiet and studied McFadden and Marino for several moments before finally speaking. "Before I answer your questions, I have to ask why a physicist and an archeologist are interested in an old story of the early church. What could make this group significant to anyone's research today?" McFadden was at a crossroad. How much do I tell this man, and would he even believe me?

"Father, our intent when we came here was to tell you as little as we could, and then, if necessary, only a partial truth. But, as a scholar, I think we owe you more than that," he paused before continuing. "If you'll tell us as much as you know about the history, or legend, of this group, I promise to share the rest of the story."

Father Cleary smiled, "That's fair enough."

The priest settled back in his big chair and looked over McFadden's head at a spot on the far wall. After what seemed like several minutes, he focused his gaze back on McFadden. "Are you familiar with the Council of Nicaea held in 325 AD?" McFadden indicated that he was, and Marino just smiled with a shrug. "In 305 AD, Emperor Constantine became the first Christian leader of the Roman empire."

Father Cleary settled deep into his plush recliner and the words came out easier as if he was reading from a book. He told of the turmoil at that time amongst the Christian leaders, and the varying beliefs and doctrines that were being preached to the many Christian sects across the empire. The pivotal question was whether Jesus was divine, and, if so, how? What was Jesus' relationship with God? In order to quell this dissent and bring peace and harmony, Constantine called for a council of the Christian leadership to be held at Nicaea in Turkey in the summer of 325 AD. More than 300 Christian bishops from across the empire came to Nicaea where Constantine was determined to finally resolve the differences of the various sects and establish a unified religion.

Father Cleary paused and looked intently from one man to the other. "Boys, this was a very confusing and violent period for the church. Christians were fighting Christians over matters of unofficial doctrine and teachings. Constantine was a brilliant leader, but, more importantly, he was an even better politician. He carefully maneuvered the council into a vague agreement that Jesus and God were of the same substance without going into too much detail as to the relationship of the two."

"This may sound like a simple solution today, but in 325 AD this was a monumental achievement and a compromise accepted by the majority of those gathered. This became known as the Nicene Creed and it was to become the focal point from which all future laws were modeled. I tell you this part of history in order for you to better understand the accompanying discussions regarding the group you spoke of."

"At this council it was also decided that the numerous gospels available would be reviewed by the assembly, and a vote would take place on which of these would be accepted for inclusion in the new Christian bible, or what we now call the New Testament. There were dozens and dozens of gospels presented. Most were written in Hebrew but there were many in Greek, and some in Coptic, the language of the Egyptian Christians. Each of the many gospels was read and the bishops voted on those that would be included, and those that would be left out.

The decision process had as much to do with politics as it did with accepted religious belief. Those that portrayed Christ as a mortal man went against the belief that he was the Son of God and were excluded." Father Cleary was quiet for a moment as if gathering his thoughts. "The bishops voted to include those gospels that painted the best picture of Jesus, His mother, and His followers."

"Amongst the gospels reviewed, and eventually excluded, was one said to have been written by an Abyssinian called Henok. The gospel talked of the crucifixion and the death of Christ and the vigil kept by His mother and His followers. The gospel spoke of the sky darkening and lightning and thunder crashing all around them when Christ finally died, just as had been mentioned in several of the other gospels. Henok spoke in detail of how the apostle Timothy walked past the confused and uneasy Roman soldiers and picked up Christ's robe from the foot of the cross. A soldier appeared ready to stop him from leaving but drew back in fear as Timothy looked up to the sky and a clap of thunder boomed directly over his head. The soldier joined the others as they went about removing the bodies of the two thieves crucified with Christ."

"According to Henok, the robe stayed in the possession of Peter for years until his arrest by the Romans. During that time, it was believed to have been used to heal the sick and injured and began to be seen as a direct connection to Jesus, who, it was believed, was healing through the robe." The priest went on as if conducting a lecture for his students, and without the benefit of any notes.

"Henok wrote that the robe transferred from apostle to apostle after Peter's death in an ongoing attempt to keep it from the hands of the Romans. No mention has ever been made in the gospels as to who finally took possession of the robe, or if it ever survived the apostles' efforts to protect its existence," he added.

"For this reason alone, the bishops voted that the Gospel of Henok be excluded, since it tended to place religious importance on an object, not unlike Pagan beliefs. Although excluded from the bible, the gospel was widely circulated amongst the others in attendance." The priest explained that many who disagreed with the bishops placed significant importance on this only known reference to a possession of Christ.

By this time, McFadden and Marino were both seated on the edge of their chairs, as if trying to get closer to the priest so as to get the information out faster.

"The Henok gospel tells of the robe being secreted out of Israel and taken to a place far enough away to hopefully keep it out of the hands of the Romans, who sought to eliminate any additional mention of the new Christian God. Since the gospel was identified as the book of Henok the Abyssinian, the logical conclusion was that the robe ultimately made its way to Africa, and, more likely, to what is now Ethiopia. The gospel ends with the robe being entrusted to a group whose job it was to protect it with their lives. They would be known as the Protectors, or in Amharic, the Tekelakayochi. Although highly unlikely, it's a great story that the church allowed to disappear from record almost seventeen hundred years ago."

Father Cleary said that, while many of the rejected gospels were bound into a book of holy writings, the Gospel of Henok and dozens more were destroyed. "This was a great tragedy since some of those documents might well have contained bits and pieces of information that today might help to answer some of the questions that still remain unanswered about Christ and His life."

Father Cleary paused. "Well, boys, that's a crash course in the selection of the gospels of the New Testament. It doesn't answer the question of whether the robe ever existed outside the imagination of Henok or not, but many would like to believe that this connection to Christ actually was once a reality.

"Now it's your turn," he said. "Tell me why you're so interested in a two-thousand-year-old story of a group of men dedicated to protecting a religious artifact that, in all likelihood, never actually existed?"

Marino and McFadden sat, unable to speak or move. Marino tried to talk but nothing came out. McFadden was the first to gather his composure enough to begin to answer the priest's question. "Father, I would ask that what we're about to tell you be kept in the strictest confidence until such a time when it can be shared with a much greater audience." Father Cleary nodded solemnly and McFadden was comfortable that their discussion would go no further.

"Before we go on, can you tell us how it is that you know so much about the Gospel of Henok if it was destroyed more than two thousand years ago? If the Council rejected it due to its content and it was ultimately destroyed with the rest of the omitted documents, where did you learn of its original existence?" McFadden looked the priest clearly in the eyes, "Father, please don't take my questioning as if we're doubting the validity of what you've told us. That's not the case at all."

Marino picked up the lead. "Father Cleary, it's just that BB and I are pretty good researchers and we haven't been able to locate anything about this group other than my uncle's diary entries, claiming that they might have existed as recently as some 70 years ago, but for what reason we don't know. Where did you learn of them?"

The priest was quiet for several moments, looking almost as if he were deciding whether or not to share a secret. Finally, he began, his voice soft and guarded as one immensely focused, appearing to carefully choose his words. "Boys," he started, "this is difficult for me to share with you, but for some reason I believe I need to be more candid with you than I have even been with myself for many, many years."

I've been a priest for almost 70 years. During that time, I have been faithful to my vows and loyal to my vocation, but I haven't been an especially successful priest or productive to any parish, church, or congregation. Early on in my life, as a young priest. I recognized that what I really wanted was to study, do research, and write. My superiors seemed to recognize that as well, and so, after several years of bouncing from parish to parish, I was given the freedom to study and teach."

McFadden sat quietly as the priest gathered his thoughts, and found he was becoming a little uncomfortable as Father Cleary spoke so candidly about his life. It was as if he were confessing his failures and limitations to the two young men who sat opposite him.

Father Cleary began again. "Over the next ten years or so, I did research and internally published papers on various topics, occasionally selecting topics that where, at times, considered controversial. Along the way, I pissed off a lot of people in the church hierarchy here in the US. Fortunately, I also gained the support of several influential men at the Vatican in Rome, who shielded and protected me from those who saw some of my writings as challenging Church doctrine, or questioning the Church's position on matters of faith or belief."

The priest paused and poured himself another cup of coffee and topped off the cups of his guests. After several small sips from the cup he seemed ready to resume his story, almost as if the coffee fortified him to continue.

"Finally," he continued, "my guardian angel, Cardinal Carmine DeAngelo, brought me to the Vatican where I was given access to centuries of old documents and writings and free rein to study and conduct research on any area that I found of interest. To this day, I still don't know what made an old Italian cardinal take a brash, opinionated young priest from the US under his wing and shield him from his detractors. Through his secretary, Monsignor Eugene Murphy —

another US born priest — doors to the vast collection of church writings were opened to me. Over the next eight or so years, I lived in dark libraries and document vaults pouring over old scrolls and hand-written letters that had not been touched for hundreds of years. Much of what I found and read had long been forgotten or misplaced. It was during this time that I came across the first mention of the Tekelakayochi."

"While the Gospel of Henok had been destroyed, as I mentioned earlier, it had been widely circulated amongst many during the Council of Nicaea, and a few of those had documented in their own writings what they had read. In several old writings, I found references by others in attendance at the Council regarding Henok's claim that the robe had been saved. While the authors of these documents didn't necessarily express a strong belief in the story, they fortunately recognized the need to include this account for later consideration. That's where I spent several years of my life going over writings from various sources, some of whom eventually became powerful influences in the direction of the church for decades following the council."

It was obvious that the telling of this story was taking its toll on the old priest, but he continued. "Without any false sense of modesty, it was during this period that I became an *expert* on the possible existence of the robe of Christ and its journey out of Israel. As I gathered together the evidence of my years of research and prepared to publish what I felt would be groundbreaking evidence, my protected existence ended. Cardinal DeAngelo died, and with his death came the end to my research and signaled my ultimate return to the States, minus my research notes which were considered too controversial to be made public." With a sigh of resignation, the priest came to the end of his story. "I was eventually assigned to Salve Regina College where I spent the remainder of my career as priest and teacher, unable to share my research with anyone."

McFadden and Tom looked at each other and Marino nodded. He turned to the priest, "Father, several months ago I came into possession of a diary begun by my now-deceased uncle more than 70 years ago. An old diary wouldn't hold much interest but this one detailed the life-threatening injuries my uncle sustained in a plane crash in Ethiopia in 1936." They could sense the change in Father Cleary's attitude. Where the priest had recently sat with an expression of mild curiosity, was now replaced by one of complete focus and concentration.

Marino recounted Angelo Colavari's experiences in 1936 and, again, those that took place 11 years later upon his return to Ethiopia when he spoke to the young Ethiopian girl who had been critically burned and then healed. He told him of the legend of the Tekelakayochi coming every 10 years to accept a new addition to their religious group.

He was silent for a moment to allow the priest to process what he had just been told. "Father, based on what you've just told us and the story recounted in my uncle's diary, this all seems to make sense. We've been thinking that the common thread between these two stories were the men who somehow healed the critically injured. But if what you've told us is true, then it's always been the blanket that was common to both accounts; the blanket that was laid across both Angelo Colavari and the young Ethiopian girl, Ayinabeba. The blanket is what was being protected. We now believe that the Tekelakayochi, the Protectors, were actually protecting the actual Robe."

"The Robe of Jesus Christ!"

CHAPTER 14

Father Cleary sat stunned by the story, speechless for some time. "Tom, I don't know what to say. Do you actually think this could be true? Could the robe of Christ be a reality and not just legend?"

McFadden looked at the face sitting across from him. Gone was the smart-talking, youthful priest. Instead, they now saw an old man of 93, confused and in shock. Here was a story that, if true, could confirm the existence of a God he had dedicated his entire life to.

"Father, I don't honestly know, but I can tell you that, if the Gospel of Henok was real, then this search has suddenly gotten new direction and commitment," Tom answered.

The three men sat quietly for some time before the old Cleary returned. "Boys, if I was fifty years younger, I would be begging you to take me along. But as it is, all I can do is wish you the very best of luck in your search and wait impatiently for your return. I hope you'll let me know how it all turns out and if you actually find the robe."

"Father, I promise we'll come back and tell you the whole story once we return. Your information is invaluable and now makes you a part of this quest. We'll be in touch regardless of what we find, or don't find." After a few minutes of Farther Cleary swearing not to tell a soul until McFadden and Marino returned, they left the priest and headed back to Boston.

Neither man spoke for quite some time as they drove back to Boston. McFadden watched the traffic around him, but his mind was thousands of miles away in Ethiopia. He replayed Father Cleary's words over and over again as if to make sure their meeting had actually occurred and that he had not dreamed it.

Tom stared out the window at nothing in particular, considering the revelations Father Cleary had shared with them. This was the real deal now. This was no longer a story in some old soldier's diary, but a real lead to one of religion's most cherished relics. The only robe that could warrant that much protection and commitment after two thousand years, the most famous robe in history. If indeed it does exist, then we would have to be talking about the Robe of Jesus Christ.

Finally, Tom regained his focus. "BB, do you realize what we're talking about? The actual robe that Jesus Christ wore. The robe that the Roman soldiers gambled for at the foot of the cross. This wouldn't be just an archeological discovery; it would be the greatest historical find of all time. It would confirm the existence of Christ, confirm Christianity as a fact-based religion; no longer faith based. If the robe does exist, it would change the world's view of religion. Not to mention that you and I would go down as the greatest archeologists in the history of man."

McFadden looked across at Marino's beaming face before finally responding, "Tom, doesn't this frighten you, just a little bit? I can't even imagine what the effects of this discovery would mean. What would it do to the belief in religion in general? What impact would this have on the Muslims, the Jews, the Buddhists, and every other religion in the world? Christianity would take on a whole new meaning, and Catholicism would become the most influential religion on earth. Nothing would ever be the same."

"You're right," Tom answered. "This would be a scientist's greatest dream. His greatest achievement, to discover something most believe never existed."

McFadden added, "But I just can't imagine a 2000-year-old cloth robe with miraculous healing powers in the hands of a bunch of monks in the mountains in the 21st century. How did it travel more than 1500 miles from Israel to Ethiopia almost two thousand years ago? Where did these Protectors come from? Who organized them, and why hasn't anyone seen or heard from them in all this time? If it does exist today, why is the robe being hidden in the mountains in Africa and not in the possession of the Vatican?"

Marino looked at his friend and smiled. "Easy, big guy! Are you having doubts about our trip before we even start?"

"No! Maybe! I'm not sure," he replied. "I'm just getting a little ahead of myself, here. I'm trying to see how this discovery would affect civilization today. The US alone is going through a period where religion is being forced out of our daily lives. First, it was prayer in school, and then the Pledge of Allegiance, and then they wanted to remove "In God We Trust" from our currency. We're in a society that doesn't want to believe in any God. What would this mean to the rest of the world?"

He thought for a few minutes. "There are just so many questions that need answering that I'm having trouble putting my arms around the whole thing." McFadden gave him a broad smile, "Okay, you're right. One step at a time! First thing we have to do is organize the trip to Ethiopia and come up with some sort of game plan for when we get there. If the robe does exist, and if we find it, then we'll have to deal with these questions. The main thing right now is that no one else can know what we're looking for or why we're going. I think the story of researching your uncle's experiences during the war and his crash and survival appear pretty sound. We'll just have to trust that Father Cleary is a man of his word and will keep everything we've told him in confidence until we can finish our search."

CHAPTER 15

The next several weeks were spent organizing what they would need, what they should bring, and what they could get, once there, that might be needed. It was agreed that they wouldn't bring too much gear so as not to attract any unnecessary attention. They applied for their visas and listed the reason for their trip as tourists on their way to research family history.

During this preparation time, McFadden began to accumulate as much data as he could that dealt with Ethiopia during Angelo's time there. He began by obtaining aerial maps of the mountain area where Colavari believed he was hit and eventually crashed in 1936. He found old maps of the area and compared them to current views he found on Google Earth. He was amazed at what could be found online if you had the time and patience to do some research. He was able to find a web site that contained the specifications of most of the planes used during World War II, including the Breda Ba 65-, the plane the Italians used during the war with Ethiopia. What followed were long nights of comparing flight plans, fuel consumption, and maximum range for the fighter plane.

About a week before they were scheduled to depart for Addis Ababa, the two men sat in McFadden's kitchen comparing notes. When they had decided that they would go to Ethiopia, they developed a list of the types of information they'd like to have before they arrived. McFadden and Marino split the list and went about their own research.

McFadden became serious. "As our departure date draws nearer, I realize that we're pretty well prepared with our basic supplies and the general location of where your uncle believes he went down. But we have to remember, he was wounded, in shock, and losing a lot of blood." McFadden stopped and looked Marino squarely in the eyes. "I don't know how much we can depend on as fact when we read his account."

Marino was silent as McFadden continued. "Initially, I thought our best approach would be to try and duplicate your uncle's flight that day and see if we can locate where they were hit by the Ethiopian machine gunners, and then go from there. But regardless of what your uncle wrote, we really don't have much information at all. He could have been anywhere, and we have no way of knowing if we're even on the right side of the mountains. I think our better approach would be to try and locate the spot where Spinoza's plane was found and then use that as our starting point," McFadden offered. "At least we'll know that we're in the general area. Uncle Angelo could only have flown so far from that spot."

"That's a lot of territory to cover. What are the odds of locating that spot after 70 years?" Marino thought out loud. "We could be there for months, or a lifetime." Marino thought for a few seconds. "I've been trying to find any mention of the 1st Flight Wing of the 2nd Fighter Command during their time in Ethiopia. There's not much out there on the Internet. I think it's because Italy doesn't want to be reminded of their treatment of the Ethiopians during the 1930's. I've found a little about their efforts during WWII, but I'm drawing a blank on anything before that. I'll keep searching."

They decided to continue their individual research and get together again the following evening. Over the next 24-hours, Marino lived in front of his computer and used every search engine available in an attempt to locate some information on the 1st Flight Wing in Ethiopia. After hours approaching the problem from one direction, he would switch his focus and attack it from another. After several frustrating and disappointing hours with no positive results, he finally found a site that contained much of the information he needed, but documented for an entirely different reason.

At 8:00 pm the next evening, the two men met again in McFadden's kitchen to compare notes once more. The table was covered with maps, reference books, and stacks of handwritten notes. Marino said that he had been able to access a lot of the war information maintained by the Italian Army and Air Force on the Internet. The Air Force, it seemed, maintained fairly thorough records on their strategic and tactical efforts before and during World War II. The record keeping seemed to have suffered significantly once Germany abandoned them late in the war, but that really didn't affect the timeline they were concerned with.

Marino appeared excited as he continued to talk about his research and what he'd uncovered. "Just by accident I found an obscure website written in Italian. Thank God my mother forced us to speak Italian in the house growing up. Anyway, I found a section that contained documents detailing the successes of the Air Force from the late 1920s right up to and through the beginning of WWII."

McFadden was caught up in the excitement. "Please tell me there was information in there that dealt with Ethiopia." Marino only smiled. "Patience, grasshopper!"

Marino went on, "It appears they accumulated mountains of data to use as educational tools for young pilots entering into service during 1935 to 1939. In addition to a logistical record of their available and required equipment, the Air Force maintained a list dealing with aircraft losses and their cause. They used this information as a training tool to help show the young cadets what types of mistakes the pilots may have made that contributed to a crash or to being shot down. Since they lost so few aircrafts in the Ethiopian campaign, they accurately documented not only where planes went down, but also what they felt was the cause for the loss." Marino looked at McFadden and smiled broadly.

He didn't speak for several seconds and finally McFadden asked, "What makes you so happy?"

Marino's smile grew bigger. "In one of the sections I found a copy of a report by a search and rescue team whose job it was to rescue downed pilots or, when necessary, recover their remains. The report was dated October 4, 1936. He picked up a sheet of paper and read. "Located the crash site - Lt. C. Spinoza: multiple bullet wounds most likely resulting in death before impact - Aircraft a total loss."

"You've got to be kidding. Does it say where they found Spinoza's plane?" he asked excitedly.

Marino looked at his notes. "All it says is that the plane was found approximately 167 miles northwest of the air base. That would place the plane somewhere in, or near, the mountains. That should be the general starting area for our search. If we can find that spot, then we have a place to jump off from."

McFadden reached across the table and pinched Marino's right cheek, "you're a good boy, Tommy," just like Momma Rizzo used to do to them when they were kids. "That's got to save us weeks of blindly searching for a starting point."

McFadden's research on the performance specifications of the Breda that the two young Italians had been flying back in 1936 would help them to limit the outbound path of Angelo's plane after being hit, especially since it was mortally wounded. He had determined what the plane's range would have been and the average cruising speed the two pilots would have flown to reach the area near the beginning of the Simien Mountain range, where they spotted the supply train.

"Once we find the place where Spinoza went down, we can try to come up with a maximum range for Angelo's plane from there," McFadden added.

"Don't get yourself wound up over this, BB, we're looking for an area that is probably overgrown or hidden under decades of Mother Nature spreading herself in all directions," Tom said.

"Are you giving up before we even begin?" McFadden challenged. He leaned back and took a deep breath. "I know I'm making this sound like an easy task, but I'm feeling a lot better about finding your uncle's crash site now that we have a lead on locating Spinoza's plane."

Marino was more upbeat. "This is no different than digging in Egypt or South America. First, we identify where we think the tomb is hidden, and then we just keep expanding our search area until we find something that points us in the right direction, one goal at a time. At least we don't have to dig under tons of sand or hack through miles of jungle trying to find a clue from thousands of years ago."

Colavari's diary said they had traveled about 150 miles when he had spotted the supply train, yet the Air Force documents recorded they'd traveled at least 167 miles. A few miles off either way could add many more miles to their search. McFadden had used the Internet to locate a site where he could view photos of the old forts and camps established in Ethiopia by the Italians prior to World War II. Using the maps and Colavari's description, he was able to locate the only airfield within 200 miles southeast of the Simien Mountains, the Pagalori Air Base, home of both the 9th and 11th Fighter Squadrons — Colavari's unit.

He printed out a copy of the map and blew it up to where he could clearly see the terrain highlights. Using the map's stated scale, he drew a line from the center of the base to an area approximately 167 miles north northwest of the airfield. The Breda Ba 65 had a fuel capacity of 1,586 liters, or 419 US gallons. She had a top speed of 258 miles per hour at 16,400 feet, and at the average fighter altitude of 13,000 feet, the plane could cruise at approximately 223 miles per hour. The cruising speed at sea level dropped significantly to 186 miles per hour.

Based on accounts written by other World War II fighter pilots, McFadden learned that, when scouting for ground forces, most pilots liked to drop their cruising speed to between 80 and 90 knots per hour at roughly 3000 feet to allow for better scanning of the search areas.

This meant that, if Colavari and Spinoza were traveling within the normal cruising speed, the search for Spinoza's plane could be somewhere within a 20-mile range; even *if* his calculations were correct, 20 square miles was a massive area. So many things could have affected their distance, weather, altitude, fuel consumption, mechanical condition of the planes, etc.

McFadden told Marino what he'd found so far, and Marino was about to mention that this would make the search more realistic, but still an imposing project, when he smiled and caught himself before McFadden could give him the dope slap.

"If we try to do this on the ground we'll be there for months, just as you said," McFadden offered. "I'm going to try and narrow the search area based on the data I've gotten on the plane's capabilities and your uncle's comments. After we've reduced the area to be covered, I think we can begin to look for sites that might generally fit the description."

"The best way for us to begin looking will be from the air," McFadden said. "If we can come up with a general flight path, we can fly the route and take pictures and try to compare them to your uncle's sketches and the terrain maps. Once we have a few likely spots we can hire a vehicle and scout the area on foot."

"Sounds like a plan," Marino agreed.

CHAPTER 16

Three days later, the men were checking through security at Logan airport in Boston and heading for the departure gate. Each had a carry-on bag containing what they thought would be necessary for their trip. Marino had his Kindle, and McFadden had his stack of research notes and maps. Once he was focused on a project, it was difficult for him to put it aside. The flight to Addis Ababa would take the two men more than 15 hours onboard KLM Airlines flight number 1132. The air fare was surprisingly reasonable at just under $1800 round trip. That was good since they were not being sponsored or supported by any university or organization. They'd be footing the entire cost of this expedition themselves. For a brief moment, they had toyed with the idea of requesting funds from Boston College, or possibly National Geographic, but had decided against it. No, they would have to share way too much information before a decision would be made and they chose not to risk losing control of the search or being delayed in leaving.

Fortunately, they both had acquired enough frequent flyer miles over the years from KLM's mileage partners to enable them to fly business class. They would need the ability to recline and sleep during the long flight so that they would be rested and ready to begin the first steps of their journey. This was especially important to McFadden, since his size would make for an agonizing trip sitting in coach in a seat that barely reclined. Actually, there would be little rest as both men were too wired to sleep. Instead, they went over their search plan step by step to make sure they hadn't forgotten or overlooked anything.

It wasn't long before McFadden realized that Tom's dark good looks hadn't been lost on the attractive flight attendant in Business class, and vice-versa. He'd flirted with the young woman, "Natalie," from the time he took his seat, until they arrived in Addis Ababa. Several times Tom got up and walked to the galley area to talk with her. The two laughed and seemed to have hit it off. McFadden was a little jealous at how easily Tom could talk with a woman he didn't know and seem to put her right at ease. McFadden's first love had always been books and he'd never been that outgoing around girls in high school, and even less so in college. That wasn't to say that he hadn't had his series of first loves. It was just that he hadn't found anyone yet who could make that spark. He needed a woman who could appreciate and share his drive and determination. Well, there wasn't any reason to think about that now.

Tom came back to his seat. McFadden just stared at him without saying a word. He watched as Marino strapped himself in and adjusted his seat belt. Marino was looking at Natalie, but he could see his friend watching him out of the corner of his eye. Finally, he turned to McFadden, "What?" he asked.

McFadden just shook his head, "You're a dog!"

Marino tried to defend himself. "She's a nice woman and we seem to have a few things in common. So, we exchanged email addresses. No big deal!"

"Does she have an older sister?" McFadden asked. "No," Tommy responded, "but her mother's single if you have some spare time."

That was the one thing they really didn't have much of. Time would be against them to a certain degree. They had limited resources and agreed that they could not afford to conduct their expedition for no longer than five or six weeks, two months at the most. If they didn't find the monastery during that time, they would have to return home and work at getting additional funding or sponsorship in order to return and resume the search. McFadden had become more optimistic about their chances ever since Tom had located the report on the discovery of Spinoza's plane. He believed that piece of information may well have saved not only their time, but the entire expedition itself.

Once they located the crash site, the real search would begin, but at least they would be within striking distance of Colavari's crash. There was quite a bit of information in the old pilot's diary to help them eliminate some of the places within the search area.

Their baggage contained the very basics of what would be needed for them to venture out of the city into the desolate and isolated countryside. Binoculars, compass, canteens, hiking boots, and the few personal items each man chose to include in his ruck sack. Other items such as the tent, sleeping bags, etc., would logically be obtained in the capital. The major items such as the vehicle for travel through the desert and air transportation would have to be carefully found after they'd stocked up and were ready to head out.

When they did try to sleep, it seemed that both men dreamt about the search, but in different ways. Tom dreamt that they discovered the location of the monastery just outside the capital, but that it was now a tourist spot. For McFadden, it was more a daydream as he gazed out the window of the plane and stared at the white clouds. He saw them finding the monastery, but, once there, the monks refused to talk to them or let them in and they ran out of supplies and had to return home. Neither man wanted to share his doubts with the other, so they just kept going over the details of the search and tried to sound upbeat.

After what seemed like days, the chief flight attendant finally announced they were descending and would be touching down 25 minutes ahead of schedule. The 15 hours in the air made them more than ready to plant their feet on solid ground. They looked out the window as the plane approached the airport and saw mile after mile of open desert. They were eventually surprised to see that, as they drew closer to the airport, Addis Ababa looked like any other city — high rise office buildings, congested highways, and housing developments surrounding the city proper.

Tom leaned back in his seat and adjusted the tightness of the safety belt. "You know, it's funny," he began, "but for some reason I expected we'd be landing in the middle of the desert and surrounded by thousands of tents."

McFadden laughed. "Now that you say that I was kind of expecting the same thing. We seem to forget that more than 70 years have passed since your uncle was here and this country, like any other country, continues to develop and grow.

The pilot made an exceptionally smooth landing and soon the plane was making its way across several runways and heading to the modern terminal. When the plane finally stopped and the seat belt light went out, the two men stretched and retrieved their carry-on luggage from the overhead bins. They had traveled in comfortable and light clothing but were pleasantly surprised at how nice it felt as they descended the steps and hit the tarmac.

It was late afternoon and the temperature was relatively comfortable. It was their dry season and it usually didn't get much above 80 degrees during the day. Looking across the runway towards the terminal, they could see the heat radiating from the black top. "Wow, it feels like autumn, but standing in the sun on this blacktop is really hot!" Tom offered.

McFadden smiled and added, "Enjoy it because once we get out of the city and hit the desert it will be a scorcher."

The next stop was customs and each man explained that he was there for vacation and sightseeing. McFadden's agent was short and slim, with light brown skin and bright inquisitive eyes. He wore a cleanly pressed uniform and looked very much the professional. After going through McFadden's bag, he stared at his passport and compared the picture with the man standing before him. He seemed to be taking quite a bit of time reviewing McFadden's papers, but eventually appeared satisfied that they matched. After a few moments, the man broke into a wide smile. McFadden noticed how sparkling the pearl white teeth were against the dark face. In careful English, the agent asked McFadden if he was an American football player. He'd never seen anyone quite as big as this man and was obviously impressed by his size.

McFadden smiled back and lied, saying that he had played football in college and had tried out for a professional team, but was considered too small. The agent laughed and asked if there were a lot of people in America as big as him. McFadden smiled back and told the agent that he was just average size.

He must have sounded just touristy enough for the customs agent because he finally stamped McFadden's passport and visa and handed the papers back. "Enjoy your stay, Mr. McFadden, and be careful in the sun," he advised. "The heat here can get to you quickly if you're not used to it." McFadden thanked the agent, gathered up his bag, and proceeded inside the terminal to meet up with Marino.

"What took so long?" Marino asked.

"The agent wanted to know if I was a professional football player," he laughed. "I lied. Anyway, we're in Ethiopia and are legal and legitimate tourists. Let's pick up our luggage and grab a taxi to the hotel and get some rest. Tomorrow we begin our adventure."

CHAPTER 17

Once they retrieved their bags, they stepped outside and were immediately met by a group of men offering taxi services to anywhere in the city. Before they could choose, a taxi further back in line pulled ahead of the others and stopped in front of the two Americans. Surprisingly, none of the other drivers seemed upset or complained about the line jumper. They merely smiled at the driver as he exited the taxi and then turned back to their various conversations. The driver opened the doors for the men, placed the luggage in the trunk, and asked where they would like to go.

McFadden answered, "We're staying at the Sheraton Hotel."

The driver smiled broadly and repeated, "The Sheraton, yes, gentlemen!" As they pulled away from the terminal the driver introduced himself, "Gentlemen, I am Mohammed and I would like to offer my services as your personal chauffeur and guide during your stay." He spoke surprisingly good English and gestured grandly with his hands on and off the wheel as he spoke. "I know every place in the city and can show you wonderful sights and take you to the best restaurants." He paused for a moment to take a breath before continuing.

"Addis Ababa is a beautiful city and nobody knows her better than Mohammed."

"Maybe we could use you in a few days, but first we have business to conduct before we have any leisure time," Marino answered.

Mohammed beamed and handed Marino a card with a phone number written on it. "When you are ready for me, just have the hotel call that number and I will be there in minutes. My rates are very cheap and I am very honest."

The drive to the hotel showed that the capital was like any big city. The traffic was congested and often bumper to bumper. Mixed in with the cars and SUVs were battered older cars and trucks with enormous loads barely secured to their truck beds. After 25 minutes, they pulled up to the entrance of the Sheraton. The taxi had barely come to a complete stop before Mohammed jumped out and raced around to open the doors for his new American clients.

The doorman gestured over his shoulder and a young man appeared to grab their bags, carrying them into the hotel. Marino hadn't exchanged his American money for Ethiopian Birr, so he wound up giving the driver a very generous tip. This only encouraged Mohammed's commitment to the two Americans as he promised to be at their disposal the moment they were ready. Amid bows and handshakes, McFadden and Marino eventually extricated themselves from their new friend and entered the hotel.

The air conditioned lobby was a welcome relief from the open windows of the taxi as it drove through the crowded streets. They checked in with a young woman at the desk who confirmed their reservations. After a quick examination of their passports and visas, they were shown to a large suite with two queen-sized beds, a large sitting room with a desk, a small area with a coffee maker, a refrigerator, and a microwave. The room was on the eighth floor and the large window provided a panoramic view of the city.

While McFadden unpacked and set up his computer on the desk, Marino took a quick shower and changed into slacks and a short sleeve cotton shirt. It was now McFadden's turn to hit the shower and he seemed to take forever before finally emerging, wrapped in a large towel. "Did you leave any hot water for the rest of the guests?" Marino joked.

"I just needed to relax my aching bones," McFadden answered. "Now I'm ready to get something to eat before it gets too dark."

After McFadden finished dressing, they went down to the lobby and decided to skip dinner at the hotel and try one of the local restaurants within walking distance. The clerk said there were three excellent restaurants within four blocks of the hotel. The one she recommended was family owned and known for its traditional Ethiopian foods. The other two served excellent lamb dishes. Although a big eater, McFadden had never been a great fan of lamb, so it was agreed the traditional Ethiopian restaurant was their goal for the evening.

As they stepped outside the hotel, it seemed that it had cooled off a bit since they arrived. Actually, the showers and clean clothes made them feel much better. With a light breeze at their backs, they headed north, away from the hotel and followed the desk clerk's directions. After about four blocks, they arrived at the restaurant the clerk had recommended and they compared the name over the entrance, to the words the clerk had written on a piece of paper. They were the same;

they had arrived at 'The Kingdom of Aksum,' named after an empire that ruled much of Abyssinia from the first through the sixth century AD.

The inside of the restaurant was dimly lit and smelled of strong coffee. A small man in a tan suit with a black bowtie greeted them in English. "I assume you gentlemen are American," he said.

Marino smiled back and asked how he knew they were from the US.

"If you will forgive me, sir, but you are so tall it made me think you were Americans. We don't see many men as tall as you unless they come from the US. I am Ahmed, the owner. May I show you to a table?" he asked politely.

McFadden answered, "Yes, Ahmed, we're hungry and the hotel said some wonderful things about your food. Besides, you seem like a good detective and you might be able to help us find a few things while we're here in Addis Ababa."

Ahmed smiled and led them to a quiet table away from the open door. "Gentlemen, you are most welcome. Please be seated. May I offer you something to drink before you order? We have an excellent Ethiopian beer, St. George Amber."

"Ahmed, we're here to experience your culture and learn about your customs, so please bring us two St. George Ambers to start with," Marino said. Within moments, he was back with two tall bottles and glasses which he filled for his guests.

McFadden, the true beer drinker among the two, took a long drink and placed the now half-empty glass on the table. "This is excellent!" he said. "When you have the chance, bring us two more bottles."

The small owner nodded with a smile. "What can I offer you gentlemen for dinner tonight?" he asked. Marino spoke before McFadden could open his mouth. "Ahmed, looking at my friend, you can see that he is a big eater, and, since we are guests in your country, we would be pleased if you would select our meal for us tonight and serve whatever you think we might enjoy."

Ahmed bowed deeply. "Relax, my friends, and await a meal you will not soon forget." With that said, he disappeared into the back of the restaurant and soon they could hear his voice as if giving commands to the kitchen staff.

An excellent salad containing olives, dates, and greens was ceremoniously brought in, followed by several types of thick meat stews known as wat in Ethiopian culture. This was accompanied by several vegetable side dishes served atop injera, a large sourdough flatbread made of teff flour. The meal was placed in the center of the table, as was the custom. There were no utensils in this traditional meal and Ahmed explained that they were to use the injera to scoop up the entrees and side dishes. He returned from another trip into the kitchen carrying a large bowl of the very popular Tihlo, a type of dumpling. He explained that Ethiopian cuisine employs no pork or shellfish of any kind, as they are forbidden in the Islamic, Jewish, and Ethiopian Orthodox faiths. As Marino and McFadden surveyed the table, Ahmed slowly backed away and left the men to dine quietly alone.

McFadden didn't realize just how hungry he was until the food was placed before him and he smelled the mixed aromas from the various plates. The two men began to eat and, surprisingly, there was very little conversation for the next few minutes. After a few awkward attempts, they were finally able to master the use of the injera to scoop up the food, despite making a small mess between them. They were in deep concentration and, little by little, the bowls were emptied and the injera slowly disappeared. When they were finally finished, they sat back and surveyed the collective damage. There wasn't much left, just a few dumplings in the bowl surrounded by eight empty beer bottles. Marino was the first to speak. "I'm never eating again. I can't believe how much I just put away. This has to be the most food I've ever eaten at one sitting."

McFadden sat with a relaxed look on his face. "I may have eaten more at one sitting, but never anything better. This was just what I needed!"

When he was certain that his guests had completed their meal, Ahmed returned to the table carrying a tray with two cups and a pot of steaming coffee. "My friends, you honor me profoundly by so thoroughly enjoying what I chose for you. Now, to finish this meal, I bring you Ethiopian coffee, strong and sweet." He poured coffee into the two cups and left the pot on the table, discreetly placing the check face down between them.

"This one is mine!" McFadden said as he grabbed the check.

"I won't argue with you," Marino replied. "I'm not sure I can even reach around for my wallet. I'm so stuffed." McFadden looked at the check and mentally converted the Birr into US currency.

"Do you know what this meal cost us?" he asked. "I'm not so sure I want to know," replied Marino. McFadden reached in his pocket and removed the roll of bills he carried. "This cost us approximately 1200 Birr, or roughly thirty-four US dollars. It's custom to leave a 1-2 Birr tip in a proper restaurant. We can't leave this man thirty-four dollars for that meal," he said as he placed two twenty's and a ten-dollar bill on top of the check. "I wouldn't be able to sleep thinking I'd robbed him."

With that, the men finished the last bit of coffee in their cups and rose to leave. Ahmed quickly appeared and saw the US bills on the table. "One moment while I get you gentlemen your change," he said. McFadden raised his hand as if to say no, "Ahmed, we would be insulted if you didn't accept the entire amount, as our way of thanking you for your hospitality and kindness to a couple of strangers. That was the finest meal I have ever eaten."

Ahmed bowed to the two men. "Your generosity overwhelms me, my friends. I hope you will honor me again while you are here and allow me to prepare an even greater meal for you."

The two men shook Ahmed's hand and stepped onto the street, with the little man's best wishes following them out the door. The walk back to the hotel took considerably longer than the trip out, given their full stomachs. As expected, they slept very well that night.

CHAPTER 18

The next morning, they had a light breakfast in their room and laid out their plans for the day. They needed transportation, both ground and air. "Do you want to give our taxi driver friend, Mohammad, a call and let him run you around?" McFadden asked.

"Normally, I'd like to just get the lay of the land on my own, but since time is of the essence, it might be best to hire a driver who could also function as our local guide while we're in the capital," Marino answered. "Although it would be nice to have our own chauffeur to do the driving and navigation, we definitely need the freedom to travel when and where we want. I think I'll let Mohammed take me to rent a car as my first stop. Once we have our own wheels, we can come and go as we want without anybody getting curious in what the two Americans are doing. After we've had a day or two moving around on our own, they should start to look at us as a pair of normal tourists. Eventually, our little sightseeing tours shouldn't attract anyone's attention."

"Since we're here and so close to beginning this adventure, I guess I'm getting a little paranoid. No one could possibly know why we're here, but I don't want to risk some clever fellow somehow putting two and two together and coming up with 'religious artifact' as the answer."

With that, Marino gathered his money, passport, and the list of miscellaneous things they were going to need. He called down to the desk and gave them Mohammed's number and asked them to contact the taxi driver.

Several minutes later, the front desk called and told Marino that the taxi would be at the door within 10 minutes. "Okay, I've got my transportation on the way."

McFadden nodded, "I'm going to take a taxi back to the airport and see if I can locate a pilot and a plane to fly us out to Spinoza's crash site. I'll meet you back here whenever."

They split up at the front door to the hotel and headed in opposite directions. Marino had given quite a bit of thought to renting a vehicle, but he wasn't sure whether he wanted to go with one of the large car rental agencies, or if it would be better to rent locally. When he asked the driver where he could find a rental car, Mohammed told of several places he might try, although "Lucky Car Rental" was the most reliable. Marino agreed to check out this local agency.

The drive took Marino south of the downtown area and out into more rural areas where there were more factories and businesses with more antiquated conditions. As they drove on the narrow-paved road, they passed fewer vehicles and began to share the road with carts being pulled small donkeys and small groups of women carrying large bundles on their heads. That had always amazed the young American. "How do they keep those bundles balanced? *It has to hurt your neck*, he thought. After about 20 minutes of weaving around the steady pedestrian and animal traffic, the taxi pulled through the open gate into a large fenced-in yard. There were a number of four-wheel drive vehicles lined up in front of a door that went into a small office. Marino asked his taxi driver to wait until he found out whether a vehicle would be available.

Mohammed smiled and shut off the engine and lit a cigarette. "I will be here, sir!" he said. "Take your time."

Marino entered the small dimly lit office. There was a counter with several chairs lining the wall. At first, Marino thought he was alone, but, as his eyes became more accustomed to the interior lighting from the bright afternoon sun, he saw there was a desk in the far corner where an older man with a beautifully-trimmed grey beard sat looking at the new arrival.

"How may I help you, sir?" He asked as he stood, gesturing for Marino to walk around the counter and join him in his little office area. Marino walked to the desk and stretched out his hand.

"My name is Tom Marino, and I'm looking to rent a vehicle for about a week."

The man behind the desk took the offered hand with a firm grip. "Well, Mr. Marino," he said in heavily accented English, "I usually only rent to the locals, and occasionally to an owner of one of the larger farms further outside the city when they want to go out and check on their investment. We don't get many tourists out this way. What do you need a vehicle for?"

Marino stuck to their original story and told the man he was hoping to track down the crash site of his uncle's plane from before World War II in order to complete a history of his family. "I've been throughout the US, following family that emigrated near the turn of the century. My father's side is pretty well accounted for, but in my mother's family we have a few gaps." He watched the man's expression and tried to determine how much of his story he was buying. "What I want to do is find the site where my uncle crashed during the war and maybe bring home a piece of the plane as a sort of symbol or remembrance of the experience he went through."

"Sit down, Mr. Marino," the man offered.

"Please, call me Tom," said Marino.

"Okay, Tom. My name is Jacob and I own this business. I'm intrigued by what you want to do. Family history is important to us here, as well. Where do you plan to look and how long would you need the vehicle?"

Marino kept to the story and knew this was the time to continue the deception and provide a little misdirection. "To the best of my uncle's recollections prior to his death last year, he believes the plane went down south east of the Great Rift Valley."

"That's a great amount of area to search, Tom. How long do you think it will take?"

Marino smiled, "I don't know how long it will take, but I can tell you I only have two weeks to locate the crash site. If I don't find it by then I'll have to put off the search and head back home and try another time."

Jacob was silent for a few moments. "I think I can help you, but, to be most honest, I will have to charge you a little more than I usually charge others because of where you are going, how long you will be gone, and the risk of damage to my vehicle traveling off-road." Jacob looked at Marino. "If you were going northwest, I would not be able to assist you. That area is home to a great tribe of bandits," he paused. "To this day, they rob and kill anyone who travels too close to the mountains northwest of the Rift. They have been there for generations and anyone foolish enough to venture into their stronghold is likely never to be seen again. There are stories of whole caravans disappearing after the war when trade was again possible and merchants peddled their goods from Addis Ababa to the seaport. Of course, that was many years ago."

Jacob seemed to be enjoying the storytelling and became very serious. "Even the army stays away. There's really nothing out there except sand and rocks, so I believe they feel there is no reason to chase the bandits from a place no one really wants. Very dangerous!"

Marino was struck by the old man's story. *There's something we hadn't even considered in today's world,* he thought to himself. If there was the possibility of crossing paths with thieves and bandits, then that created a whole new area of concern. He pushed the thought out of his head and looked seriously at the owner.

"That's quite a story for the 21st century," he said. Jacob smiled.

"It's not as big a problem now, since so much is moved by trucks or flown by plane over the mountains, but we still hear of the occasional traveler who ventures out and disappears."

Jacob seemed to take Marino's silence as acceptance of the story. Calling them back to business, Jacob said, "I will let you have a vehicle for fifty American dollars a day plus a $300 dollar deposit to cover any damage. In advance. Does that seem fair?"

Marino tried not to show his surprise. He had expected to pay as much as $100 or more a day. He kept his expression blank as if trying to calculate the total cost, and then held out his hand. "I think that's very fair. I don't have a lot of money with me, but I can afford that, and I promise to bring your vehicle back safe and sound."

Jacob smiled and shook Marino's hand to seal the deal. "Good, let's go outside and choose the one that will serve you best."

Jacob led Marino out of the office and over to the row of four wheelers. "Considering where you will be going, you will want the option of having air conditioning," he said. Marino was a born mechanic and could usually spot a problem right off. The vehicles consisted of a Land Rover, three Jeep station wagons and several Toyota Land Cruisers. "Let me show you the best one on the lot," Jacob said. "This Land Rover is the oldest vehicle I have, but she will run forever. Everything works and I usually drive it as my personal truck."

Marino looked at the newer trucks first, checking under the hood for leaks or signs of damage. Surprisingly, they were all in very good condition. Jacob seemed to read his mind. "These are what feeds my family. I treat each one as if it were the only one I owned. "

After a few minutes examining each of the newer vehicles, Marino worked his way down the line to the 1987 Land Rover Defender. The odometer showed only 74,000 miles, but Jacob volunteered that it had been around at least once, so it actually had at least 174,000 miles, but the engine had been rebuilt 30,000 miles ago. The engine compartment was as clean as could be expected, considering the terrain the vehicle traversed. It was obvious that the truck had recently received new or rebuilt parts. The suspension was the old-style Rover had used for years before going to a less impressive system to reduce cost and remain competitive. He started the engine and the truck sounded quiet. It idled easy and the AC worked. It was fitted with a front electric winch and the tires were good with plenty of tread. "You're right, this is the best," Marino finally said.

Jacob smiled, "I told you so. I do not keep junk and I do not rent junk."

Marino shut off the engine and went out to pay the taxi driver who had been sitting patiently, watching the whole process. He paid the stated fare and gave the driver a handsome tip for leading him to Jacob.

Mohammed thanked him and drove off back to the city, making a mental note to stop back later that night and see his cousin so that Jacob could thank him properly for delivering the American to "Lucky Car Rental."

Jacob gave Marino the keys and included three 5-gallon gas cans and a 5-gallon water can. He checked the oil and the spare tire and placed a small toolbox on the floor behind the driver's seat, "Just in case!" he added.

"Thank you, Jacob!" Marino said as he fastened the seat belt. "I'll take excellent car of her and should see you in about a week."

Jacob shook Marino's hand once more. "Good luck, Tom! I hope you find what you're looking for." With that, Marino put the old truck in gear and eased himself onto the road, heading back towards the city.

Marino was pleased with his find. The old Rover handled well on the return trip. The steering was tight and the brakes responsive. He saw a small sand dune off to his right, so he pulled off the side of the road and engaged the four-wheel drive. He turned towards the dune and gently pulled the vehicle to the beginning of the incline. The Rover dug into the soft sand and steadily climbed up to the top and then descended the opposite side without the slightest hesitation.

"Jacob, you were right," he said triumphantly to himself. "You don't rent junk." He disengaged the four-wheel drive and returned the truck to the roadway.

Within a half hour, he pulled up to the front door of the hotel and handed the keys and $5 to the young valet parker. He smiled, "Take good care of her, she's a rental." The young man stared at the bill before quickly putting in his pocket. "As if she were my own, sir!" he said as he slowly pulled away and headed for the garage.

Jacob waited until the Rover had pulled onto the road and disappeared heading towards the city before returning to his office. He picked up the phone and dialed the familiar number. "I think I may have one," he said. He listened for several moments, and then said "Yes, of course."

After he hung up, Jacob removed the laptop from the top drawer of his desk. Once the screen lit up, he clicked on an application and watched as a map of the roadways around him suddenly appeared. His eyes followed the small blinking light, as it moved slowly away from his yard and made its way towards the capital. The transmitter was working just fine. After about a half hour, the light stopped moving.

"So, my friend, you are staying at the Sheraton. That should make things a little easier for us." He sat back in his chair and smiled. He would be able to follow every turn of the Rover right there from his office.

CHAPTER 19

While Marino was off successfully renting their transportation, McFadden was heading to the Addis Ababa airport. He had to locate a private pilot and plane to start them on the search. It turned out that there were very few planes that were available for hire. Most were large cargo carriers, with the occasional private jet parked nearby. The cargo planes were too big and too fast for the type of search they needed to do, and, aside from the cost of hiring a jet, they were even much faster than the cargo planes. No, they would need something smaller with the ability to fly low and slow if needed.

After several false leads, he was finally directed to Desert Air, a small passenger and cargo hauling company that flew primarily from the capital to the seacoast. Desert Air turned out to be a two-plane one-pilot airline. The owner — the pilot, mechanic, and flight attendant — was a small, barrel-chested Israeli man in his mid-sixties called Aaron Pierce.

He was short and stocky with bright alert dark eyes. He was balding and what was left of his salt and pepper hair was tied into a small ponytail. He reminded BB of a bulldog — broad across the chest with a large flat fighter's face. He sat in the small office, the air-conditioner humming as it worked to keep out the worst of the afternoon heat. The King Air and DC-3 were parked in the attached hangar at the far end of the airfield where private jets parked amongst the numerous small cargo planes that covered the west end of the tarmac. McFadden had immediately noted that the two aircrafts were sparkling clean, and that the hangar was uncluttered. He was impressed and felt Pierce was an attention-to-detail man. A good thing when you make flying your way of life.

"Mr. Pierce, my name is Francis McFadden and I was wondering if your King Air was available for hire for several days?" Pierce didn't immediately answer. He sat and sized up his visitor.

Finally, he said, "Well, Mr. McFadden, I'm very particular about what I haul, where I haul it, and for whom. I don't haul anything that's illegal or that I'm opposed to, such as guns, drugs, explosives or people wanted by the law. That said, what do you want moved and to where?"

Pierce's voice was deep and spoke with a heavy Israeli accent. McFadden evaluated the little Israeli more closely and realized that he liked the man's candor and honesty. But, more importantly, he liked the man generally.

"Your cargo will be me and a friend, and we want you to haul us out to the Simien Mountain range and cruise for a few hours, then haul us back to the airport. Nothing illegal, and the worst thing you'll face will be our potentially boring company for a few hours. We're looking for something, a place actually, and we believe we can only locate it from the air. Are you available?"

"Sit down, Mr. McFadden and you can tell me what you want us to find in the desert. And please, call me Aaron. Mr. Pierce makes me sound older than I care to admit." McFadden took a chair close to the window and looked out at the busy comings and goings of the private and business planes.

He extended his hand across the desk, "Well, Aaron, my friends call me BB and we're trying to find a little bit of history."

McFadden and Marino had decided that the best story to explain their expedition was the truth, to a certain extent. "My friend Tom Marino and I are college professors by trade, and archeologists and historians by avocation. Tom's uncle was a pilot with the Italian Air Force in the mid-thirties here in Ethiopia. He was shot down in September of 1936 and survived the crash and the war. We're hoping to locate where his plane went down as part of family history research. If we can locate a few likely sites for the crash by air, then we'll drive back and begin our research. I'm thinking that if we can't locate a likely spot in two to three days then we won't locate it at all and will call this off." McFadden paused and waited for Pierce to speak.

"Well, BB, I'm not so sure that I understand what's so important about finding the remains of an old war plane from 1936, but it doesn't sound illegal, so I'll fly you both out there for one day and if we don't find evidence of a crash then you can tell me what you're really looking for. If that sounds fair to you, then I'll haul you and your friend."

McFadden smiled and held out his hand, "You've got a deal."

After agreeing on a daily rate, McFadden spread his map of the mountain range on Pierce's desk and showed the general area he thought might lead them to their objective. "Tom's uncle wrote that he thought they had traveled about 150 miles northeast before spotting the supply train. On the other hand, the S&R unit said they found Spinoza's wreckage about 167 miles north."

McFadden paused while Pierce studied the map and traced the route with his finger. "Depending upon whom we believe or whose navigation was the most accurate, we're faced with roughly a 17-20-mile-deep search area of unknown width," McFadden added. "Tom and I both agree that the most logical point to start will be where Spinoza went down. According to the report, Spinoza's plane didn't burn when it crashed, so there should be a significant amount of debris at the site, although 70 years of forest growth may well have buried most of it."

Pierce was silent as he studied the map. McFadden could see that he'd gotten the pilot's attention as the man ran his finger back and forth across the flight line BB had drawn. After a few minutes Pierce stood back and crossed his arms while his eyes remained on the map.

"You've got my interest, BB," he said finally. "Assuming your information on the first crash is fairly accurate, I think this is doable. Give me until tomorrow to come up with a search pattern and we can hit that area grid by grid." He sounded excited as he kept looking at the map. "I don't care how long it's been since that plane went down, there has to be some evidence of the crash. Nature can only hide so much." He went on, "And you're right. The best way to find a crash site is from the air. If you try to do it on the ground, you could walk right by or drive over the top of it. Okay, I'm in," he said as he finally looked away from the map and faced McFadden.

"You and your buddy show up here tomorrow morning at about 9:00 and I'll show you what I've come up with, and, if you're satisfied, we can be in the air before 10:00."

McFadden smiled back at the battered face. "I'm feeling better about this already," he said. "With you on board as a member of the team and not just as the pilot, I think our chances of finding the first crash site have increased significantly. Alright, Tom and I will see you in the morning, and thanks!" They shook hands and McFadden left the map with Pierce and walked back to the terminal to grab a taxi for the ride back to the hotel.

This is looking better all the time, he thought to himself. They had the plane and a pilot who appeared eager to participate in the journey. Tom would have a vehicle so they would have the freedom to move on the ground once they located the crash site — the starting point. McFadden smiled to himself. Now he was saying "once" they found the site, and not "if" they found it. "The power of positive thinking at its finest."

McFadden arrived back at the hotel before Marino and looked over his notes for the thousandth time. Things were starting to fall into place. Hopefully, tomorrow would put them on the path towards the answers to the questions in Angelo Colavari's diary. "Why did I survive? How did I survive?" Although, closing that book would set up a whole new series of even tougher questions. Did the robe of Jesus Christ exist 2000 years after his death, and, if so, did it possess the power to heal broken bodies?

Marino's return brought McFadden back to the moment. "How'd you do? He asked as his friend flopped on the other bed.

"We've got a good Land Rover that should get us where we want to go and bring us back again." Tom told McFadden of his luck in finding the local car rental agency and the deal he had worked out with Jacob, the owner. He also told him about the bandits that were supposed to occupy most of the area they planned to search. McFadden was quiet as he digested this latest bit of information.

"That's not good. It won't be an issue until we're ready for the search on foot, yet that's a variable we hadn't planned for," he said.

Marino thought for a moment, "I guess we could get ourselves a couple of rifles and say we were going hunting, in case we saw anyone."

"No, that won't work for two reasons," McFadden answered. "First, you need a permit to hunt in Ethiopia, and they are very strict as to where you can hunt and under what conditions. There are certain areas where hunting is permitted and your name and permit number are given to the local game wardens so they know who is going to be out there and what they're looking for. That would raise a lot of questions as to why the two young Americans stopped being tourists and suddenly became big game hunters. No, that would bring us under the government's attention and possibly limit our ability to move freely."

He was quiet again for a few moments before looking Marino in the eyes and saying, "Besides, we're here looking to confirm the existence of the Robe of Jesus Christ. I don't want to find myself in a position where I might have to shoot someone in order to find it. It goes against everything we're setting out to do."

Marino smiled and nodded. "You're right. I was just thinking out loud. I don't want to be there either. Okay! No guns. What do we do if there really are bandits in the mountains?"

Now it was McFadden's turn to smile. "You're asking the wrong kid. I didn't even play Cowboys and Indians when I was growing up. I guess we play it by ear and hope that either they don't really exist, or that we can sneak in and move quietly enough so as not to attract anyone's attention."

McFadden reported on his success that afternoon and brought Tom up to speed on what he'd been able to arrange for the plane. "I like this guy, and I really think he's excited about being involved with the search for the planes. Anyway, I hope he is. He's planning on developing a grid pattern for the search, which should make it more efficient and more productive."

"What if he's so interested that he wants to come along with us when we drive out to the site?" Tom asked.

"We'll worry about that if it happens and find a way to head out on our own," McFadden answered. "You can always tell him that this is a really personal and sensitive family journey that you want to keep this to yourself and me, your very best friend in the whole wide world." he finished, feigning bashfulness at the ending of his statement.

"Okay, that's all I can take on an empty stomach," Tom said laughing. "Let's change and go downstairs for dinner. I really don't want to go out tonight. There's too much going on tomorrow!" They both showered and dressed casually for dinner in the hotel restaurant. They went over their plans again while they ate and toasted each other on their good luck at finding just the right truck and the perfect plane and pilot. Neither of them noticed the man at the bar across the room. He sat with his back to the men and watched their every move through the reflection in the mirror.

CHAPTER 20

At 7:00 am, the phone in their room rang and, when McFadden answered it, he heard the voice of Aaron Pierce. "Good morning, BB," came the pilot's gruff greeting. "Whenever you guys are ready you can come out. I worked on the search grid last night and I'd like to get airborne before mid-morning, if possible. We have a lot of area to cover and I'd like to be there while the sun is still high."

McFadden smiled to himself. Pierce was on board! "Alright, Aaron, give us a little while to dress and grab something to eat and we'll be out there." Before he could say another word, Pierce acknowledged, "Roger!" and the phone went dead. By now, Tom had opened his eyes and was looking at McFadden questioningly.

"Our newest team member wants us out to the airport so that we can begin the search. I had a feeling he was a 'no nonsense' type of guy. Get dressed while I call room service and have them throw some lunch together for us. We can pick it up on the way out." Tom called out from the bathroom, "You might as well call the desk and have the valet bring the Land Rover around. We don't want to keep our new team member waiting."

Forty minutes later, loaded down with a dozen bottles of water and half a dozen sandwiches tucked away in an Igloo cooler, Tom pulled the Rover away from the front of the hotel and pointed her towards the airport. The traffic was moving, but the roads were crammed with a variety of vehicles heading out to begin their day's work.

After maneuvering through rush hour traffic they arrived at the offices of Desert Air. They parked next to the building and were about to walk in when they heard a whistle come from the hangar. They looked in and saw Pierce walking around the King Air doing his ground check.

"Good morning," he called. They walked across the clean hangar floor and met up with Pierce as he made his final check of the engine cowling and front struts. McFadden shook his hand and then introduced Tom to their new pilot.

"Nice to meet you, Tom," Pierce said. "I'm through here. Let's go inside and you can look over what I've come up with."

The office was still cool from the night air. When the temperature drops at night in the desert, it can get really cold, but it wouldn't be long before the air conditioner would be struggling to keep out the early morning heat. Pierce led them to a coffee pot sitting on a small table next to his desk. They each grabbed a mug and passed the pot around. McFadden and Pierce both drank theirs black. He nudged Pierce as they watched Marino pour a steady stream of sugar from the jar into his cup.

"Kid, you're going to die a hopeless diabetic if you're not careful," Pierce said with a smile.

"Not you, too?" Marino answered, "This is my only vice in life. Let me suffer quietly." Pierce slapped Marino on the shoulder and laughed, "Just kidding, Tom. Make yourself at home."

Pierce took his cup and led them to a large table in the back of the office where he switched on an overhead light. The fluorescent light illuminated the table and McFadden could see that his black and white map of the mountain area had been replaced with a large multi-color map, showing an aerial view of the Simien Mountains and the surrounding terrain. The map had been marked with a series of longitudinal and latitudinal lines which created boxes of varying lengths and widths.

Pierce was quiet while the two Americans put their cups down and leaned over the table to take a closer look. "After we spoke yesterday, I gave this a lot of thought. Since you guys are hiring me to help you find something or someplace in the mountains, I figured it was my job to come up with some sort of game plan."

He waited for either of them to speak, but it was clear that he had their attention. "The Simien Mountains cover a vast range. Almost 137km north to south, and more than 412km east to west. In coming up with this grid system I had to make a few assumptions. We can always revisit these, but I think this might not be a bad way to start the search."

Marino spoke first. "Aaron, you are way ahead of where we hoped to be. We originally planned to just cruise up and down the mountain range and hope to find something that looked like a crash site. Your map looks a whole lot more professional and I think we're more than willing to accept your assumptions at this stage. Go ahead with your plan."

"Okay! The first assumption I made had to do with the S&R unit. BB, you remember yesterday when I told you it would be easy to walk around or over a crash site and never even see it?" McFadden nodded. Pierce continued, "Well then, we have to assume that the search team was probably led to the site by the aerial observation of another plane. It's unlikely they would have driven that distance and then have been lucky enough to find the plane on their own."

By now, McFadden and Marino had found something to sit on or lean against and Pierce could see that they were taking this all in. Pierce went back to the map and pointed at the long grids he had marked traveling north to south. "Given that we accept the possible distance from the air base to the crash site as being roughly 167 miles, we have to decide whether those are road miles or flying miles; "as the crow flies," so to speak."

He went on, "If we're talking about 167 miles as the crow flies, then we should be able to initially narrow the search area to about 20 square miles," he leaned over the map and circled a four grid square. "If that's the case, the pilot could have clearly seen the spot from about 3000 feet. There would have been a hole in the tree cover where the plane crashed through. If they found it that way, then the search pilot would have had to lead the S&R people back to the site and direct them from the air." He stepped back from the table and took a long drink from the coffee cup. "That's just a theory, mind you."

McFadden and Marino continued to stare at the map. "In the 1930s, planes had only been in service for a little over 20 years and were considered a valuable addition to the war machine. It was considered a dashing and dangerous profession which allowed very little room for error. If a plane went down, the Army, or Air Force, depending on what country we're talking about, wouldn't want to totally lose a valuable piece of hardware. I can see the Italian Army sending up another plane to locate a valuable piece of equipment.

If parts of it could be salvaged, then they'd send a crew to retrieve what was left. The logical course of action would be for the search plane to pinpoint the crash site, give the S&R unit the coordinates, and then plan to fly out once they'd driven to the area and guide them by air." Pierce looked at the two men and waited for any questions or comments. When none came, he continued.

"I like the idea that the crash site may have been discovered by another plane. If that's the case, then we would actually be looking at 167 miles as the crow flies. Of course, the area that they were looking for would have been pretty well torn up even if the plane hadn't burned. They may have only been made of aluminum and sheet metal, but they still made a hole when they hit the ground. If we go with this theory for now, then we have to assume that the plane came down fairly close to one of the few roads or trails that follow the edge of the mountains throughout the desert. The S&R unit would never have been able to drive their truck through the trees that cover most of the area."

"For today, I'd like to fly to the old air base and then head north, follow the edge of the mountains where they meet up with the desert, along the general flight path your uncle might have taken. At about 150 miles out we can begin a low-level search and see if we can spot anything between there and, say, 170 miles out. What do you think?"

Neither man spoke for a few moments, then they both started talking at once. Tom laughed. "After you," he gestured to McFadden. "I think Tom and I are both trying to say that we like what you've come up with and are ready to hit the skies."

The route was now official. Pierce called the tower and filed his flight plan. He told Air Traffic Control that he was taking several tourists on a sight-seeing tour of the mountains and desert northwest of the Rift. Not an uncommon destination for many of the visitors to Addis Ababa this time of year. He saw no reason why he shouldn't tell the tower where they were actually going, since they were doing nothing wrong or illegal. He only made the trip sound a little vague to protect his client's ultimate objective. No need to have some locals out there searching for the wreckage before they could find it. If someone else got there first, the Americans might wind up having to buy their souvenirs.

As Pierce taxied the King Air out of the hangar, McFadden and Marino grabbed the cooler out of the truck along with binoculars and a large metal case. They loaded their cargo onboard and Marino took the co-pilot seat next to Pierce, while McFadden spread out on one of the four seats that lined each side of the passenger section. Promptly at 9:45 am, the small plane lifted off from the runway and made a slow bank northeast as it headed for the site of the old Pagalori Air Base.

CHAPTER 21

It was a beautiful day for flying. There was a light trailing wind and Pierce kept the plane on a steady heading across the desert. Within 20 minutes, they had left any sign of civilization behind and saw nothing below except sand and the occasional truck traffic traveling north or south as they made their way to and from the capital along the only paved road for miles. The men were quiet as they flew into the rising sun and closer to their first objective. After about 45 minutes Pierce pointed below to his left and began a slow banking turn. "Here's what's left of the old air base," he said.

Marino looked out the windshield while McFadden leaned against the glass on the left side of the aircraft. The first thing they saw as they approached was the remains of the control tower. The tall metal frame held what was left of the traffic tower. The roof and sides of the small building had long been removed and used for other projects by the desert inhabitants so now only a shell remained. The buildings that had once housed the Air Force — barracks, offices, supply buildings, and hangars — were in pretty much the same condition. The metal frames held in the air by long skinny steel supports reminded Marino of his old erector set.

The other structures had long been stripped as well, and, in some areas, the only things visible now were the concrete foundations, although they wouldn't have been surprised if those were stripped, too.

The two runways, one headed north/south and the other east/west had long since been reclaimed by decades of desert storms and drifting sand. In its empty condition it presented an eerie image. Almost like looking at the remains of a lost civilization. Marino found himself unconsciously looking for signs of the hospital where his uncle had spent so many weeks after his return.

Pierce flew a lazy circle around what was left of the base, and then turned the nose of the plane northwest towards the mountains visible in the distance. "Okay, guys, this is where we start the clock. One hundred and fifty-five miles as the crow flies!" He gave the plane a little more throttle and leveled off at 5000 feet as they left the base behind.

McFadden removed the aluminum case from its place buckled into one the spare passenger seats and took out the high-tech video camera from its padded pocket. Pierce looked over his shoulder at McFadden as the American assembled the camera and attached the lens.

"I'm going to try and take as much footage of the search grids as I can. We can look at this later and slow down the images so that we can concentrate on any area we think might be worth looking at again," he said as he laid the camera on the seat across from him.

Pierce nodded. "If you're going to get video footage then we have to increase altitude. Video won't be much help if we're skimming the trees. We'll need to be fairly high to get any shots worth keeping. I'd say we fly the first pass on each grid at about 3000 feet and then film the second pass at about 5000 feet. If you're going to be reviewing this film in reduced speed later then you really want to be looking straight down and not off at the horizon."

Pierce kept them entertained over the next hour or so with old stories of life in the 1960s Israeli Air Defense Force. McFadden passed around bottles of cold water and sandwiches and time passed quickly. Pierce was an interesting and informative guide. Finally, he pulled back on the throttle and slowed the plane to a cruising speed of about 90 miles an hour, while slowly descending to his search altitude of 3000 feet. They were just approaching the lowlands as the desert began its climb to meet the first signs of growth. The mountains began to loom to their left and Pierce let the plane drift east so that it hung just over the beginning of the mountain's tree line.

"Okay, we're at just about 140 miles from the base. This looks good! We haven't flown over any heavy forest area yet, so this is consistent with your uncle's account of the incident that they were beginning to turn away from the mountains. It really depends now on how much further they flew along this path before they saw the pack train." All eyes were transfixed out the windows as the plane continued to fly along its path.

Every few minutes, Pierce would call out the distance traveled. "145 miles, 150 miles, 155 miles," until he finally banked away from the trees. "160 miles!"

The time to cover the first 20-mile grid had passed so quickly that Tom and BB both realized they had been doing more sight-seeing than searching. From now on they had to concentrate on why they were there. Where did the plane go down?

Pierce leveled the plane after completing the turn and they headed south back along the route they had just come, only this time he flew a little further away from the desert and more over the tree line. "I'm going to make three passes each way. That will allow us to cover six north-south sections on the grid map. BB, after that I'll climb to 5000 and you can video the same runs," he said over the steady drone of the engine. For the next 5 passes, McFadden and Marino studied the trees' canopies as the plane alternated its north then south routes.

It was a monotonous trip, looking below at the never-ending tree canopy and not knowing what it was they were actually hoping to see. It took almost 15 minutes to complete each leg of the 20-mile search grid. In a little under an hour and a half Pierce swung the small plane east and headed towards the open desert as he gained altitude. At 5000 feet, he leveled off and brought the plane's speed back to just over 90 knots an hour before repeating the first northern pass along the grid line.

While Marino and Pierce searched the tree cover from both sides of the cockpit, McFadden steadied the camera and began to film the area below. An hour and a half later they had completed the second pass over the entire area and now had it digitally recorded.

"Well, I think we've pretty much covered everything we can for today," Pierce said as he circled the plane west in a slow turn towards the capital. We've covered about a third of the grid area and we'll have to be patient. I didn't expect us to find very much on Day 1," he said. "Although we didn't find any evidence of the crash site, we did cover about 7 square miles of our grid."

They hadn't really seen anything worth looking at again, so McFadden disassembled the camera equipment and placed everything back in the padded case. He was initially disappointed with their lack of success, but then realized how much closer they were to hopefully find Spinoza's plane from the air, even if it took a few days. The decision to hire Pierce had been a good one, and Pierce's enthusiasm was proving to be a real benefit. With him outlining a search area and monitoring their progress mile by mile, they had a real good chance of making this all come together.

"Aaron, how much longer do you think it will take us to cover the whole grid?" McFadden asked.

Pierce seemed to calculate the distance before answering. "When we come back tomorrow, the GPS settings will enable us to pick up where we left off. For the next section of the search area I think we climb a little higher, maybe to 4000 feet. Although we won't be able to see as clearly at 4000 as we can at 3000, we'll have longer to view the areas," he said confidently. "Too low and we can shoot right over a potential crash site and then have to hope that BB picked it up with the camera. I'm guessing we need about two more days to cover the area completely." Neither BB nor Tom could fault his logic, and besides, they wanted to take advantage of his years of experience.

"You're the boss, Aaron, until we find the spot or until the money runs out," Tom offered. Pierce looked across at Tom and smiled, "I'm certain there's more to this story than you guys are telling me, but I have a good feeling about you two. If that time comes, we can work something out, as far as flight time is concerned. Until then, we keep on our course and schedule. We'll go back up tomorrow morning, but I'm committed for the day after with a couple of my steady clients."

Tom had been quiet for a while before sharing his thoughts. "I hate to be a wet blanket on this whole expedition, but we're basing all our hopes on this one area, the description of an area written down over 70 years ago. What if Angelo wasn't such a good navigator? What if he was off by a couple of miles in estimating how far he'd traveled? We could be miles away from where they went down." The other two men were quiet for a while as they considered Marino's concerns.

Pierce was the first to speak. "Tom, you might well be right. We could be miles off course, but I don't think we are. I'm thinking your uncle was a pretty sharp kid, and besides, he had every reason to be as accurate as he could be. He planned to come back and find his plane. I'm willing to bet he took everything into consideration when he laid out his ideas on where he had been, and where he wanted to go."

McFadden offered his opinion as well. "Aaron's right. When we find the crash site, wherever it's actually located, I'm sure we'll find the area around it just as Angelo described it. We're close, Tom. I can feel it!"

Tom wasn't sure whether it was Aaron's logical approach to the problem or BB's enthusiasm, but he began to lose his doubts and again found himself caught up in the adventure. "Thanks, guys. I think you're right. We're on the right trail and we can't expect to find everything on the first day. Tomorrow is a new start and we've already eliminated a good chunk of the grid."

With that settled, Pierce put the plane into a slight bank and pointed the nose back towards the airfield. He felt they'd had a good day, but he decided to go over the area he'd laid out just to be sure he hadn't missed anything. Tomorrow would be the day, he told himself.

CHAPTER 22

After landing and taxiing to the hangar, the men split up. Aaron went to service the plane while Tom and BB made their goodbyes. BB took the wheel of the Land Rover and they headed back to the hotel. The ride back was quiet, as each man reviewed the day's experience in his own way. McFadden was optimistic. They hadn't found anything useful, but hopefully they had eliminated a large portion of the search area. He believed in Aaron's approach and was confident that they wouldn't go home empty-handed.

A few cars back, a beat-up dirty Toyota cruised along the highway watching the roof of the Land Rover tower over the rest of the traffic. "This is too easy," he thought to himself.

Tom's thoughts took him back to the day that the two young fliers went down. What must that experience have been like? One minute you're king of the skies with nothing to fear, and the next your plane is breaking apart beneath your feet as you're speeding towards the ground. His uncle must have thought he was going to die right there. Instead, he survived a crash that should have killed him. If not dead then, the injuries should have been enough to ensure he died quickly on that spot. But he didn't die. He was saved by a miracle, a group of priests covered him with the 2000-year-old robe of Jesus Christ and he was healed. Even now, Tom had his doubts about the robe and what they might find.

He was suddenly aware that they'd stopped and was surprised to find that they were back at the hotel. The young valet ran to meet them and McFadden gave him the keys, asking him to fill the tank and put the gas on their bill. He gave the boy a $10.00 bill to ensure that everything was taken care of. For $10.00 the boy would have sat up with the car all night. He thanked McFadden profusely and promised that the car would be standing in front of the hotel ready to go at a moment's notice.

They both seemed to loosen up after a quick shower and a change into fresh clothes. "I think we need to celebrate one successful day down, and several to go," Tom said with a smile. "How about we go back and visit our friend Ahmed and let him choose another great meal for us?" McFadden offered, "If he can top the meal we had the last time, I'll have to move here for good." With that decided, they headed down to the lobby and began the evening walk to the restaurant.

Ahmed seemed to race to the door as the two Americans entered. "My friends, I am honored that you have chosen to visit my restaurant again. Please be seated here where it is quiet. I will bring you beer while you look at the menu." And he was gone as quickly as he came. In what appeared like seconds, he was back with two tall bottles of St. George Amber beer and two cold glasses just like the last time. He poured for his guests and waited silently while they took their first drink.

McFadden easily drank half the glass before placing it back on the table. "Excellent, Ahmed. That was exactly what I needed this evening," he offered to the smiling owner. "Two more of the same." Tom spoke for them both. "You served such a wonderful meal the last time we were here that we would like for you to select our menu again."

Ahmed flashed a wide smile and his bright white teeth seemed to glow under the lights of the dining room. "The first meal I served was very good, but this shall be the meal you will talk with your friends about for years," he said with a bow. Before they could respond, he was off and moving. Just as before, they could hear his voice in the kitchen sounding so much like a general barking commands. There was the sound of pots and pans moving, doors opening and closing swiftly, and then it was over as quickly as it started, and Ahmed was back on the floor. He bowed to his guests and asked them to be patient, but the meal would be well worth waiting for.

While they waited, McFadden and Marino enjoyed their second two bottles of beer as they went over the day's events. It really had gone very well and they agreed that Pierce's map really should make the difference. One third out of the way, assuming they didn't strike gold tomorrow. If they found Spinoza's plane on the next flight, they could then begin the real search on the ground. That was the way they wanted to hunt for treasure; on the ground and able to reach out and touch it.

As they discussed their plans, Ahmed exited the kitchen and was followed by several of his staff carrying covered trays. As they reached the table, several of the busboys quickly arrived and set down tray stands where the trays were arranged in a semi-circle facing their table. With a smile, Ahmed began to take the lids off the trays and slowly reveal the feast he had prepared. The mixed aromas reached them before they had a chance to even look at what lay before them. Ahmed began to identify the plates and talk about how they had been prepared, but McFadden didn't hear a thing. His eyes grew big and his stomach began to grumble in anticipation.

Finally, Ahmed began to place the dishes before his guests, and watched with satisfaction as the two big men began to make the food disappear amid several additional bottles of beer. He left them to their banquet and returned to find Tom leaning back with a satisfied look upon his face. McFadden, meanwhile, was taking the opportunity to finish the last of several of the dishes. Ahmed had never seen anyone eat like this big one.

When the last plate had been finished, McFadden looked up and saw Ahmed looking at him anxiously. "What can I say," McFadden began. "Our first meal was excellent but couldn't come close to matching what we have sampled tonight. You are a master in the kitchen."

Tom smiled and seconded his friend's comments. "Ahmed, thank you so much for this experience. This is a meal I will never forget." After several cups of extremely strong coffee, it was time to go. McFadden didn't even look at the bill and just handed Ahmed two fifty-dollar bills. Amid the bows and smiles and promises of an even greater meal the next time, McFadden and Marino finally made their way to the street and headed back to the hotel.

A short ways back, across the street, a small dark man kept close to the buildings to avoid being seen and walked towards the Sheraton Hotel.

The next morning began much like the day before. At 7:00 am the phone rang. Marino was awake, but still lying in bed. "I'll bet I know who that is," he said as McFadden rolled over to grab the phone. "That's the Captain calling to make sure his crew is up and ready to go."

McFadden barely had time to say hello before Pierce shouted that he was ready to go and they'd better get there within the next hour or he'd take off without them. A proper military-oriented fellow in all his dealings, Pierce wasn't going to be delayed by a couple of "tourists."

Within 45 minutes the two Americans arrived at the air field where Pierce was impatiently waiting for them, only stopping to order a quick breakfast at the hotel.

Although Tadele felt certain he knew where the Land Rover was headed this morning, he didn't want to assume anything. Even though the vehicle had been fitted with the tracking device, he didn't want to fall too far behind, in the event they suddenly changed plans and drove off towards the desert. He would keep his place five cars back and hope they continued to the airport.

When Tom pulled the Rover up to the front of Desert Air, they saw that the King Air was already outside the hangar and the steps were down. Pierce met them at the door and greeted them warmly. "Morning, guys! Grab a cup of coffee and come on over to the map. I've been thinking a little about our game plan for today," he volunteered.

As they walked to the table at the rear of the office, Pierce continued. "If it's okay with you, I'd like to make some adjustments to our search plan for today. I went over the grids that we flew yesterday and I think we may be off just a little." McFadden and Marino looked down at the map and saw that the search area had moved slightly north, and a little east of the old rectangular grid system they had followed yesterday.

Pierce was silent as the two men looked at the new map. When they looked up, he continued. "BB, I went over the specifications you have on the Breda's capabilities and fuel consumption. As I said before, these planes were pretty basic and not necessarily identical coming off the assembly line. Considering this, and the fact that ground/air speed instruments were pretty primitive at that time, I decided to discount Angelo's estimate of how far they'd traveled. He could have conceivably been off by several miles. I still think he was a pretty sharp kid in 1936, but he was dependent on instrumentation that was evolving each day. In reality, I would imagine he made his estimates on distance traveled based on fuel consumption, and the plane's fuel gauge. I believe we'll have more success if we use the mileage reported by the Search and Rescue team."

The two men were listening intently as their pilot continued his review. "Even though I still think they were led to the crash site by another plane," Pierce went on, "they would have been much more accurate in determining distance using the odometers in their vehicles. They would have known almost to the tenth of a mile how far they'd traveled." He paused a moment and looked at the faces of the two men standing across the table. Satisfied that they were still with him, he leaned over the map and used a pencil as a pointer as he explained the reasons for the change in strategy. "Part of the reason for the change is mine. I flew us to the search area based on miles flown, and not miles driven. It may not seem like much, but one hundred and fifty air miles could be quite a bit different than one hundred fifty road miles just from an instrumentation standpoint. By plane to that area would be straight, "as the crow flies."

"If the team had driven to the location" he continued, "we have to take into consideration the road conditions they would have had to face. Having to deal with difficult terrain could have added many more miles than the plane would have experienced.

McFadden recognized where Pierce was taking them, and it made sense. Going with the best available measuring equipment for the time could be quite different from the basic ground to air instruments used in airplanes of the early to mid-1930s. Marino seemed to have the same question that McFadden was considering and asked, "Where do you think this takes us?" The two men just stared at the map and waited for Pierce to answer.

"If I'm on the right track, and I truly believe I am, the worst-case scenario is that we've wasted one day cruising an area that was unlikely to be the site of either crash. That's not really a bad thing since we now have a little experience in how this whole effort is going to unfold. We take this knowledge and move it to a new location and continue what we've been doing."

Although initially a little disappointed, as Pierce explained the reason for the new strategy, McFadden was feeling a little better since their focus now appeared to be based more on facts than on the interpretation of a 70-year-old diary. "I understand what you're saying, and I agree with your thought process. How far does this take us from where we searched yesterday?" McFadden asked.

Marino was more direct with his question. "How much more time does this add onto our search?" he asked.

Pierce smiled and raised his hands. "Relax, Guys, this isn't the end of the world. By making our adjustments today, we avoid another day in the wrong place. Actually, I think we're going to save a little airtime. The grids of the new area are smaller and closer to the 167-mile trip that the S&R team reported." He could see he still had their attention. They weren't upset or angry, but they did seem a bit uncertain of what this all meant to their search plans.

"In considering this new search area, I saw more opportunity for identifying the crash site of Spinoza. I'm willing to bet that we find him in this general area," he said as he circled an area in the grid with his pencil.

Marino looked at McFadden, who nodded back to him. "Aaron, yesterday we said you were the boss and I don't think that's changed in 24 hours. We're counting on your experience to get us to Spinoza's plane, and if we need to make some changes then we make some changes. My only question is why we're still on the ground?" With that, the tension was gone and the men grabbed their gear and headed out to the King Air.

CHAPTER 23

This flight started much like their time yesterday, although there was no need to fly past the old airfield. Within an hour, they were circling the area that Pierce had shown them on the map earlier. As he cruised north of the old search area, he looked off to the side and appeared to be studying the trees.

"Remember I said that a plane crashing through the trees would leave something behind. That's still true! Regardless of how long ago the crash took place, there should be some visible damage on the trees. Keep your eyes open for anything that looks different from one tree to the next."

Pierce then made a slow bank south and leveled the plane for the first of their runs. This time, McFadden had the camera equipment out and ready before Pierce had even leveled the plane.

For the next several hours, Pierce crossed and crisscrossed the search area with no success. They were sure they would find what they were looking if they just followed the grid areas. As Pierce reached the end of their northern boundary, he banked the plane to the left and overlapped a section they had already completed and an area still to be searched. He leveled the plane and increased speed to get them up to flying altitude.

"We might as well…" The plane suddenly banked hard left and McFadden was thrown back in his seat. "What the hell happened?" he shouted.

"Sorry, guys! The reflection of the sun hit a section of the trees and I thought I saw a glint of metal. It may be nothing, but I'd like to make another pass." The King Air continued a wide swing until it was again headed south. "Look out to the left and watch the light hit the tops of the trees as we come parallel to that path. Three sets of eyes searched the trees as the plane came full circle. "There! Did you see it?" he asked. McFadden and Marino exchanged looks.

"The only thing I saw were miles of trees," Tom answered.

"No, I'll make another pass," Pierce said. "BB, get your camera ready and start to shoot as soon as I tell you." Pierce banked the plane in another wide circle and leveled the wings for another pass. "Okay, everybody, look out the left and concentrate. Focus the camera on the area just behind the port engine. I'm going to fly us right over the spot I'm talking about. Ready, keep watching… keep watching… THERE!" This time, McFadden did notice a difference in the pattern of the treetops and thought he, too, saw something shiny.

"I think I saw what you were talking about," he said. "Maybe it was because I was sitting right behind you, but the sun did make the trees look different."

Marino looked from one man to the other. "I have no idea what you two are talking about. It all looked the same to me. Maybe the video will show some piece of information the naked eye missed."

"I just punched the coordinates of this spot into the plane's GPS so we know where we saw this," Pierce said, as McFadden carefully entered the coordinates into his handheld Garmin GPS just to be sure they had the exact location. "That's all we can do for now. I'll be interested in seeing what the video picked up when we get back." As if in a hurry to view the video, Pierce put the plane into a gradual climb and increased speed as he raced in a straight line for their home base.

In less than 2 hours, Pierce received ground clearance to land and lined the plane up for his approach. She touched down lightly and, with a small bounce, settled on the ground. He reduced power and headed for the exit lane leading to Desert Air's hangar. No sooner had he pulled up in front of the building and cut the engines than Pierce was out of the plane and walking quickly towards the office. As he walked he looked over his shoulder to the end of the end of the hangars.

By the time, Marino and McFadden entered the building, Pierce had the air conditioner on full blast. McFadden uploaded the footage to his laptop while Pierce attached the cable to a larger monitor for easier visibility to view what they had spotted. Within a few seconds they were looking at an endless view of the trees they'd flown over earlier that day. They would have had quite a bit of video to review if McFadden hadn't left the audio on while he filmed.

McFadden fast-forwarded through minutes of video, stopping every so often to listen to the background conversation. The camera view stopped for a second before resuming. This time they could hear Pierce's voice. "Ready, keep watching... keep watching... THERE!" McFadden hit a key and the frame froze on the monitor. He zoomed in on a spot and stared at the picture. At first, McFadden and Marino didn't see anything special, but, as he continued to zoom in and out, they saw what looked like a rectangular shadow in the trees.

"Remember, I said that despite being made of aluminum and sheet metal those planes made a hole when they hit. Well, there's the hole! When Spinoza's plane went down, it must have come in at an angle and shaved the limbs and branches right off the trunk of the trees as it crashed to the bottom. Nature may have taken decades to close the gap and recover the ground, but those were old growth trees and their trunks never recovered. It looks like a couple may be dead. There may be new growth at the very tops of these trees, but the trunks have been damaged so badly they probably can't repair and regrow the missing limbs. At just the right angle, the afternoon light showed the path of the dying plane as it sliced its way through." The more they listened to Pierce's explanation, and the more they looked at the picture on the monitor, the clearer the image became.

"I'm willing to bet that if you use the GPS coordinates I plugged into the plane's computer this afternoon, it will take you to the wreckage of a 1936 Breda Ba 65 at approximately 169 miles northwest of the air base." With that, Pierce went to the refrigerator and removed three bottles of beer and passed them around. Then he sat down and plopped his feet on his desk and appeared to be waiting preparedly for the questions.

The two men continued to stare at the frozen frame as Pierce leaned back in his chair and took a long swig from the beer bottle. "Now that you pointed it out, I think I can see a straight line about the width of the old fighter," Marino finally said. "It does look like a section of the trees have been sliced out underneath the top branches. I can't believe we hit a likely spot to search on our way back at the end of the day."

McFadden repeatedly adjusted the frame back and forth, first far away and then zooming in right over the spot Pierce had observed. He had to agree with Tom. Considering their budget and limited time available to search, they were exceptionally lucky to get a possible hit so soon. Tomorrow they would drive out to the site and hope the coordinates led them to the plane.

Pierce finished his beer and tossed the empty bottle into the wastepaper basket. "What do you want to do?" he asked.

"I think Tom and I will have to take the next leg of this journey by truck. We'll use the coordinates you have for the site and follow them to where you saw the hole." He paused and looked at Pierce before speaking. "Once Tom and I have found the wreckage then I think we use the plane to hunt for the final location, where Angelo had crash landed."

Pierce sounded almost disappointed when he offered, "I'd like to shut down for a day or so and ride out with you guys, but I have two scheduled flights over the next couple of days I can't get out of. Returning customers and too much money to risk losing."

McFadden looked at Marino and saw relief in his eyes. They'd almost had to come up with a story to tell Aaron why he couldn't come with them. Fortunately, Pierce had excused himself. "We understand.

By the time you finish with your trips we should be ready for the next flight. We'll check back with you on Thursday." It was agreed.

As they were finishing their beers, Pierce casually asked, "Do you guys know anyone else here in Addis Ababa? Have you told anybody what you're trying to do?" The men across the table looked at one another and shook their heads. McFadden said that he hadn't spoken with anyone other than Pierce.

Marino thought for a moment and then said, "The only one I mentioned this to in general was the guy who owns the car rental agency. Why do you ask?"

Pierce looked over his shoulder and said, "Go look out the window to your right at the end of the row of hangars and tell me what you see." McFadden and Marino cautiously approached the window and looked down the long line of hangars. Before they could answer his question, Pierce said, "A beige Toyota." The two men turned back to Pierce and McFadden asked, "How did you know it was there?"

"It was there yesterday when we took off, and it was there when we landed. It was gone after you left yesterday afternoon. This morning when we were boarding the plane I saw it again, and it was here when we landed. No one around these parts owns that car."

"Boys, I don't know why, but someone is tracking your every move."

CHAPTER 24

As Marino and McFadden left the office and walked to the Land Rover, they tried not to look at the Toyota parked about 100 yards from Pierce's hangar. As they drove back to the hotel, Tom kept looking in the rearview mirror to see if the car was indeed following them. He didn't see it anywhere behind them and chalked it up to Pierce's suspicious nature. "Why would anyone want to follow us?" he asked out loud.

Tadele was playing it safe and decided to give the Americans a little more room, since the traffic wasn't as heavy going into the city at this hour and it would be easier for them to notice a car following them. Besides, they were going back to the hotel anyway. He was quite a few car lengths back, when the Land Rover passed the turn leading to the hotel and proceeded further west towards downtown. "Where are you going now my friends?" he asked himself out loud as he maintained his distance in the rush hour traffic.

Instead of going directly to the hotel, the men had decided to make a detour. With directions provided by the desk clerk, they were headed to a mall where they would find Addis Ababa's answer to Wal-Mart. They found a parking space close to the entrance and stopped to check the locations of the various departments. Not surprisingly, everything was written in Amharic so they just began to walk through the store until they found a store selling Sporting Goods.

Rather than follow them into the store, Tadele found a parking spot several cars back in the next row where he had a view of the Rover and decided to wait for the men to return. Obviously, they wouldn't be going anywhere without their transportation.

McFadden and Marino took the escalator to the second floor and each man grabbed a shopping cart. They walked down aisle after aisle, picking up the items they'd probably need for the next several days. They had decided to allow themselves up to three days in the field for this part of the search. That meant they would have to sleep outdoors, so they filled two shopping carts as they walked aisle after aisle. They picked up a three-man tent, two sleeping bags, two back packs, a Coleman lantern for light at night, insect repellent, four cases of bottled water, and a case of the civilian version of the military's MRE (Meals Ready to Eat). They added a few more odds and ends to the carts, and then went for their one big purchase — a metal detector. After examining what was available and comparing their capabilities, they decided on a Garrett AT Pro Metal Detector with Headphones. There were a few that were less expensive and a few that cost more, but this would do nicely for the type of searching they would be doing.

"Whatever we forget for this trip," Marino said, "we'll know what to include for the next one. After all, it's only 3 days." The Rover had a 28-gallon gas tank, so they would have more than enough gas to get them out there. Besides, the two extra 5-gallon cans would ensure they had enough to get back. After a final inventory, they headed to the checkout and Tom put the $675 bill on his American Express card. "Never leave home without it!" he said as if endorsing it for a commercial.

Their supplies filled the storage area behind the rear seats in the Rover and flowed onto the seat behind McFadden. While Tom drove, McFadden plugged the adapter for the GPS into the cigarette lighter and entered the coordinates Pierce had given them. The GPS calculated the distance and then showed the trip at a little over 300 hundred miles. A trip like that back in the States would have taken a little less than 4 hours, but here in Ethiopia, without a country-wide road system, there was no telling how long it might take them. But they were prepared.

As Marino exited the parking lot, he made a left turn onto the road to the hotel. He looked in the rearview mirror again and saw the Toyota about four cars back. "He was right!"

"Who was right?" McFadden asked.

"Aaron! I think there is a car following us." Marino wouldn't have even noticed the Toyota behind them if Pierce hadn't directed their attention to it before they left.

Tadele wasn't paying as close attention to the cars in front of him as he should have. With cars changing lanes and turning off the road, there was suddenly only one vehicle separating him from the Rover. Before he could change lanes or fall back the car in front made a quick left-hand turn and Tadele was suddenly right behind the Rover.

McFadden adjusted the mirror on the passenger sun visor. He saw the Toyota behind them and reached for the bag at his feet. Tadele saw the movement in the Rover and suspected that he might have been spotted. He cursed to himself. There was no reason for him to be so close to the Rover, but he was boxed in and wasn't able to turn for about a minute. He tried to conceal himself behind the steering wheel and hoped the men could not get a good look at him.

Tadele had seen McFadden move a bit in the front seat but he never actually turned around to look behind. After several moments, he saw a break in traffic and was able to turn at the next intersection. He had been careless in allowing himself to get so close. He would be more careful going forward. He made the decision that they were most likely headed back to the hotel, and there was no point in risking them spotting the old car again. He would drive directly to the hotel and find a place where he could watch them without risking being spotted again.

McFadden saw the car turn and felt a sense of relief. "Maybe it was just a coincidence that he was there. It could have been just another Toyota that looked like the one from the airport. What would prompt anyone to want to follow the two of us? Anyway, he's gone. He turned right at the last corner."

Marino was silent for a few minutes. "I can't figure why we'd be followed either. I mean, the only one I told about the crash is the guy who owns the car rental where I got the Land Rover. Why would he be at all interested in what we were doing?" Gone was any excitement they might have had over their find this afternoon. Marino focused his attention back on the road, "But just to play it safe, I think we should keep our eyes open and be more aware of who, or what, is around us."

About 25 miles away, a small light continued to blink on the screen of the laptop and appeared to slowly head back towards the city. "How was your day, Tom? Did you have any luck?" Jacob asked out loud.

Hopefully, when Tadele returned he would be able to provide more specific details of their day.

After a quick meal at the hotel restaurant, McFadden and Marino returned to their room. Despite the suspicious car behind them today, the mood again was upbeat. They had accomplished in two days what they had thought might take them a week. Finding Aaron Pierce had been the best bit of luck they'd had so far. He'd be ready for them when they returned and then they'd hit the sky again with hopes to have the same success further north. They did a quick inventory of their gear and then went to bed. Tomorrow would be an early start of a very long day.

CHAPTER 25

The front gate to the Lucky Car Rental grounds was closed and locked. Several spotlights shown down on the row of parked rental vehicles. Anyone approaching them at night would be clearly visible to one of several security cameras trained on the vehicles and the office building. The cameras were carefully concealed so as not to draw any suspicion from the locals. Someone might question why a small car rental agency would have such a sophisticated security system. It would be immediately suspected that it was the base of some shady underground illegal operation. No need to attract any unnecessary attention. Looking at the building from the street, you could barely make out the lone light burning inside. Jacob had spent a good part of the afternoon monitoring the travel of the blinking light as it left the hotel earlier that morning and proceeded to the airport. Once there, the Rover did not move again until late in the afternoon. On its way back, the blinking light had stopped for about an hour, before starting again and finally arriving at the hotel.

Three men sat at the small table in the rear of the darkened building. The single light bulb hanging over the table provided just enough illumination for the men to see the map spread out before them. Jacob sat facing Tadele and appeared to be watching a spot over the other man's shoulder. Tadele sat in front of an old wooden cabinet that hung on the wall behind him. The two unpainted doors would not have attracted anyone's attention, as it looked like an old medicine storage cabinet.

The doors were open now and revealed four expensive monitors. Three were closed circuit TV monitors showing various angles of the building and the parking lot. Every few seconds, the images changed, allowing Jacob to see the entire area in real-time images. The CCTV system was also motion sensitive. It would lock the nearest camera on anything moving outside the building larger than a dog. No one could approach the building undetected. Jacob watched the three monitors as the cameras scanned and recorded everything in the parking lot. The fourth monitor revealed an overlay of the city and showed a stationary blinking light, which indicated that the transponder hidden in the Land Rover the Americans had rented was working properly. The vehicle sat parked at the Sheraton.

To Jacob's right, a third man sat quietly. He had said very little since Tadele had picked him up earlier that evening. As always, the man would be found standing quietly alone on a secluded stretch of road just outside the Capital. He would enter the car, greet Tadele warmly and then there would be silence, until they arrived at the car rental office. Later he would be taken back to the same spot and left standing alone in the dark as Tadele drove off.

As the three men sat drinking coffee, Jacob turned first to Tadele and asked, "What happened this afternoon?" Tadele smiled and told them how he had followed the Americans from the hotel that morning to the airport and finally to Desert Air.

"They never knew I was there. There was no reason for them to even think anyone would be following them. They went into the office and were there for about an hour before taking off in the plane headed east. I left but came back there later before they landed."

He provided the missing information as to why the Rover had stopped moving for almost an hour on its way back to the hotel. He explained that, after leaving the airport, the two men had stopped at the El Alegia shopping mall and bought a variety of supplies and equipment before returning to the Sheraton.

"I think they may have seen the car at the airport. After leaving the mall, they headed in the direction of the hotel and I kept my distance in traffic, but I think they may have become suspicious. I could see movement in the car but nothing to indicate they had seen me. Rather than run the risk of being spotted, I turned off and drove directly to the hotel."

"Do you think they got a good look at you?" Jacob asked. They had gone this far and he didn't want to put the Americans on the alert.

"No, I was only behind them for a few seconds and then I was gone," Tadele responded. "As I said, they didn't slow down or turn around and look behind them. In that traffic they couldn't have gotten a good look at me. I think they just saw the car and thought they'd seen it before. But the Toyota cannot be used again."

He explained that he had left the car a block from the hotel and took up a position under the shade of a tree where he could watch the entrance. A short time later the Rover arrived and the one called Marino gave the keys to the valet before going inside.

After the valet parked the Rover in the garage, Tadele said he had made his way unseen to the vehicle and, looking through the windows, observed much of what had been purchased. He confirmed what they had already suspected. The Americans were going into the desert and appeared well-prepared for several days away from the city.

The third man at the table was much older. A tall and thin individual. He was clean shaven and had a quiet air of authority about him, like he saw what others were not seeing. He wore a robe and sandals, much like any of the other thousands of desert inhabitants. In a crowd he would disappear; a nobody. There was nothing exceptional about him except for his eyes. They seemed to look right through you as you spoke. Not a threatening gaze, but rather that of someone paying close attention to every word you spoke. It was like he ran an extremely quick study of everyone and everything with whom he interacted.

They called him Brother Anteneh, but with an obvious tone of respect. While Tadele spoke like the city dweller he was, Anteneh's speech was soft and intelligent — a man of education. "How is it he came here rather than to one of the other rental agencies?" he asked softly. Jacob smiled, "All of the taxi drivers working at the Sheraton and the Hilton, including my cousin Mohammed, always recommend Lucky Car Rental and bring any foreigner looking to rent a vehicle here first. I tip them well for "bringing me the business. It is a very efficient way of keeping track of the visitors."

"I do not rent to any of the tourists or businessmen, but this gives me the opportunity to see who is in the city and why they are here. As I spoke with this American and he told me the story of his uncle and I decided it would be best to have him in a vehicle we could keep track of and know his every move. I gave him a price he could not resist. We could not afford to have him traveling without us always knowing exactly where he was, and, hopefully, what he was doing."

Anteneh nodded and smiled. "Excellent, Jacob. As always, you make the right choices. We are fortunate to have men like you and Tadele amongst our friends," he stated. The two men smiled broadly at the compliment. "How much do you think they really know, Jacob?" he asked. "Do they know anything solid or are they just guessing?"

Jacob turned to the older man and was silent for a moment. "The one who rented the Rover is called Tom Marino. The story about his uncle's crash sounded like he could be talking about either Colavari or Spinoza, but, since he said his uncle survived the war, I realized Colavari was probably the most likely person. If it is Colavari, then there is a chance they may be searching for the Spinoza crash site, as well. Without that spot as a starting point, they would have no way of calculating in which direction Colavari flew the plane after being damaged."

The older man was quiet and looked at one of the security monitors as he spoke. "They should have cleaned up everything at the Spinoza wreck years ago," he said to himself. "If they had done that there would be no place from which to start. They could have searched a hundred miles in any direction and found nothing. Who would have thought that someone would come back here after more than 70 years? Well, it is too late now. There is too much debris at Spinoza's site and not enough time to remove it all. Besides, it is too far for us to travel without fear of being seen, especially if they continue their air search. The only thing we can do is to make sure that the Colavari site is picked clean. There can be nothing left there for them to find."

Satisfied with his decision, he turned back to the other two men, resting his hand gently on Tadele's shoulder as one might touch a child, the little taxi driver beaming with pride. "Tadele, please drive me back so that I can tell him what we have discovered." He embraced Jacob. "Peace be upon you, loyal friend," he smiled. "And upon you," replied Jacob.

Jacob unlocked the gate and pulled it open wide enough to allow the battered Toyota to pull out onto the road and watched it slowly disappear into the night. Tomorrow would be a long day if the Americans left to search for the spot where Spinoza had gone down. He could not go home tonight. He would have to sleep in his office so that he would be ready to track the Land Rover's journey as soon as it left.

An hour later, Tadele pulled the old car to the side of the road where he had picked up the older man hours before and watched as his lone passenger quietly exited. As Anteneh walked slowly into the black night, he softly called back, "Blessings be upon you, Tadele." Before he could respond, the night closed around the old man and he was gone. As he drove away towards the city, Tadele wondered how Anteneh would get back. He had never seen or heard another vehicle, but knew it was too far for the man to travel by foot.

As Brother Anteneh stood watching the old Toyota disappear down the lonely road, he heard the engine of another vehicle start in the distance and then saw the shaded headlights come on as it pulled up next to him. The old Jeep pulled to a stop and the young driver smiled at the older man as he quietly got in and buckled his seat belt. They drove several minutes before the young man spoke. "He is waiting up for you," he said quietly. Anteneh smiled and nodded. His mind was considering the options available to them and the consequences they faced if a wrong decision was made.

Finally, the young driver could wait no longer. He had to ask the question for which so many awaited the answer. "Do they know anything, Brother? What will we do if they come and search?"

Brother Anteneh merely smiled and squeezed the young man's hand. "I'm not sure what they know, or suspect," he answered. "We will leave it up to him to provide the guidance needed to deal with this." For the remainder of the ride, neither man spoke; the young man curious and the older man frightened.

CHAPTER 26

McFadden awoke at 5:00am and jumped out of bed, ready to start their long trek into the wilderness. He called room service and had them send up a light breakfast with a large pot of coffee. He also had them prepare another package of sandwiches for the road. There was no way of knowing how long it would take them to reach the coordinates he had punched into the GPS. He wondered to himself what they would find when they got there. Would the crash site be easy to find, or had nature buried the evidence under decades of growth? He kept thinking of Aaron's comment about walking right over a site without noticing it.

Breakfast arrived and the two men ate in concentrating silence. As McFadden drank his second cup of coffee, his mind began to wonder. What if another group from the base had come out later after they'd returned with Spinoza's body and salvaged what was left after the crash? McFadden caught himself and stopped asking the "what if" questions. Those could wait until they reached the mountains.

Tom looked at his friend and could tell his mind was someplace else. "What are you thinking about?"

McFadden snapped back to the present. "Just daydreaming about whether we'll be able to locate Spinoza's plane today. It's funny, but as we get deeper into this, I have my occasional doubt over where this will all end up. Forget it, I'm ready."

Tom was quiet himself. "I sometimes have the same nagging doubts, but then I think about what my uncle wrote and what Father Cleary told us, and I find I'm able to refocus. We need to take this one day at a time and try not to think too far ahead." Marino finished and stood up. "Okay, let's get going, big guy!"

McFadden nodded and they grabbed their gear and headed down to the lobby. While McFadden picked up their food, Tom had them bring the Rover to the front door. All their equipment was just the way they'd left it. Tom added their personal items to the stockpile as McFadden returned with their food.

At 6:00 am, the roads were quiet leaving the city, and there was little traffic as they headed north and left Addis Ababa behind. McFadden used the suction cup on the GPS to attach it to the center of the windshield, so that they could both follow their progress.

Jacob had had a restless night and was also awake early. He hadn't been able to sleep and was drinking his third cup of coffee as he watched the blinking light head north and away from the city. They wouldn't be able to follow the Land Rover by car today. There would be no way to avoid being seen. With the aid of the hidden tracking device and the computer monitor, Jacob would be viewing their progress from the comfort of his office.

It wasn't long before the Rover was cruising along the two-lane paved road. They watched as the horizon to the east began to turn red, waiting for the sun to rise and begin its slow journey towards the west. With only desert before them and nothing to obstruct their view, they stared at the blossoming sunrise and the beginning of a new day. A day that brought with it the promise of a great adventure, and hopefully the greatest ever known. It was invigorating to be starting the day on such an aesthetically pleasing morning. It had been cool in the city when they left, but they knew the sun would change that before long.

The Rover was a comfortable ride and the air conditioner would prove invaluable as the day dragged on. During the first hour they saw only one vehicle on the road. It was an older truck with stake body sides that approached them from the opposite direction. It moved slowly and revealed a load that was stacked high above the truck's cab. The assortment of boxes and barrels appeared to be tied tightly. Two men rode on top of the mountain of cargo and waved as they passed them. Tom honked the horn twice in acknowledgement and watched the truck in his rearview mirror as it became smaller and smaller until it disappeared.

As Marino directed his attention back on the road before them, McFadden gazed at the surrounding desert and allowed his mind to drift back to a time over 70 years ago. Angelo Colavari wouldn't have found much difference between his Ethiopia in 1947 and the version of today. The hard-top road would have been an improvement but everything else would appear very much the same. The sun was just as fiery and the blazing sand still stretched endlessly in every direction.

They were about two hours outside the city when the GPS directed them west and off the paved road. They had covered a little over seventy miles, but now they were forced to reduce speed. Progress would be much slower from now on, but Tom found what looked like an old caravan trail and they would follow this for as long as they could, providing it headed in their general direction. They would try to avoid making their own trail in the soft sand for as long as possible.

Tom engaged the four-wheel drive on the fly and the Rover seemed to handle the desert without any difficulty. It was good that they had the GPS and hadn't relied on any of the maps McFadden had obtained. They wouldn't have been able to travel in a straight line from the city anyway. The terrain just wasn't compatible for a regular vehicle. They probably could have gone directly northwest to the crash site had they been traveling by camel, but that trip would have cost them several days they couldn't afford.

"How does she handle?" McFadden asked.

"Not too bad. Kind of like driving a dune buggy, but the rough road is a little tough on the arms. Despite the good suspension system, I can still feel every rut or bump," Tom answered.

"I can relieve you anytime you want," McFadden offered.

"Let me go for a while longer and then I'll change spots with you." Tom had always enjoyed driving and being the pilot, as it helped pass the time.

After two hours off-road, they had traveled an additional 70 miles. McFadden looked at the screen on the GPS and commented, "One hundred fifty down – a little more than one hundred fifty to go. It was a smidgen past 10:00, and it had taken them almost four hours to cover

150 miles. At this rate they wouldn't reach the mountains for another 3-4 hours. That would mean they wouldn't be able to start looking for the plane until maybe three or four in the afternoon, the hottest time of the day.

"Depending on what time we arrive, it might be a good idea just to set up camp for the night and start looking first thing in the morning when it's cooler," Marino suggested.

"It sounds logical, but I'm willing to bet that, once we get there, neither one of us is going to be able to wait until tomorrow to start our search." McFadden smiled. "But you're right! I can just see us walking around the woods at night with flashlights."

During the next hour they were able to add another 35 miles, but then the terrain appeared to flatten out and Tom was able to increase his speed to almost 45 miles per hour. One hundred and eighty-five down. Tom had been behind the wheel for almost 5 hours, but he wasn't ready to hand it off to McFadden. They each drank several bottles of water and had some of the sandwiches the hotel had packed. Tom ate his while he drove.

As the Rover bounced over the sand, the men watched the little arrow on the GPS continue to slowly move north. Two hours passed and they subtracted another 90 miles from the total left to cover. The soil was turning harder as they approached the mountains, and Tom was able to get a little more speed out of the Rover. After a quick roadside pit stop, Tom changed places and McFadden took over the wheel.

The trees were getting closer, but now the terrain appeared to get rockier as they approached the base of the mountains. McFadden was forced to reduce speed and carefully choose his path. This meant they were no longer traveling in a straight line. They drove back and forth, east to west, west to east, looking for the angle that presented the least amount of obstacles. Finally, at a little after 4:00 pm, they reached the base of the mountains. It had taken them upwards of 9 hours to travel 316 miles. They were beat and the sun was beginning its descent to the west.

Tom stretched as he exited the Rover. "As much as I was willing to bet against it, I have to agree with you. Let's set up camp and get a good night's sleep before we go traipsing around in the forest. Besides, I'm hungry for something more than a sandwich. Let's heat some water and have an MRE."

McFadden agreed, but suggested that they set up before eating. The night came quick in the desert and the last thing they wanted to do would be pitching their tent in the dark.

McFadden began to unload their gear while Tom looked for a flat spot to make camp. Actually, the best place seemed to be about 30 yards back down the path they had just driven. The ground was mostly dirt, so they would be able to drive in the tent pegs. They stockpiled their gear at this site and, within 15 minutes, the tent was up with their sleeping bags rolled out inside. The stove was soon on and a pot of water sat on the burner. The hot water would be added to the foil packages of dehydrated food in the MREs. McFadden went to gather wood for a campfire to keep away any four-legged visitors they might have during the night.

Darkness would soon set in. Tom lit the Coleman lantern and hung it at the opening of their tent. McFadden returned with a huge armload of wood and kindling. He placed the kindling in a pile and built a circle of dirt and rock around the wood, to prevent any embers from rolling away and starting the grass on fire. He left again, and this time returned with a large piece of wood under each arm. "We have to have seats," he said before dropping one on each side of the campfire.

The stove was just bringing the water to a boil. They each chose an MRE out of the case. Tom chose beef tips and noodles while McFadden selected the chili and beans. They poured hot water into each pouch and let them sit for a while before starting to mix the ingredients. The MRE's were designed to provide more than 2400 calories to the active field soldier. They contained an entrée, a drink, dessert, and a snack. If necessary, they could even be eaten cold out of the package. After the long day's travel, the two men quickly consumed their gourmet meals.

The campfire provided just enough additional light to illuminate the area so that they could clearly see one another. "That was quite a ride," Tom finally said.

"It was harder on you since you drove the lion's share of the trip," McFadden acknowledged. "I don't know how you drove for so long without a break."

Tom smiled. "You get the honors on the return. "I'm going to catch up on my beauty sleep when we head back."

"The trip's not that long," retorted McFadden.

They sat and watched the flames of the fire for a while before Tom finally looked up. "BB, just think about it. We could be 100 yards from

Spinoza's plane right now. Tomorrow we could walk into those trees and find the crash site. From there, we could drive a few miles and locate my uncle's plane. We could conceivably find both of them in the same day."

McFadden thought for a moment. "You're right. We could be just yards from the plane. But then again, the Italians may have come back here after it was located and cleaned everything out." This time McFadden was the realist. "Tomorrow will tell."

The effects of the day's long drive were finally catching up to them. McFadden backed the Rover down the path and parked it next to the tent just in case. Tom turned off the lantern and threw a few large pieces of wood on the campfire, just to keep the area bright for a few more hours. Before long, both men were sound asleep.

While the two men slept and dreamt about their search, a few miles to the northeast, there was another group of men working steadily through the night with small propane-powered floodlights to illuminate their surroundings. Brother Anteneh was in charge and urged his companions to be thorough in their work and to try not to miss even the smallest piece of the wreckage. He had chosen the youngest men from their group, since this would be heavy and demanding work throughout most of the night. He needed the strongest and healthiest to complete this task. They moved in silence. Everyone seemed to sense the importance of their work and they were focused on removing anything that could identify the place as a crash site.

They were just inside the tree line and had to haul the pieces they found to the waiting truck parked on the hard ground. There was no need to worry about being seen, as there was no road nearby, the trees were thick, and the moonless sky made the area outside the crash site so dark that as they brought out items to load on the truck, Tadele had to use a flashlight to show them a clear path. Jacob had sent Tadele with the truck and the lights soon after Anteneh had left. He knew there would be much to move, and his friends had nothing in which to haul pieces of such varying size and weight.

It was amazing how much weight these men were able to carry, lift, or push as they went about the task. If there was anything good to be said about the work, it was that the crash so many years ago had been of such impact that the plane had literally broken into hundreds of manageable pieces. Fortunately, there were no sections of the plane so large that they could not be moved. As the hours passed and the truck body began to fill with the remains of the plane, Anteneh kept watch of the crash site itself. When they were finished, it had to look as if nothing had ever happened there. The forest growth that had hidden the plane for so many years was carefully pulled away as the various parts were discovered so they could be removed, but none of the growth was pulled from the ground.

When all the obvious debris was located and removed, the men got down on hand and knee and felt for objects hidden beneath the underbrush. It took hours but, as the sun began to light the horizon to the east, Anteneh agreed with the men that the area had been swept as clean as possible and that nothing remained that could likely be identified as part of a plane. Any pieces remaining would be so small that no one would stumble across them.

Several of the men climbed aboard the truck and fastened a canvas tarp from behind the cab over the entire contents before securing the end of the canvas to the rear of the truck bed. Anyone passing this truck would see piles of rusted metal and assorted pieces of wood and aluminum. Nothing to attract anyone's attention.

As the men made their final inspection of the area, they slowly walked from the site and disappeared behind the green wall of the mountain. Anteneh was the last person to leave the site and prayed that nothing had been left that would help the two Americans.

When everyone had gone, Tadele started the truck and headed for a place further out into the desert where another group from the mountain had dug a hole large enough to conceal everything found. The truck had a dump bed so that it could be backed to the edge of the hole and then released. Men climbed into the hole and began to pull items from the top of the pile and distributed the debris evenly throughout the hole. A short time later, everything would be covered over and the desert would hide its new treasure for all time. Tadele loaded the diggers onto his truck and, within an hour, they too disappeared behind the trees and bushes that was the forest.

There would be no following the Americans tomorrow. It would be impossible to trail them without being seen in the wide-open desert. They would have to watch their movements on the monitor from the comfort of Jacob's office and try to determine if they found what they were looking for.

CHAPTER 27

The two men slept soundly and woke early to find that the temperature had dropped significantly overnight. McFadden reached over to his bag and search around until he found his Boston College hooded sweatshirt. He'd only need this for a few hours, until the sun rose and burned off the chill. "Nature calls," said McFadden as he pulled his boots on and then unzipped the tent flap. He was only gone for a few minutes before reentering the tent. "Damn it's cold out there. It would have been a long and uncomfortable night if we hadn't bought these sleeping bags."

Tom pulled on an old wool sweater and watch cap and disappeared off towards the trees.

The campfire had burned out overnight. There was no reason to relight it. McFadden set up the small propane stove and placed a pot of water over the top of the flame. While he waited for the water to boil, he brushed his teeth using one of the bottles of water to rinse. He could do without bathing for a few days, but there were some things that could not be ignored. Tom returned and took care of his own oral hygiene. By now, the water was beginning to boil so the men chose their next MRE from the case. Breakfast was still the high calorie meal, but not quite as tasty as dinner had been the night before.

They made a pot of coffee and were looking at the trees before them. "Well, after we finish, I think we should get the GPS and double check our location," McFadden suggested. "Assuming our climb didn't throw us too far off course, we should be able to start our walk through the forest from somewhere around here. I'm only hoping that it brings us to where Aaron first spotted the change in the trees, and that the anomaly we saw is actually the results of the crash and not just Mother Nature screwing with us."

The sun was visible off to the east and was already beginning to warm them. After tidying their camp site, they loaded their backpacks with water, some energy bars, and an extra MRE just in case they got stuck overnight. They brought insect repellant, flashlights, and an Army entrenching tool – a small folding shovel. They were ready for the search. McFadden took the GPS and turned on the power. Within a few seconds, it had connected with whatever satellite was being used to transmit the signal. He called up the GPS's coordinates from the previous day and the blinking light on the monitor indicated that they were about a half mile east of the recorded site.

That seemed to make sense. They were just at the edge of the tree line and looked to see what the most direct route would be for them to reach the coordinates. After walking back and forth a few times, they chose an area where the brush wasn't quite as thick, although it would lead them parallel and not in a straight line. As they made their way through the brush and shrubs, the area seemed to widen and appeared flat.

Tom carried the metal detector and waited for his opportunity to sweep a likely area. As the two men made their way deeper, McFadden suddenly stopped and appeared to Marino to be thinking of something.

"What's the problem?" Marino asked.

"I was just remembering something your uncle wrote in his diary about the attack. He said that, as he lined up on the supply train and began his dive, machine guns on both sides opened up on him and Spinoza. If this is actually the entrance he saw them using, then the machine guns would have been on either side somewhere in front of us."

Marino looked at him waiting for him to reach the point of his comment. McFadden looked around before turning back to his friend, "We could probably confirm this site before we go much further. If this is where it all began, there would have been machine guns firing from both sides of the path. There should be an awful lot of metal shell casings lying around. Why don't you try the metal detector on the right side of this area and see if we find anything. If we find the spent brass, we'll know we've hit the right spot. If not, then we should probably move east or west and try to find another likely spot."

Marino smiled at McFadden, "Brilliant idea, Mon Capitan!"

With this new search pattern in mind, both men walked back a hundred yards and turned to look at what they thought could have been the beginning of the trail Angelo Colavari saw so clearly in 1936. They stared at the brush and trees in front of them and tried to envision a natural opening wide enough for horses and camels to walk through, but all they saw were trees. McFadden said, "You stay here and let me try and walk through that mess and see if I can find anything, any clue that this might have been a trail. If I do, then you can come in with the detector and see if there's anything around."

Marino agreed and watched as his friend began to work his way back through the wall of growth. After some twists and turns, and an appropriate amount of colorful language, McFadden eventually disappeared behind the wall of vegetation. "Do you see anything?" Marino called out. "Any luck?"

"I really can't tell if there's anything here," he answered. "Turn on the metal detector and try walking towards me. Walk to your left and right every few yards and see if you pick up anything. We'll try this for a little while and, if we don't find anything, we can move to another spot. This is too big an area to expect to hit it at the first shot." McFadden looked around. "There has to be several potential areas that look like they could be a trail. If we don't find anything here, I think we just keep moving west and look for another likely spot."

Marino turned on the metal detector and adjusted the earphones. He began a slow walk towards McFadden while moving left to right every few feet. After a half hour, it was apparent that there was no significant metal anywhere around them. "Okay, let's move to the next spot," McFadden said.

The two men continued this approach at three more spots without any improvement in their luck. McFadden continued to monitor the GPS to make sure they weren't drifting away from the possible crash site they had identified the previous day. "Let's give this another shot and if we don't find anything then we hike in and try to find the spot Pierce saw yesterday."

They moved another 50 yards west and repeated the process. McFadden would try to walk in towards the trees looking for any sign of a path. "Any luck this time?" Marino called.

McFadden didn't immediately answer. The ground cover was the thickest off to his right. It became difficult trying to walk at an angle, so he walked back towards the flat area in what looked to be the middle. As he reached what he thought was flat ground, his foot sunk about six inches through the underbrush before hitting bottom. He struggled forward a few feet and turned to his right, and then bumped against a rise in the ground about 4 or 5 inches high.

He went to the left and found he still had to step up slightly to get out from where he stood. He stepped back down and moved a few feet further in and realized he was walking in what seemed to be a rut in the ground. He walked straight along the rut and then turned right and found himself again walking up a slight incline. He turned back to the rut and then walked to his left and felt as if he was walking slightly upward. "This could be what's left of the trail into the mountains," he thought to himself. Mother Nature may have reclaimed the trail, but she couldn't fill in the rut that was the road; a path that may have been beaten into the ground by countless feet over several generations.

He finally heard Marino calling him. He shouted back, "Tom, come on in here and bring the detector. Try and work yourself directly back here to where I am. I think I may have found something."

It took Marino several minutes to maneuver himself through, over, and around years of forest growth. "What do you have?" Marino asked as he finally worked his way over to McFadden. "I don't see anything," he said as he looked all around where they stood.

"Come over here and stand in front of me," McFadden instructed. "Stand directly in front of me." Marino did as instructed. "Now follow me for a few feet. Okay, now turn to your right and take a few steps."

As Marino turned and took a step, his foot hit the elevated side of the path and he stumbled forward almost losing his balance. "What's the idea of that? I almost took a header into all of this." Marino regained his footing and stepped back to where McFadden told him to turn right. This time Marino was prepared when he turned left and raised his foot in order to step up. Marino was a little confused. "I thought we were looking for a place where machine guns could be placed to shoot planes out of the sky instead of…" He stopped and smiled. He finally understood what McFadden was trying to show him. "A road! A path into the mountains worn deep by a steady caravan of men and animals during the war. You found it," he said with a broad smile. "You're good! I never would have put this together without you. Regardless of what's out here, we now know there was once a pathway leading in here."

McFadden smiled. "You'd have gotten it if you walked in here first," he said to downplay the discovery.

"Thanks, but I'd have walked right over this," Marino answered with much conviction about his abilities.

"Well, never mind how we found it," McFadden replied. "Now we have to find a place where machine guns could be placed on a level surface." McFadden went on, "Finding the path wasn't too bad. Finding the spent brass can be an entirely different problem. It could literally be under a couple of feet of growth. Let's hope the metal detector can penetrate deep enough to find 70-some year-old bullet brass."

After looking around, Marino began to climb the slight incline off to his right while McFadden climbed up the left. After about 8 to 10 feet, Marino thought he felt the ground level off. "It feels somewhat flat here if you can disregard the vegetation," he offered. "I'm going to walk back towards the way we came in and see if it stays flat." He turned the metal detector on and adjusted the headphones over his ears.

Movement was slow as he fought his way in a straight line back towards where their camp was. Every few steps, he swung the base of the detector right to left, carefully listening for any indication that there might be metal around him.

"Who knows what direction I should be moving in? The guns, if this is the right place, could have just as well been behind us or off to the right or left. Suddenly, Marino yanked the headphones off and yelled, "Wow, that hurt!"

McFadden forced his way over to Marino. "Are you okay? What happened?"

Marino shook his head before answering. "Two important things to remember for the future. Number one, turn the volume on the metal detector down to its lowest setting when sweeping the underbrush while wearing headphones. Number two, never place the detector flat on the ground. These are words to live by," he stated. "I don't know what I just found, but it's metal for sure."

Squatting over the spot where Marino thought he had found the metal, McFadden began to dig a small hole with the entrenching tool. For the first several shovelfuls of dirt, he found nothing, but then hit something solid, but it could have been a rock. He dug the shovel deeper into the ground around the hole and pulled up a small pile of dirt. When he flipped the dirt off the shovel and onto the ground, he saw several long green objects mixed in with dirt. He picked one up and wiped the dirt off, observing it in his hand. "If we polished this little baby up, we'd have a nice brass .303 British shell casing. Actually, the type of machine gun most readably available to the Ethiopians at that time. The same caliber that your uncle and Spinoza were facing that day."

Taking the empty shell in his hand, Marino brought it up close to his eye, looking at it carefully before speaking. "BB, this could have been the round that brought down my uncle or killed poor Spinoza. It's kind of eerie looking at these so many years after they probably shot down two planes."

"Try to stay objective on this, Tommy. The important thing to remember is that your uncle lived, and, as a result, may have experienced something few people in history ever have, or could ever believe."

Dropping the shell back on the ground, Marino regained his composure and adjusted the volume on the detector and began to slowly sweep the head back and forth over the ground in front of him. "This place is filled with shell casings. This is definitely one of the positions where a machine gun was set up." He smiled, "We're in the right place, big guy!" He stepped down and worked his way to what they felt was the other side of the trail, climbing several feet until the ground appeared to level off. "I don't think I'll need the headphones," he said and pulled them off and placed them around his neck. "If the area I hit on this side is anything as large as the first one, we'll be able to hear the alarm clearly." Slowly, he began to walk back towards what they believed was the beginning of the trail, but only picked up an occasional "blip" from the detector.

After a few more steps, he turned around and began to backtrack towards where he had started. After he crossed that point, he continued to walk slowly, moving the detector in an even arch. Suddenly, there were a few blips, followed by a few more, and, before long, it sounded like a fire alarm. Marino turned off the machine and McFadden appeared with the little shovel. He began to dig through the brush towards the ground itself. When he reached the dirt, it only took two shovels full to uncover a small mountain of brass.

"Well, we've found a trail and shell casings, so we could be in the correct general area," Marino said with a smile. "Now all we have to do is find Carlo's plane and then the real search begins."

McFadden again looked at the monitor of the GPS and saw that the arrow was pointing off to the northeast and the distance from the site had dropped to a little over a quarter of a mile. Marino rested the metal detector on his shoulder and followed McFadden as he blazed a new trail east. After a while, the area became less brush and more trees, so they were able to negotiate a much straighter path. They continued to walk for about a half hour. "I think we've seen the worst of the terrain," McFadden declared.

He held the GPS out in front of him as they walked, watching the distance from the spot become smaller and smaller: 700 feet, then 600, 500, 400 and then the area seemed to get brighter ahead. When they reached 125 feet, they were entering a small clearing and there was no longer any doubt of finding the plane. They stopped at the beginning of what was about a 40-square-foot clearing. Sticking out of the ground, at about a 45-degree angle, they saw what was left of a Breda Ba.65, single engine fighter. At this point, they didn't need the GPS to tell them they had found the crash site. There were pieces of the wings and the engine strewn about with large sections of the fuselage partially stuck in the ground. The numbers on the tail section matched those listed by Search and Rescues in their report on Spinoza's plane. There was evidence of the force of the impact as Spinoza's plane smashed into the ground. McFadden looked up and could see the damage the tree trunks had suffered as the plane came in and shaved dozens of feet of limbs and bark, as it plummeted down. Several of the trees in the area had died as a result, and others had never fully recovered.

As he surveyed the damage, McFadden remembered Pierce's words. "I don't care how long it's been since that plane went down, there has to be some evidence of the crash. Nature can only hide so much." He smiled to himself. "How right you are, Aaron. How right you are!"

While McFadden was reviewing the overall crash area, Marino had been checking out the cockpit area of the fuselage. Even if Spinoza had survived the machine gun fire and it was only his plane that had been hit, there was no way he could have lived through this crash. The pilot's seat had been crushed up against the control panel by the fuel tank, which was positioned directly behind the pilot. When the plane struck the ground, the sudden stop in momentum broke the tank free and threw it forward. He never had a chance. It was probably just as well that he had died before the plane hit the ground. There was evidence of where the Search and Rescue team had to cut the side of the cockpit in order to remove the pilot's body.

"Well, we've achieved the first milestone," McFadden said.

Marino was suddenly back to the present. "Right, now what do we do?" he asked. "This may be the first milestone, but now comes the really hard part. Which way did Angelo's plane go from here?"

After spending some time examining the crash site and picking up various pieces of debris for a closer look, the two men settled against a large tree to drink some water and replenish with an energy bar. McFadden got up and took several dozen photos of the site from different angles using his cell phone. "This is the critical find," McFadden said. "Without this spot, we'd have no idea which way to begin any semblance of a search. Knowing the performance specs of the plane, and the details Angelo recalled from that day, we can approach this logically. From this site, and considering the damage to his plane, Angelo could have only flown for a short period before he, too, went down. From here, I think we draw a semi-circle of about 180 degrees east to west and utilize both Pierce's planes and his flight knowledge to branch out from here."

Marino sat quietly for a while as he looked up through the trees to where the plane must have first struck as it raced towards the ground. "I have a really good feeling about this, BB. Carlo has shown us the way. Now it's up to us to put this all together. We could be really close to solving this mystery in the next few days if we're lucky." They could see that evening was fast approaching and they needed to get back to their camp site before dark.

After a few more drinks from their canteens, the two men were up and ready for the trip back to their vehicle. Reversing the GPS coordinates, they arrived back at the tent in a little over and hour and still had enough daylight to gather some additional wood for their fire and prepare their meals before the cold black of night slowly closed in on them. The evening was a repeat of the night before, except that the excitement of their find made sleep a little more difficult.

Three hundred miles away, the atmosphere was not nearly as happy. "They found Spinoza's plane," Jacob said to no one in particular as he, Tadele, and Brother Anteneh watched the monitor. "They're either very good, or very lucky," he added.

Anteneh's expression hadn't changed during the past several hours. Based on his knowledge of the area and where he determined the Americans had stopped, he knew it was only a matter of hours before they located the crash site. "Alright, my friends, it is done," he said calmly. "We've faced this possibility for years and now it is here. Let us hope that they are indeed just lucky."

CHAPTER 28

The following morning found both men awake early and in great spirits. McFadden was up and rummaging through their supplies. "Would you like breakfast in bed?" he joked to Marino.

"Sure, but just brown my French toast and make the bacon crispy," Marino replied. Fadden casually threw an MRE and hit him right off the top of his head. "Is the bacon crispy enough?"

There was no dragging their feet this morning. Both men were eager to get back and begin the next phase of their journey in the search for Colavari's plane, which they hoped would lead them to the Robe of Jesus Christ. After their usual two cups of coffee, they were ready to move. They quickly packed their gear and cleaned up the campsite, making sure the fire was out and that all their trash was picked up and bagged. McFadden took the first shift driving and the Rover seemed to bounce a little more as he pushed harder on the pedal.

"Slow down, big guy!" Marino cautioned. "Getting back quicker won't be so good if we have to replace the suspension on this baby."

McFadden eased off the gas and the truck settled back to about 40 mph and the ride smoothed out. It would take them less than 9 hours for the return trip to the hotel, since they were free to follow the best path and not be concerned with straying too far off the road. The Rover seemed to handle even better on the return trip, but that was probably because their spirits were much higher.

"As much as I hate to admit it, but without Aaron's help who knows how long it would have taken us to find that plane," McFadden said.

"And we're going to need him just as much going forward to find Angelo's plane, as well," Marino added. They were both thinking the same thing – "How much are we going to have to tell Aaron going forward?"

After about three hours, McFadden relinquished the wheel and Marino drove the rest of the way back to the hotel. They left all their equipment and camping gear in the Rover, each just carrying in their backpack. There was no argument as to who got the shower first. They graciously offered each other the first use of the bathroom so that the other could lie across the bed and catch a few winks before it was his time. As it turned out, neither of them even saw the bathroom. They laid across their beds for just a few minutes, and the next thing they heard was the obnoxious ringing of the telephone in their room at 6:00am. Marino was the first to find the receiver and mumbled a, "hello?"

Aaron Pierce's voice boomed on the other end. "Well, tell me. Did you find the plane?" he hollered. By this time, McFadden was also awake and could hear their new friend's voice clearly.

"Tell him we'll be out to see him in about an hour or two," McFadden said as he rolled over and put the pillow over his head.

Pierce heard him and yelled, "Don't give me that hour or two crap! Did you find the plane?"

Marino's head was immediately clear. "Aaron, we found it just where you told us it would be. Thanks!"

His voice calm now, "Alright, then. Come out as soon as you can and tell me about the trip," he said.

"We'll see you in about an hour," Marino assured him.

"Come on, BB. We really need to go see Aaron. I'll order some breakfast while you hit the shower. Up, big guy! Up!" he said loudly.

McFadden sat on the side of the bed and lazily pulled his extra-large frame upright. Shuffling towards the bathroom, half asleep, his only comment was, "lots of breakfast, lots of food."

Twenty minutes later, it was Marino's turn and room service arrived as he headed for the shower. The small waiter pushed the cart into the room and maneuvered it next to the table. He then began unloading covered tray after covered tray onto the table, and when the table ran out of room, he placed the trays on the closest bed. He had never brought so much food to any room in the previous 10 years he had worked there. But seeing McFadden towering over him, he now wondered whether there was actually enough.

After signing for the meal, and still without having converted his US cash to Ethiopian Birr, McFadden gave the waiter a $10 tip, and, in doing so, gained the young man's undying gratitude and devotion. After several bows and a half dozen, "Blessings be upon you!" McFadden finally led the man out the door. He was on his second cup of coffee and halfway through the large Spanish omelet, or whatever they call it in Ethiopia, when Tom came out. They were both starved and conversation quit until they had eaten at least the first round of breakfast.

McFadden leaned back in his chair and poured himself and Tom another cup of coffee. "I think we're really at a cross-road here. How much, if anything, do we tell Aaron at this point?" he asked. "We owe the guy and we still need him for the next part of the trip, but we really don't need a partner, or a potential liability. We didn't come this far for some well-intentioned guy to tell the world we think we found the Robe."

Marino nodded. "I think we're good for a little while yet. We tell him about how we found Spinoza's plane using the information he provided. He knew what we were trying to do, so there are no surprises there. We're just continuing with the search we originally hired him for. It should take us at least another couple of days before we can narrow down where we need to look." He looked relaxed and confident as he stretched his legs and put his feet on the coffee table. "Let's wait until the very last minute before we decide how much Aaron needs to know."

McFadden agreed. There was actually still more than enough left to do before they reached the real reason for their search. In a little more than an hour after Pierce's call, the two men were on their way to the airport.

Traffic was the same as it had been each time they drove out in the morning — fairly light leaving the city, and stop-and-go entering. Tom checked the rearview mirror every few seconds trying to see if there was anyone following them. There were no vehicles that appeared to be sticking with them as they worked their way through what little traffic there was. All clear.

Yes, there was no one following this morning, at least not on the roadways. Jacob had decided that since Tadele had probably been spotted, and since they pretty much knew where the Americans were headed, they would stay in the office for now and track them on the monitor. The homing device on the Rover was still functioning perfectly.

Tom pulled into the area where the private airplane hangars lined the far side of the main airport and made his way to Desert Air. When they pulled up, they saw that both planes were still in the hangar. "Maybe we're not going up today," Tom questioned. Just then, the door swung open and Pierce appeared holding a bottle of champagne.

"I know it's early, but we still need to celebrate," he shouted. "Come on in, the glasses are chilled. Besides, I want all the details on what you found, and where."

They followed Pierce back into the office and walked to their usual meeting place at the table in the back of the room. Pierce filled the chilled glasses and handed one to each of his new friends. "Here's to the next find. May your uncle's plane be where we can see it," he said and raised his glass. They all tapped glasses and wished each other good luck. "Alright, give me the details," he finally said.

McFadden and Marino took turns briefing Pierce on the various steps they had taken to finally locate the plane. Pierce was hanging on every word and smiled as Marino said they wouldn't have been as successful without his advice and suggestions. Finally, McFadden explained how they had found the machine gun brass that should've been there if they'd found the right spot.

Pierce smiled and nodded. "Nice going, kid. You really used your head!"

"We owe you, Aaron," McFadden said as he looked the older man square in the eyes. "We'd never have gotten this far without you and we really appreciate all your help."

Pierce shrugged his shoulders at the compliment and then seemed to become more serious. "Okay, now I think I'm entitled to the rest of the story about why you two are really out here, and don't give me any crap about wanting to find an old crash site. No one's going to invest this amount of time and money to look at a pile of old plane debris." He stopped and looked at the two men as if to say, "Well?"

Marino and McFadden exchanged looks and McFadden took the lead. "You're right, we do owe you the truth," he said. Tom flashed a panicked look at his friend as if to say, "You can't tell him."

McFadden merely nodded back and settled on the edge of the desk. "We are looking for Tom's uncle's plane, but not as part of a family history." Marino attempted to speak, but McFadden interrupted, "It's alright. He needs to know." He could see the anger brewing in his friend's face as he turned back to Pierce.

"Aaron, everything we've told you about the crash is true. But the reason we're looking is because of something else that drives the historian and archeologist in us. When Angelo Colavari crashed, he was seriously hurt, and some men, whom we believe were monks or priests, found him and nursed him back to health. There's no record of any monastery having ever existed in this area. We want to locate that monastery and determine how old it is and the last time it was inhabited." He paused to let Pierce take this all in. He looked at Marino and saw the tension leave his friend's face and a small smile appeared in the corner of his mouth, acknowledging his quick wit.

Marino jumped in, adding his own bit of misinformation. "Aaron, this is actually sort of a religious exploration and we didn't want to share the find with anyone. I'm sorry we weren't up front with you from the beginning."

Pierce smiled back at the two men. "I knew you guys were holding out on me, but I understand why you wanted to keep it to yourselves. You can relax. I'm not a very religious guy, so I'm not interested in getting my name included in your story," he laughed. "Besides, this has to do with Christians or Catholics and Muslims, and I am neither. I still want to help, but I'll leave you on your own once we find the plane." With that said, they shook hands in agreement.

"Now that that's out of the way, we can get moving on to your uncle's site. Since we have the location of the first plane, I think we can begin work on identifying several directions Angelo could have gone after being hit; how fast he could have flown and how far he could have gotten before the plane crapped out beneath him?" He took a breath and stared down at their search map on the table. "You guys go have lunch or go back to the hotel and give me a few hours to re-work the search pattern."

They agreed and the two Americans left to run a few errands. "You'll never know how close I came to killing you back there," Marino said when they'd pulled away from the office. "I really thought you were going to tell him everything."

"I know, and I'm sorry I couldn't let you know where I was headed, but I really didn't know myself. We need his help and I feel sorry for deceiving him, but we've come too far to risk this becoming public knowledge. Besides, we know he didn't believe our story anyway, so this provides just enough mystery with just the right amount of BS to satisfy him." McFadden found himself checking the rearview mirror out of habit now as they drove, but it didn't appear that anyone had followed them from the airport.

"It's just as well," Tom said. "At least now we don't have to worry about accidently mentioning the monastery, or monks, or priests in front of him. They drove back to the hotel and killed several hours going over the notes and pictures of their previous day's find. They looked at the map McFadden had originally drawn and shown to Aaron and speculated on which direction they thought they'd have to head if they were on their own.

"We laid out a big area to search and that was before we found the plane yesterday. With that spot located, I'm hoping Aaron can come up with a smaller grid."

Marino agreed. "Knowing as much as he does about the plane's capabilities and the information that we gave him based on Angelo's description in his diary on the extent of the damage it sustained, it only makes sense that there are just so many ways it could travel, and for just so long."

CHAPTER 29

It had been three hours since they had left Pierce when the phone rang. They both reached for it, but McFadden was closet. "Marino and McFadden Explorations," he answered, hoping it was indeed Pierce and not the front desk.

"Marino and McFadden?" came the voice they were expecting. "Where the hell does Pierce fit into this corporation? Come on back when you can. I've come up with a little bit of a change to the game plan," he said confidently. "If you get back here quickly enough, we can probably get a couple of hours of flight time before it gets too late."

"We're on our way," McFadden said as he nodded to Marino that they were heading out. Neither man was hungry, so they called for the Rover and found it waiting at the entrance when they reached the lobby. During the ride back to the airport, the conversation was upbeat and positive. They were ready to hit the skies and begin the next leg of the search. How quickly would they find the other plane, and, thus, the way to the Robe?

The ride to the airport went quickly. They were so used to the drive by this time that they felt comfortable maneuvering through the busy traffic and pushing the speed limit a little.

As they pulled up in front of the office, they instinctively looked behind to see if the old Toyota was following them again. No, nothing back there this time. When they entered the office, they could see Pierce was bent over the table looking at his map. He didn't look up, but rather told them to grab a cup of coffee and come on over. Once they'd filled their cups, they joined the little man, picking their own spot at the table and joining him to peer down at the map.

"I don't know how lucky we're going to be today," he started, "but we're going to have to make some assumptions again. I know I said there's always evidence left over after a crash, but finding this one won't be as easy, since your uncle came in on his belly and slid quite a distance before things started to break up." He looked at the two men and continued. "Any evidence would be on the ground and certainly covered over after all these years. I think the best we can hope for is to identify several likely spots from the air, and then you two can check them out on foot." He waited for a response, but neither man spoke so he continued.

"Based on what you've told me about the last minutes of the flight and what I've read about the plane, I'm guessing he couldn't have gone more than three, maybe four miles before the engine began to die and his air speed dropped so low he couldn't maintain altitude." He was on a roll and kept talking. "A couple of relevant pieces of information we have to remember are that the spot where he went down was an opening, high ground on both sides. That shouldn't have changed over 70 years. The other piece is that he was flying parallel to the mountain and that's how he was able to spot the opening off to his right side."

McFadden jumped in before Aaron could continue. "So, we should be focusing on any area where we've got high ground or hills with some sort of a depression, or low land, that breaks it in two."

Marino was following McFadden's logic. "You're right! It won't be that easy, but at least we have an idea of what we think it should look like. If we can identify a few spots like that, then we can really cover a lot of ground using the Rover." You could feel the excitement in the room as the two Americans looked up at Pierce and smiled.

"Alright, I'm with you," said Pierce, "but trust me, there will probably be a lot of spots that meet that criteria when looking down from the air. We're going to have to look at them closely at ground level and try to prioritize your best shots right off. It's doable, but you're going spend a lot more time on foot. And remember, the three or four miles he traveled before he crashed are just a guesstimate on my part, although I feel pretty good about the distance." He waited to see if either man had anything to add before continuing.

"Let's take a few hours and fly the route I think he took and see how many likely spots we can find. It could be a few, or it could be dozens or more, but we should have a look anyway. Check the map while I pull the plane out and do the pre-flight." He was up and out the door before either of them had a chance to speak.

"I like this approach," Marino said quietly. "We'll be on the ground and by ourselves and won't have to worry about what Aaron sees or thinks. We can go as fast or as slow as we want and really go over these areas with the metal detector."

McFadden was staring at the map of the mountain range. "We got spoiled with finding Spinoza's site; second day out and there it was. Look at these mountains. Unless we can spot a few decent possibilities, we could be out there for weeks. That's assuming we ever find it. I don't want to sound like the voice of doom, but, while the search plan sounds pretty straightforward from the air, it's going to be daunting on the ground."

He stood up and shook his head. "Never mind, we have to start somewhere. The plan's good and we'll make the most of our airtime. Let's hope we can find at least a couple of likely spots today and maybe hit the ground tomorrow." As they took another look at the map, they heard the engine on the King Air come to life and knew it was time. McFadden grabbed the bag with the food and water out of the Rover and the two men climbed aboard. Marino pulled up the steps and took one last look before closing and locking the door. There was no old Toyota anywhere to be seen.

By this time, both men had grown accustomed to the flight of the plane and McFadden found himself starting to doze as the plane leveled off for the trip north. Pierce settled in and looked over at Marino, who was in the co-pilot seat again. "We'll do this the same way we did the first search, except this time we use Spinoza's plane as the starting point and fly our three to four-mile swing from there. This time we're not interested in searching by grid. This time we cruise parallel and look for anything that could be considered flat ground. Once we find something, I'll punch in the GPS coordinates and you guys can head out there later and take a closer look."

After almost three hours flying up and back, with the mountains alternating from their right to their left side, they'd found six spots that were worth taking a closer look at on the ground. Once back at Desert Air, beer in hand, they stood around the map and circled the areas they'd identified from the air.

"Okay, guys. It's time for you to hit the road again," Pierce said. "Since the spots are within a mile or two of each other, you should be able to cover them in a day or two. Just be careful and stay on your guard in case you run across anybody."

"We'll leave in the morning," McFadden offered. "When we get back, we'll let you know how we did and whether we have to go up again and take another look." Pierce wished them good luck and, within a few minutes, they were back on the road leading into the city.

Tadele sat with Jacob in the office as they watched the computer monitor and saw that the men were leaving the airport. "I wish I knew if you found anything today, Tom," he said. "We will have to pay close attention to their movements tomorrow, Tadele. We have to be in a position to give advance warning just in case." They followed the movement of the Rover until it arrived back at the hotel. "I think we can call this a day," he said to Tadele. "Come back early in the morning so we can pick them up again and see what direction their search takes them tomorrow." Tadele shook his friend's hand and went to the old Toyota parked out front. He opened the gate and let himself out, closing and locking it behind him before driving away slowly towards his home. Jacob stretched out on the couch in the back room. "No going home tonight, either. When will this end so that my life can get back to normal?"

Having made this trip before, they knew what they would bring along and what could remain in their room. The next morning found them repeating the same routine they'd followed when they went searching for the first plane. They called room service who delivered food and a dozen bottles of water. Then, just in case, they stopped and filled two of their 5-gallon gas cans and attached them to carriers on either side of the rear door, along with a five-gallon water can on the front bumper. They were ready!

Their destination was in virtually the same direction, only this time they would be traveling north several more miles before beginning their search at the first location they'd plugged into the GPS. The hours passed quickly and Marino was more prepared for the drive across the sand than he'd been the first time. He'd learned not to fight the wheel and let it move to the contours of the desert. This took a lot of the bouncing off of his arms and he didn't seem to tire as quickly.

As they approached the spot where they'd found the old trail and the machine gun brass, Marino began to clock the mileage on the odometer. They arrived at their first location, just before the three-mile marker. They got out of the car and went in for a closer look. As they worked their way through the vegetation and got about 30 feet in, they found that, although the hills rose on both sides, the middle ground was too high and a plane would have struck it head-on rather than fly over it. One down, five to go.

The second area turned out to be another no-go as well. While the ground between the hills was flat and wide, it barely went a hundred feet before stopping at a sheer vertical wall. Any plane coming in would smash into the side of the mountain before it ever had a chance to slow down and stop. The final two locations proved just as useless as the first two had. They'd covered almost two miles and had nothing to show for it, and the sun would be sinking shortly. This was as good a spot to set up camp as any. They were on flat ground and there was plenty of firewood. Besides, they had a clear view of the desert and could see anyone approaching from miles away.

The tent was up and a small fire burning in a few minutes. MRE's would be their meal again. As they ate, neither had much to say. Finally, Marino broke the silence. "What do you think, BB? Do we head back and go up with Aaron for another look?"

McFadden seemed to ponder the question before answering. "If we go back and fly over this area again, we're only going to come up with a few more sites to check. We can check out sites tomorrow without going back. I say we stay out here and search on our own. We know what we're looking for anyway without wasting at least two days in travel." He waited for Tom to consider their options. They were a team and each could contribute their own ideas.

"When you look at it that way, it makes sense just to go looking on our own," he said after a few moments of thought. "We can cover an awful lot of territory in two full days and can always fall back on the plane if we strike out completely." Once that was settled, both men seemed to relax and enjoy the desert sunset. Tomorrow may be the day!

Back at Lucky Car Rental the atmosphere was tense. After watching their progress the entire day, Jacob was a little concerned over what direction the two men would head come morning. If they turned back, then there was nothing to worry about. But if they continued north, then they would become more of a risk with each turn of the car's wheels. He decided to call and pass along the information he had so far. The phone was answered on the first ring.

"They've stopped for the night," he said, listening to the voice on the other end before continuing. "I can't tell exactly how close they are, but I can tell you that they are headed in the right direction. If they continue heading straight in the morning, then decisions will have to be made." He waited again before speaking. "Yes, I will call tomorrow as soon as I see which way they are going. We can only pray," he added in response to some comment on the other end. "Yes, as soon I know, you will know," and with that, the conversation was over and the phone went dead.

CHAPTER 30

McFadden and Marino decided to break camp each day rather than drive north and, thus, have to retrace their steps back to the campsite. Besides, even though they'd seen no one so far, there was no point is risking all their gear to some wandering nomad. After their usual quick breakfast, they began their slow drive north, stopping every so often to check out a potential location. None of the areas looked like a plane could have crashed and slid along the ground for any distance. They were all either too narrow or too short.

It was approaching 11:00 am, and they were thinking of stopping for lunch when McFadden saw another potential spot. "We might as well take a look at this one before we stop to eat." By now, they'd become somewhat pessimistic and seemed to expect to come up empty at every stop. They grabbed the little shovel and their canteens and approached the land visible between the two ridges. This didn't look too bad, they thought. The opening between the side walls appeared fairly flat, except for an occasional tree that could have grown there during the past 70 plus years.

Marino stopped and surveyed the distance between the natural walls. "This is the widest place we've seen so far. I'm going to try and walk off the distance from side to side and see if there's enough room for a plane to get through." With that said, he made his way left and placed his back against the rocks and then began to walk across to the other side. He stepped off as close to a yard as he could, depending on his footing, and by the time he'd reached the other side, he had paced off a little over 75 feet. This was more than enough room for the Italian fighter to pass through without hitting either side.

While he was measuring off the width, McFadden was walking further in and checking to see how far back this spot went. There was quite a bit of vegetation and fallen limbs, so it took him a little while to get through and around all the obstacles. When he finally reached the end, he had walked several hundred feet. Finally, this stretch was probably long enough for a small plane to crash land on its belly and skid to a stop before reaching the end. He turned around as Marino appeared behind him. "This looks pretty good," he told his partner. "This is the most promising area we've seen so far. My only concern is there's no sign of any wreckage as far as I can determine. It may well be under all this growth, but you'd think some of the bigger pieces of the fuselage would be obvious."

Marino looked around as if trying to find something McFadden had missed. "I know I didn't find anything about my uncle's crash on the website where Spinoza was listed, but what if they came and cleaned everything up? Better yet, what if some roaming desert people found it and hauled everything away for scrap or to use it for something else?"

"Yeah, I guess that's possible. And if they did it 70 plus years ago, anything they left would be covered over," McFadden added.

Looking back from and from side to side, Marino finally said, "Why don't I get the metal detector and do a few sweeps of the area and see if there's anything underneath all this stuff?"

"Let's go a little further and see what's up behind those trees, before we get down to the real searching," McFadden suggested. "This area might look a little different if we're looking down on it. We might even locate evidence of a path or trail leading higher up."

They picked out what looked like the most likely way through the trees and started to work their way higher up and away from the new spot. The climbing was slow and they had to choose their footing carefully. Every so often, they stopped to look down in the hopes of seeing something different at this height and angle. It all looked the same and they still couldn't see anything that looked like plane debris. They had climbed about 50 feet up when there came the clear sound of gunfire. That was followed by several more shots and, when they looked in the direction they thought the shots were coming from, they saw 5 or 6 men quickly working their way down towards them. The shots continued but failed to hit either man. It was probably because they didn't stop to take aim but just fired as they came down.

It only took a few seconds before McFadden and Marino realized they were the targets of all that shooting. They hesitated just briefly before turning and stumbling their way back to level ground. "Don't look back," Marino yelled. "Run straight through this crap and head for the Rover. We have to get there before they reach the bottom."

Marino was moving fast towards the open ground and was surprised to see McFadden match him pace for pace. "I've got the keys," he yelled, "just make for the passenger side and keep your head down." They finally broke clear and raced towards the Rover as the shots continued behind them. Their pursuers must have reached solid ground as well because the shots were coming faster and the shouts of the men sounded like they were getting closer.

They reached the Rover before the men cleared the trees. Marino turned the key, slammed the shifter into drive, and floored the accelerator. The truck jumped forward and was gaining speed. They saw the men come into view where they could afford to take more careful aim with each shot. Both men sunk down into their seats as if trying to make as small a target as they could against the incoming fire.

"Well, now we know that all those stories about bandits in the mountains weren't just old wives' tales," Marino finally said, as the sound of gunfire died out and he realized they were out of range of the rifles.

As Tom kept the pedal pressed to the floor and the Rover raced through the desert, McFadden was lost in thought. He seemed to be pondering the solution to a problem; working an equation in his head. This whole thing was bad. Suddenly, he sat up and looked at Marino. He'd found an answer.

"Tom, slow down! Something's not right, here." Marino reduced his speed, but dared not stop entirely for fear of who may be close in tow. "What's not right?" he asked.

"Doesn't this whole thing seem a little odd?" McFadden asked him. Marino looked at his friend and now it was his turn to look puzzled. "These mountains are home to bandits, who for generations are said to have preyed upon travelers, whole caravans, and anyone who strayed too close to the paths; bandits who for hundreds of years should have honed their skills on how to rob or kill anyone who ventured into the mountains. Yet, we walk into an ambush, unarmed, and these bandits chase us back to our vehicle, firing who knows how many shots at us and we're able to escape."

After a few moments, Marino too began to question the encounter. "Did we escape, or were we allowed to escape? Better yet, were we forced to flee? They used man's strongest instinct against us — the instinct for self-preservation. It was this instinct that caused us to turn and run when we thought our lives were in danger. It happened so quickly we didn't have a chance to think about what we were doing. At least I can say that about myself. When I heard those guns firing and saw the men coming out from behind the trees, my instincts took over and I was ready to haul ass. When you started to run, too, I knew I was doing the right thing. Fight or flight!"

"Here we have these people who, supposedly, "live by the gun," yet they fire all those rounds and never hit us; never hit anything. They didn't even hit the Land Rover as we drove away. We have to be the luckiest bastards in the world, or they have to be the worst bandits in history. Maybe there's another option here. What if they never wanted to catch us? What if they were only trying to keep us out of that area? Otherwise, why not wait until we walked into their ambush and take us prisoner? Why not wait until we were really close and shoot us then? Why shoot as soon as they did and allow us time to escape? I don't think we were ever in any real danger. I think they knew we were coming and were waiting for us so they could spring their 'ambush' and drive us down the mountain and back to the Rover."

"Of all the places we could have come, we show up where someone is waiting for us. I just don't believe in that many coincidences. If you wanted to keep track of someone's travels, what would be the best way?" he asked. "Sure, you could try and follow them like the guy in the Toyota did, but even then, there's a chance someone recognizes you're being tailed like Aaron did. How did they know we were there? What could have tipped them off?"

It suddenly dawned on Marino. "We're driving it! I'll bet there's a tracking device hidden somewhere on this Rover. That's the only way they could have known our every move. That's why the taxi driver took me to Lucky Car Rental that first day when I was looking for a car."

The more they talked about it, the angrier Marino became. "My good friend Jacob made sure I took the "best car" on the lot; the one with the homing device. By now the Rover had slowed to about 30 mph while the men tossed the idea back and forth. "How else could we travel 300 miles across the desert and find the 'bandits' just happened to be at that very spot? They have the whole mountain area and are lucky enough to stumble across the two Americans just as they arrive."

McFadden looked at Marino for several seconds before speaking softly. "If that's true, then we must have been close to where the monks still reside and where the Robe is being kept. We were probably too close." The more McFadden talked about the attack and their escape, the more Tom began to see the experience in a different light. Maybe this was all just for show and they never faced any danger at all. If that was indeed the case, what do they do now?

McFadden seemed to read Marino's mind. "Tom, I think it's time for us to take a giant leap of faith here and assume the attack wasn't for real. We know of at least two times in recent history when the monks helped people who were facing certain death from their injuries. I can't imagine a group of men, who for generations have dedicated their lives to protecting Christ's Robe, would allow the murder of innocent people who simply stumbled upon a path or who appear to be walking in the wrong area."

"In order for us to prove that, we're going to have to go back and try to search the mountain again. But this time, if we're attacked, we try a different strategy. Namely, we don't run. The next time we let them capture us."

Marino brought the Rover to a stop and looked at his friend with sheer disbelief. "I was with you right up to the part where you said we let them capture us. That's a great idea unless they really are just bad shots and lousy bandits and wind up killing us both. How would you feel then?"

McFadden looked at Marino and said, "How would I feel if they kill us? Mmm, let me think. Oh yeah, I'll be DEAD! Won't be thinking about much of anything."

"Okay, let me rephrase that. It would really be a waste of two promising young lives if we're wrong and they do kill us. No one will ever know what happened to us, and that could be pretty tough on our folks." McFadden was quiet for a moment as he thought of how his parents would react to his death. It would kill his mother.

"Tom, I can't see any other way to approach this than we agree it's too dangerous and head back to the states." After a moment, McFadden became serious as he spoke. "This is our only chance to find the Robe. If we leave now, just like your uncle did in 1947, we'll never come back and we'll never know if the Robe does exist 2000 years after the death of Christ. Tommy, we're just too close to walk away from this now."

Marino had taken his fair share of chances in the past and had been mostly lucky. But at those times he was usually facing the risk of breaking a bone or two. Now he had to ask himself if he was willing to actually risk his life, on the chance that bandits and killers weren't really bandits and killers. Did he really have a choice? BB was right. If they left now without knowing if they were right, he'd never be able to live with himself. He'd always be wondering what they would have found if they'd gone just a little further.

"Alright, what is it they say? 'In for a penny, in for a pound.' I guess we have to see this thing through to the end," he finally said. McFadden seemed relieved. He and Tom would go on together. "Okay," he said, "we head back to the city and make a few changes before we come back out here again." This time they made it back in less than 8 hours. Tom wasn't worried anymore about damaging Jacob's Land Rover.

When they arrived back at the hotel, they retreated behind closed doors in their room and came up with a new plan and a new list of things that would need to be done if they were to make another attempt at the mountain. They knew they'd been really close before the attack.

The first thing they needed to do was to cut themselves free and get rid of the tracking device, and hopefully anyone trailing them.

Marino went downstairs and spoke to the young valet parker he'd given $10 to earlier. He explained what he wanted to do the next day and asked if he was willing to help him. The boy was willing to do whatever the American asked in exchange for the $50 bill he produced. They spoke for a while and the boy nodded his understanding. He smiled to himself as the American went back into the hotel. It sounded exciting to him. Almost like being in an adventure movie and he was one of the stars.

While Marino was working out the details with the valet parker, McFadden was on the phone arranging the rental of a Toyota Land Cruiser from Hertz. They had an office near the Hilton and agreed to hold the vehicle until McFadden came by and completed the necessary paperwork. When Marino returned to the room, he briefed McFadden on what he'd arranged with the valet parker. It was now McFadden's turn to check a few things off their to-do list. He needed a ride to Hertz but decided against taking one of the taxis parked at the entrance.

Instead, he went out the rear of the hotel and soon found himself on a busy side street. He was wondering where to get a cab and had just stepped off the curb, when a car screeched to a halt in front of him. The smiling driver asked if he needed a taxi. It was an older cab and in need of body work and paint. It was not the kind that you would find parked outside the hotel. Those cabs were the newest, shiniest cabs which typically shuttled tourists and businessmen around the city. This taxi was for the locals and had probably never had a westerner as a passenger.

He quickly got in and asked the driver if he knew where the Hertz office near the Hilton was. He told the driver there was an extra $10 if they made it in less than 5 minutes. No sooner had he spoken than the driver hit the gas and began weaving through the city traffic at highway speed. If anyone had seen him leave and was trying to follow, they were in for the ride of their life. After about six minutes, the driver came to a skidding halt in front of Hertz. McFadden made the gesture of looking at his watch, "Close enough," he said with a smile and handed the driver a $20 bill.

Once inside the office, McFadden completed the rental paperwork and put the deposit on a credit card. He explained that he and a friend were taking a photo tour of the area for National Geographic and planned to spend a day or two shooting in the desert. He said they hoped to be able to meet some of the desert inhabitants and see what life was like as a nomad. The tall young girl behind the desk was especially interested in their travels, warning him to be careful of the mountains. "There are bandits out there, so be very careful, Dr. McFadden," she cautioned.

Before long, he was driving the year-old Land Cruiser off the lot. He slowly drove their new transportation along with the evening traffic and headed to the El Alegia mall where there was activity going on 24 hours a day. Once there, he parked on the west side of the lot, close to an entrance door. He looked around and was satisfied that he was parked near enough to an exit to reach the car in a matter of seconds. He locked the doors and went into the mall and began to basically repeat many of the purchases they had made the last time they were there. Some of their things they could sneak out of the Rover, but they didn't want to take a chance that someone might see them.

After paying for all his new supplies, he wheeled the shopping cart outside and loaded everything into the rear of the Land Cruiser, covering it with the retractable cargo cover. Satisfied that everything was ready, he walked to the front of the mall and quickly found another local cab to take him back to the Sheraton, making sure he was dropped off at the rear of the hotel. One more item to check off their new list.

That night, they ate in the hotel dining room and spoke quietly of their adventure so far. Marino appeared confused and agitated. He said that, on second thought, he'd had enough and wanted to call the whole thing off. Almost being killed by mountain bandits was more than he had bargained for. McFadden tried to persuade him to take a little time and think it over before making his final decision. There was tension between the two men, and they barely talked for the remainder of the meal. McFadden finally asked Marino to give it two more days, at least until they spoke with the man in the city of Jimma. He might have information that was worth the trip. Reluctantly, Marino agreed to meet with the old man before making a final decision.

As they spoke, Tadele sat several booths away and listened to the whole conversation. He smiled to himself. They were frightened and confused and close to leaving. The bandits' attack had gone just as had been expected. Jacob would be pleased with this information. His only concern was this new man they spoke of; whom he could be and what information could he possibly provide? Jimma was more than a six-hour ride southwest of Addis Abba and no one from that area had ever been associated with the crashes or even mentioned by any of those involved. He waited until the two Americans left the dining room before leaving and then headed to Lucky Car Rental to tell Jacob the news. This was a new development that would require some guidance and direction.

As McFadden and Marino rode the elevator to their floor, McFadden asked, "Do you think he heard it all?"

Marino smiled back, "Every word! I'll bet he can't wait to tell his buddies that the Americans are fighting. Although, he's got to be really confused about our trip to Jimma to speak with the "old man.""

They had finally identified the mystery man who had been following them. The day Pierce had pointed him out and they later spotted the old Toyota behind them McFadden had carefully pointed the camera with the auto zoom lens back between the two front seats and used the automatic shutter to quickly shoot a series of ten pictures of the car and driver before the man turned off the road. The movement was so subtle, McFadden was confident the driver never realized he was being filmed. McFadden had downloaded the pictures to his laptop and revealed several clear photos of Tadele. The two men studied the face and were confident they would be able to quickly pick him out of a crowd. The hunter's existence was now known and he could easily become the hunted.

Once they were back in their room, McFadden was immediately on the phone to room service. "We just ate, what are you getting?" Tom wanted to know. "We had such a big disagreement at dinner that I never did get a chance for dessert. I'm ordering a quart of ice cream. You want anything?"

A short while later, Tadele was sitting across from Jacob explaining the argument between the Americans. Jacob smiled and dialed the number he had long ago memorized.

"It looks as if our friends have finally had enough of the desert. They may be leaving within the next several days. Our only concern is that they are driving to Jimma in the morning to speak with a man who they believe may be able to provide them with information about the crash. No, I have no idea whom they could meet with that would be able to provide any information. Tadele will follow them in the morning and report back to me as soon as they arrive in the city. Yes, I will call as soon as there is something definite. Thank you. May there be peace and happiness in your house as well!"

CHAPTER 31

McFadden and Marino were awake at a little after 5:00 a.m. and went over the details of the day's departure. They ordered breakfast and again had the kitchen prepare sandwiches and include bottles of water. When they were ready, Marino called the front desk and asked that the Land Rover be parked outside the front door, since they would be leaving for the day within the next half hour. As they exited the front door, Tadele could see that Marino wore a baseball cap this morning. The two men walked to the where the Rover was parked, and Marino took the driver's seat while McFadden sat in the passenger seat. There was little conversation between the two men as Marino started the vehicle and pulled out into the morning traffic. As they drove away from the hotel, Marino saw a Jeep station wagon pull away from the curb and proceed in the same direction.

"You were right," he said to McFadden. "We have company. Since we may be leaving in the next day or two, they can't afford to lose sight of us now. They certainly have to know whom we're meeting in Jimma," he nodded towards the mirror, "and I'm willing to bet that's one of the Jeep's from Jacob's lot trailing us."

As they drove south, Marino carefully looked back between the seats at the blanket lying on the floor. "Are you okay, Abraham?" he asked. The young parking attendant raised the blanket just enough to look at Marino and smile. "I am very fine back here, sir!" he answered.

Going with traffic, Marino maintained a speed that made it easy for the Jeep to keep pace with them. After a while, McFadden lowered the backrest of his seat and disappeared from sight, as if catching up on some sleep.

Further back in traffic, in the Jeep, Tadele maintained his distance for several miles, before allowing the morning traffic to pass him by. He had decided to stay far back this time and depend on the blinking arrow on the vehicle's dash as it kept moving with the traffic. He felt confident that they were pretty much at the end of their journey. In another day or two, they would leave, and things would return to normal. Then they could finally clean up the Spinoza site, and no one would ever again be able to locate where the planes had gone down.

Pedestrian traffic on the sidewalks increased as they approached downtown, and the stores and shops along the way showed plenty of activity. This would be critical if they were to be successful this morning.

"I've got the food, and the only other thing I'll have to take out of here is the metal detector, McFadden said. "I dissembled it so that it fits in the backpack."

"We're going to have to make this really fast," Marino said as he looked for the Jeep in the morning traffic. He couldn't see it, but he knew it was there. "If I can't see him, he probably can't see me." That would give them the few seconds they needed to make their move. Marino kept pace with the morning traffic and watched for the right moment to present itself. After about 15 minutes, the traffic slowed and Marino saw his opportunity. He waited until he approached a traffic signal and, as it turned red, he made a right turn against the light and proceeded down the busy street. It was now or never!

McFadden had been watching the traffic behind them through the passenger side rearview mirror. "Remember, Abraham," he continued, "once you're in the driver's seat I want you to head out of town and drive south and away from the city. There will be a Jeep station wagon following you, so don't let him get close enough to get a good look at you. Do you understand?"

The young man again pulled the blanket back and smiled up at Marino. "I will drive for hours before I turn around and come back to the city. He will never know he is not following you and Mr. BB." Marino pulled the $50 bill from his shirt pocket and handed it back to the valet.

"Here's a little something extra," McFadden said as he slipped a $20 bill between the seats into the little man's open hand. "We really need a few hours, Abraham, so we're counting on you."

The boy was speechless for a few seconds. "I will drive into the night. I have relatives outside of Jimma and will drive to their home. By the time I get there it will be too dark for the man to see who is driving," he assured them.

The Jeep was stuck behind several cars stopped at the light. Tadele wondered why they had made this turn but was unconcerned since he could still follow the movements of the blinking light on the screen.

As the streets became more crowded, Marino slowed. "I think we're about ready. This is as good a place as any. The Jeep hasn't made the turn yet. Okay, BB, go!" McFadden grabbed the bag with the metal detector and was out of the Rover and heading into the nearest store before it came to a stop.

Still not seeing the Jeep, Marino stopped the Rover and was out and quickly lost in the crowded sidewalk. He had left the hat on the driver's seat. The driver's door had no sooner slammed shut than Abraham slid behind the wheel and put on the baseball cap and put the car in gear. The entire switch had taken just a few seconds. The car was again in motion and moving with the morning traffic. Marino walked into the closest store and stood back from the door while watching the traffic pass by. Within a few seconds, the Jeep passed the store and appeared to be in no hurry. They'd done it. Now it was time to put all their planning into action. The clock was ticking.

As Tadele finally made the right turn, he was just able to make out the roof of the vehicle about a block ahead of him. He slowly worked his way through traffic until the vehicle was several car lengths ahead. He still wasn't sure what the Americans hoped to find in Jimma, but he backed off and followed the slow-moving traffic as it continued south. In a few hours, they would reach the city and hopefully he would learn what the Americans hoped to achieve.

Once the Jeep was lost in the traffic, Marino exited the store and walked back the way they had come until he spotted McFadden having coffee in a small restaurant. "Are you kidding me?" Marino smiled as he joined his friend. McFadden had ordered two coffees and was eating a large pastry.

"I figured we could use one more blast of caffeine before we head north." They quickly emptied their cups and were back on the street looking for a taxi. Within a minute, they hailed a local cab and were soon on their way to the mall and the waiting Toyota. The Land Cruiser was just where McFadden had left it the night before, and all their supplies were safe in the back. They were soon back on the road and heading out of the city towards the mountains.

The Land Cruiser turned out to be a much better vehicle than the Rover had been and took the bumps and ruts almost as if they were on a highway. "These are designed to take a beating and handle anything that you could throw at it," McFadden offered. "If it's good enough for the Paris to Dakar race, then it should handle anything we might encounter."

Because of that, they were able to maintain a better speed for most of the trip. There was no hesitation as to where they were going this time and they drove the straightest and most direct route. The trip took a little less than seven hours, arriving at the spot where they'd been chased the day before, shortly after 2:00pm. If this spot turned out to be a dud then they would have to start from square one all over again.

Rather than go directly to where they had parked the day before, they found a spot under some overhanging tree limbs that would provide a little cover and hopefully shield them from anyone looking down. They were parked about a quarter of a mile away from yesterday's spot and each man began to scan the area through binoculars, looking for any sign that they might have been spotted. Everything was quiet and they appeared to be alone. If their plan with Abraham had been successful, then nobody would be expecting them to be anywhere near here, at least not yet. After watching and listening for about a half hour, they felt that their luck was holding out. There didn't appear to be anyone else around. McFadden drove back to where they had made their escape two days earlier.

When the GPS told them they had arrived at their destination, McFadden turned the Land Cruiser around and backed close to the beginning of the flat ground they'd found the first time. If they had to make another quick getaway, the vehicle would at least be parked facing the safest direction — back out into the desert. Quietly, they removed the tools they would need to give the area a thorough search. They had their metal detector and a brand-new entrenching tool.

"Let's start by trying to walk this whole area first and see if there is anything visible after all," McFadden suggested. "We might even step on or stumble across something underneath all this growth." Marino nodded his agreement and walked to the far-right side of the rise to the very beginning of the flat ground, and started walking towards the rock wall straight back.

"If I stay at the very edge of this stretch of ground, I may find some debris." With that, he began a slow shuffle towards the rear, trying to bump into or step on something hidden underneath. His feet got caught in the brush every couple of steps and caused him to stumble a few times. *This isn't going to work,* he thought to himself. *I might just as well try to walk over all this crap.* That was a better plan and he covered more ground with less effort.

Meanwhile, McFadden had begun to walk across from one side to the other. The more he looked at his surroundings, the more he thought that everything was a little too neat to be natural. It almost looked as if someone or something had gone over this whole area and flattened everything down.

"How does this all look to you?" he called over to Marino. "It looks to me as if somebody drove over all this ground."

"It does look a little too smooth and even. Could animals have trampled this flat?" he answered.

McFadden stopped and looked from front to rear and from right to left. "It would have to be a lot of them, and they'd have to be pretty big to cover this much area. Besides, how would they get in, and where would they go? They didn't come in from the desert side or go out that way since there's no path or tracks in the sand over there. If they came down the mountain, there'd be some evidence of a trail leading down from the high ground."

"I'm going to get the metal detector and see what's underneath all of this," Marino said as he began to walk back to the Rover. Within a few minutes, he had the headphones on and was adjusting the sound level before beginning his sweep. He started in what he considered the middle and began working his way out. If a plane had gone down here, there should be more stuff in the center than on the outskirts. Every few steps he'd get a small beep through the headphones.

By now, McFadden had grabbed the entrenching tool and was following behind, waiting for Tom to stop and point to a spot. Each time he'd pull back the brush and dig around with the little shovel, and every so often he'd find a small sliver of metal that couldn't be determined as to whether it was part of a plane or not. It took several hours, but they finally completed the sweeps from front to rear, never finding anything larger than the size of a baseball, and never with any type of markings. They could have been parts of a plane, but they could also have been left from some group who had camped or stayed there over a period of years. Nothing conclusive and none of it marked. There wasn't much of anything around and it looked like their most promising spot was going to turn out to be another bust.

"If there's nothing in this line from the desert to the rocky wall at the far end, then I think we may have struck out," McFadden finally admitted.

"This had such great potential," Marino added as he pulled the headphones down and rested them around his neck. "If this doesn't have anything to do with my uncle's crash, why were the mountain boys waiting for us? Maybe we're wrong and they just stumbled across us and they really are lousy bandits." As he walked out of the center and approached the far right of the search area, he heard several beeps coming from the metal detector. They were there for a moment and then were gone.

"Hold on! I just got a short beep, but it was louder than any of the other spots we've checked. Come over with the shovel while I try to find it again." He pulled the headphones back over his ears and adjusted the volume a little higher. McFadden crossed to where Marino stood and watched him move slowly to his left while making short swings back and forth in front of him. After he'd taken several steps, he stopped swinging the receiver and held it steady over one area. "The beeping is pretty steady here. Give this a try and see if you come up with anything," he said over his shoulder.

CHAPTER 32

McFadden knelt down and began to dig. He broke through some vines and began to scoop little shovelfuls of dirt out. As he stuck the shovel into the ground for the third time, he hit something solid. It could have been a rock, but the sound was different, almost metallic. He put the shovel down and began to dig with his hands. He had to make the hole a little wider so that he could get his hands underneath whatever was down there.

After shifting his position to give himself a little more leverage, his hands closed around something solid and hard. He pulled it out of the hole and they both stared at their find. It had an odd shape and was caked with dirt. McFadden slowly began to work the object back and forth between his fingers, and, more and more, dirt began to fall away, revealing a familiar shape. It was an old handgun. It was a pistol, and he recognized the markings. It was an Italian Beretta.

McFadden stood and the two men began to examine it more closely. "What's an old gun doing out here?" Marino asked. McFadden didn't answer. He gave the old pistol to Marino and began to walk back and forth, appearing to be deep in thought.

"I know what it's doing here," he finally said. "Think about your uncle's account of the crash and something he mentioned almost in passing as he wrote about the men who suddenly appeared."

"He wrote that, when he awoke after the crash and found men near him, he 'reached for the pistol in my shoulder holster, but it was gone.' He was probably lying right on top of it when they found him, and it just got pushed into the ground. It's been lying there for the past 70 years until today. Lying in the exact same spot it landed after coming out of Angelo's holster."

He smiled. "If you'll pardon the pun, what we have here is the proverbial *smoking gun* that identifies this as the exact spot where your uncle crashed. We've done it, Tom! We're within walking distance of the last place the Robe of Jesus Christ was seen."

Now that they had confirmed the actual location of the crash, it was time to try the climb again. If they could get a couple of hours on the mountain without running into anyone — namely, the bandits — they felt they'd at least be able to locate a trail that could lead to their prize. They each carried a small backpack with extra water and some basic first-aid gear. You never know what could happen walking around strange places and climbing jagged mountains. McFadden carried the shovel and Marino had a compass and the GPS.

They'd search for a few hours, and, regardless of what they found, they would be out and in the desert long before nightfall. They agreed that the best time to really search would be early in the morning, just after sunrise, hopefully before anyone else was up and about. If they were successful that afternoon, then tomorrow morning could begin the final search.

As they were ready to start the climb, McFadden suddenly became quiet. After a few seconds, he looked Marino square in the face before speaking.

"Tommy, regardless of what we find, or don't find, out there, I just want you to know how much I appreciate you letting me be a part of all this. You didn't have to ask me to come along. You could have done this on your own, but I'm glad you didn't."

Marino smiled at his friend, "Listen, Big Guy. I couldn't have done this without you. I'd never have gotten this far on my own. You're the one that kept me focused on the prize. This has been, and will continue to be, a partnership whether we're successful or not." He held out his hand and it disappeared into the big mitt at the end of McFadden's right arm that was his hand. "Let's get going, partner," Marino said with a smile, and began walking towards their objective.

Without another word, the two men turned and began to make their way to the rock wall at the far end of the crash site. Once there, they separated and each man began to look for the best approach up without having to rely on climbing gear. If the bandits could walk this mountain, then so could they. They walked a few yards in opposite directions, constantly looking for some indication of a safe route up. Marino finally found what he thought was the faint trace of what might be called a path.

Looking up, he could just make out what appeared to be a switchback; a path that first went diagonally one way at a slight incline, and then switched back in the other direction, still at an incline. This would allow a man to make his way higher on the mountain, without having to climb straight up. No gear required, just stamina and strong legs.

The humidity under the trees late in the day was stifling as they began the slow climb. They quickly found themselves drinking more water than they thought they'd need. Every so often, they'd stop and listen. No sounds. No birds or other animals, and, better still, no sound of voices or gun shots. After almost an hour, they'd climbed over a hundred feet and could no longer see the spot from where they'd started. They looked for signs of travel or signs that someone had been there before them. But they found nothing. The path was mostly stone and left no marks. There were no broken branches indicating someone had walked there before them. Looking back down the path, there was nothing to indicate they'd just walked through.

The sun was continuing its voyage west, and the woods began to get darker. There was no point in getting stuck up here for the night. They'd go back down and drive out onto the desert for the night and attack the trail again early in the morning when it was cooler. Besides, they knew they'd need more than a couple of hours to really cover this rock face.

The descent was a lot quicker and they were quickly back on the ground. They looked back after they'd loaded their gear into the Land Cruiser. "Tomorrow we're going to find you, my elusive little friends," Marino said as they got in the truck and drove east and away. It was 5:15 pm.

At the same time, back on the road heading to Jimma, Abraham kept his speed steady and looked in the rearview mirror every few seconds to make sure he hadn't lost the Jeep. He was enjoying playing his role as "Thomas" in the great action movie in which he was starring. Occasionally, he looked to his right and nodded his head as if talking to the other man as he lay on the reclined seat beside him.

He'd been on the road now for almost seven hours and was determined to get to his uncle's home before stopping, hoping to arrive after it had grown dark. That way, the man behind him would think that both men were staying there for the night. It would also give his new friends almost 24 hours before it was discovered that they were not in the Rover.

Tadele was puzzled as he tried to think of where these two strangers to his country might be going. To the best of his knowledge, they knew no one except for the old pilot. It was now a little after 5:00 and they hadn't even stopped for a rest or for gas. He tried to calculate how much gas the Rover held and whether he had enough in the Jeep to continue to follow as the day grew late. He watched Marino turn and appear to say something to McFadden who was still lying back in his seat.

The other man hadn't moved from that position since they left the hotel. "That's odd," he thought. "He hasn't sat up or looked out the window once in all these hours." Tadele began to get a bad feeling about it. "Maybe McFadden isn't even in there and Marino is taking me out of the city while his partner goes back to the mountains." He drove another half hour and finally decided there was no point in trying to hide from Marino now. He had to know if McFadden was with him.

He waited until there was no oncoming traffic and then pulled out as if to pass and stepped on the gas. The Rover didn't alter its speed and he was suddenly alongside the driver's door, looking in to see if Marino was alone. What he saw was the smiling face of young Abraham, wearing Marino's baseball cap.

"They're not there!" he yelled, slamming the steering wheel with his fist. "They're not there," he repeated softly. He took his foot off the gas and hit the brakes hard enough to fishtail until it came to a halt.

I have to let Jacob know they've gone back, he thought to himself. *All this time wasted and they are probably back at Colavari's site by now.* He pulled the car to the side of the road and reached for his cell phone. "No bars!" He was out of range of the nearest cell tower. He put the car in gear and began the race back to the city. Every few minutes, he would check his phone to see if he had reception yet. "How long before I get in range?" he asked as the car began to pick up speed.

Racing back towards the city it took almost an hour before he was again in cell phone range. He hit the speed dial number and waited impatiently for Jacob to answer. Finally, he heard his friend's voice on the other end. "Lucky Car Rental," said Jacob.

"They're gone!" Tadele yelled into the phone. Before Jacob could say a word, Tadele screamed again, "They're not in the Land Rover. They never were. I followed it for almost eight hours before I saw that there was some kid driving and wearing Marino's baseball cap." He was breathless after having given Jacob his report. He tried to slow down, but he was too excited and nervous. "They must be back at the mountain looking for Colavari's plane. They won't find it, but it still worries me to have them walking around out there. What are we going to do?"

Jacob was just as shocked, but he'd had a chance to think while Tadele was rambling on about where the Americans could be. First things first, he had to call and let them know to be on the lookout for the two men. It was unlikely that they would find anything at the crash site, but you couldn't be sure some little piece of the plane wasn't left that would provide a clue. Finally, Tadele slowed down long enough for Jacob to get a word in.

"What's done is done, Tadele. Make your way back here and we'll figure out what to do next. In the meantime, I'll make the call and warn them." Tadele was out of breath. All he could mutter was, "I'll be back as quickly as I can. Wait there for me." The phone went dead, and Jacob made his call.

When the phone was answered, he said, "I don't know how, but they apparently figured out that they were being tracked. They went through an elaborate exercise to fool us into thinking they were ready to leave. They even switched vehicles and had Tadele follow the Rover out of the city for hours before discovering someone else was driving. I know you can't be everywhere, but may I suggest you station someone to watch that area just in case? Of course. As soon as I know anything, you will."

Now he had lost them, and he could only imagine how close they were to uncovering the secret that he and the untold number before him had protected for two thousand years. "Where did we go wrong?"

Several hours later he received a call and the voice on the other end told him they had checked the area and found nothing. There was no sign that anyone had been there.

"Is it possible they are still in the city and working on a plan to come back out?" the voice had asked. "It's possible," Jacob speculated. "Since they already have a new vehicle, they would have had more than enough time to get back out there by early afternoon. If they're not there now, then maybe they plan to leave in the morning." He paused. "I'll have our people in the city be on the lookout for them just in case."

CHAPTER 33

As Jacob was trying to determine how to go about finding their whereabouts, McFadden and Marino were heading out to find a new campsite in the desert. They had agreed that they would need a hot meal and a good night's sleep in preparation for the following day's climb. In order to be able to do that, they had to drive a few extra miles southwest until they found a sand dune high enough to provide shelter from any prying eyes back on the mountain, just in case.

They finally came upon two large dunes with space between that was large enough to park and conceal the Land Cruiser and even set up their camp without being visible to anyone from the mountains. The sun was beginning its final descent towards the western horizon, but they were old pros by now and their camp was quickly set up and they soon had water boiling for their MREs and coffee. There would be no wood for a fire tonight, but they didn't really care. McFadden had his Boston College sweatshirt and Tom pulled his old wool sweater from his pack. They had warm clothes, a tent to protect from the wind, and coffee heated over a can of Sterno to face the chill of the night.

Together they sat outside the tent, each holding a cup of hot coffee in their cupped hands. The heat from the cups provided just the right amount of warmth to keep them comfortable. Lost in thought, they were silent for some time before Marino spoke.

"I've been thinking. We've been talking about how we would search for the monks and then finally find the Robe." He paused while looking off into the dark and slowly took a sip of the hot brew. "What we haven't talked about is what we're going to do if we do find it. They're certainly not going to give it to us, and they most certainly won't let us take pictures. And I highly doubt that they're going to give us the exclusive for our scientific paper on how it got there and how it healed a critically injured Italian pilot prior to World War II in Ethiopia."

McFadden looked into his cup before speaking. "You're right. This isn't like discovering an ancient tomb or city where there's nobody to object to the expedition and people eager for you to succeed. If the whole idea of the Protectors is legitimate after 2000 years, it's a safe bet that they will be more than a little determined that this secret goes nowhere." He took another drink from his cup. "I have to ask myself what I would do if I were in their shoes, or, more likely, their sandals, and someone suddenly appeared wanting the twenty-five cent tour of the hiding place of Jesus Christ's Robe."

"Without the Robe or some solid evidence that it really exists, there's no way we could ever discuss having found it without being laughed out of the scientific community as idiots at best, and liars at worst," Marino answered. "This may be something that only you and I will just have to share. We may have to settle for just knowing that it's still here after 2000 years and that we both saw it. But I can live with that!"

"Actually, neither could I," McFadden responded. "I know we're talking like we've already found it, but that may be all we'll ever have. We're certainly not going to publicize the location of the Robe after all these years just to see our names in print. We've both already had that and I'm not ready to give away a 2000-year-old secret."

"So, the goal of our mission doesn't really change that much," Marino said with finality. "We search for the monks, find the Robe, try to determine if it is Christ's robe, and then we leave with this secret, if they let us."

"Good afternoon, Hertz Car Rental. How may I help you?" the young woman asked on the other end of the line. "Yes, thank you. I am Lt. Tamat Kebede with the Ethiopian Customs Office and we are attempting to locate two American tourists who may have rented a vehicle from you. We have been contacted by the U.S. Embassy. There has been a death back in the United States and, on behalf of the family, we are trying to locate a Mr. Thomas Marino so that we can advise him of the very sad news. They are registered at the Sheraton, but do not appear to be there at the moment."

"Of course, Lieutenant, I would be more than happy to help you. Such terrible news to have to deliver." The officer continued, "They would have leased the vehicle either under the names of Thomas Marino or Francis McFadden."

The clerk answered quickly, "Yes, Sir. I rented a Toyota Land Cruiser to a Dr. Francis McFadden just yesterday afternoon. He said he and another driver, Mr. Thomas Marino, would be traveling for several days and we don't expect them back until the day after tomorrow."

The clerk gave the caller the year, make, model, color, and registration plate on the Land Cruiser. "Is there anything else we can do for you Lieutenant?" the clerk asked eagerly.

"Thank you, but no. You have been a great help," the officer replied. "If you should hear from them, please, do not mention that the Customs Office is looking for them. I think Mr. Marino should hear such sad news first-hand from someone in our office."

The young woman was more than happy to help the officer. "Yes, sir, Lieutenant, I will make sure that no one from Hertz mentions anything when they return. Would you like us to contact your office when they get back?"

"No, thank you," he answered. "We'll have our people and the police on the lookout for the vehicle and should be able to locate it before they even return." The officer thanked the clerk again for her help and then hung up.

It had taken Jacob just four calls to locate the car rental agency that McFadden had leased their new vehicle from. Being from the Customs Office and having the sad duty of reporting a death to an American tourist seemed to be just the right story to elicit the help and information he needed. At least now they knew what they were looking for. His next call was to his cousin, Mohammed the taxi driver. Jacob told him that he needed to know if this Land Cruiser was still in the city. There was a handsome reward for the first driver who found it. Mohammed assured Jacob that every taxi driver he knew would soon be on the lookout. If it was in the city, they would find it.

CHAPTER 34

When McFadden and Marino woke early the next morning, it was still dark and the horizon to the east was just beginning to glow. It would be some time yet before the sun was finally visible. They were both quiet as they ate their small breakfast. The meal seemed to energize them, although each man appeared lost in his thoughts as they contemplated the potential impact of the day before them. With little conversation, they broke camp and began the drive back to the search area. They didn't use their headlights. No point in advertising they were coming. The GPS provided the route and they knew that there were no obstacles in the path that they were concerned with. They parked the vehicle further down from the crash site and tried to conceal it behind some tall bushes just in case. Once the vehicle was camouflaged, they worked their way back into the tree line and began to make their way towards the face of the mountain, a short distance further east from where they'd been yesterday. If they were lucky, they might find another way up without having to worry about someone spotting them.

The sun was just starting to rise and beginning to filter through the trees as they waited to embark on their climb. High above them, they could see the face of the mountain clearly. It would be just a few minutes before everything was bright enough for them to begin their search for an alternate route up. After hundreds of years walking through the mountains, the monks had to have made quite a few paths up and down. The two men just had to find one that would lead them up and to the secret hiding place. It would have been almost impossible, had they not been attacked several days ago and allowed to escape. The attack itself told them they had to have been close.

The climb from this new location didn't seem quite as steep as the one yesterday. They stopped every so often, constantly looking for any sign of a real path. The trees were spaced close together and relatively thin around, so they were able to use them to pull themselves up. After climbing for about 45 minutes, Tom stopped short and raised his hand as if to tell BB not to move or speak. They listened carefully and heard what sounded like voices coming from below them. Marino signaled for McFadden to wait while he moved forward.

He looked down and saw two men who appeared to be dressed like the bandits who had chased them several days before. They were sitting on a small piece of flat ground behind several trees. One man leaned against a tree smoking while the other held a pair of binoculars and appeared to be watching something further down the mountain. Marino straightened himself just slightly to try and see what they were engrossed in and was surprised to see it was the crash site they had searched just yesterday.

He sat back behind the tree and then made his way back to McFadden. "Looks like they found out we weren't in the Rover yesterday," he told him. "I think a couple of our buddies from the other day are waiting for us. They're about 100 feet below us and to our right, and one of them is watching the crash site through a pair of binoculars. My guess is that somebody, probably my 'friend' Jacob, alerted them that we were on our way out here again and these two were sent to watch and warn the others when we showed up." He looked around their position before speaking. "If we go back the way we came and make the most of the trees, I think we can work our way up higher and pass them without being seen. We just have to be really quiet and watch our footing; no stumbling and no rocks sliding down."

McFadden thought for a moment. "I guess we could just wait until they give up and then follow them back," he said, "but then it would be harder to stay hidden. Yeah, let's climb." He smiled. "I'll be like a cat. They'll never know I'm here."

"Okay, Garfield," Marino answered sarcastically, "just don't trip over your tail or we'll both be in the trap."

After backtracking about 50 feet, they chose a route that would take them almost straight up and put some extra distance between them and the two men down below. The incline was steep, but not too much for them to climb with the assistance of the trees. When Marino couldn't hear the two men talking any longer, he signaled BB that it was time to try and move across and past the lookouts. McFadden followed Marino and moved easily through the trees, watching his footing to make sure every step was on solid ground. They had moved to a point where they were now immediately above the two men, about 150 feet up. There were still no sounds and they felt they had made it halfway. Now they had to move past them and decided not to try and climb up, but rather just move horizontally until there was no longer a chance they could be seen.

Just before they began the final move, the man with the binoculars put them down and moved over and sat with his back against a tree. He was facing up the mountain and, for a moment, Marino thought they had been heard. They froze and didn't make any attempt to change their positions just in case they hadn't been discovered. Any movement on their part might be just enough to attract the attention of one of the men sitting below.

After several minutes, the other man apparently said something to his partner who moved back to his original spot and resumed watching the ground below. McFadden felt his heart start to beat again and waited for Marino to make the next move. Ever so slowly, they began to move north and away. After moving at what felt like the proverbial snail's pace, they were far enough past where they felt safe to stop and talk again. In a low voice, McFadden sat back and exhaled softly.

"I thought he had us back there. When he just sat looking up, I was sure it was only a matter of time before he spotted one of us."

Marino had done quite a bit of hunting growing up and knew that the eye rarely saw something in the trees or brush unless it moved, however slightly. "Fortunately, we just blended into our surroundings. Lucky you weren't wearing your Boston College sweatshirt. They'd have picked you right out, Garfield."

They had met their first challenge and had passed, and it was good to smile again. "We got past these two, but there's still the chance of running into some of the others, maybe two more coming down to relieve them," Marino added.

"Let's move back down a little and get off this incline. It's too difficult to try and move through the trees up this high," McFadden said as he looked around. "There's got to be some more level ground around here." Moving down from their hiding place amongst the trees, they suddenly came across a path immediately below them. "We couldn't have done this if we'd known it was here," he said in amazement. "This is clearly a path worn into the rock. It's probably taken hundreds of years to wear this down so flat."

While they were happy to finally find a path worth following, they realized that it was also a path used by the men who had worked so hard to chase them away. Although their travel would be easier now, they also faced a greater chance or running into the very people they had worked so hard to avoid.

"We have to move especially slow and quiet now, less because we don't want anyone to hear us, but more because we want to make sure we hear anybody coming our way from either direction," Marino suggested. Their travel would be slightly quicker on this path than it had been when they were sneaking through the trees, only now more dangerous.

CHAPTER 35

Jacob received a call early that morning asking if there had been any luck in locating the two Americans. He advised the voice on the other end that he was fairly certain they were no longer in the city.

The voice replied, "We have two of our young people in position to observe the site in case they return, but so far they have seen nothing. Jacob, we are all concerned over how this will end. We have never come across anyone who appears to be so determined." Jacob knew what they were going through and cursed himself for having allowed the two men to get so close.

"Brother Anteneh, I think they are as determined as they appear and I believe we cannot make any false assumptions as to what they will, or will not, do. They were bright enough to figure out not only that we were tracking their movements, but how. Because of that, they were able to lease another vehicle and disappear right under our noses. I blame myself for this present situation."

The voice on the other end was quick to respond. "My son, no one is at fault here. If blame is to be assigned then we must take the greatest share, since we failed to anticipate the possibility that someone might someday come looking for, or stumble upon, one of those crash sites. Had we done as he suggested all those years ago, we would not be going through this now. I spoke with him this morning and he asked me to tell you how much your efforts in this are appreciated. You have been our eyes and ears out there for many years and have never let us down. We shall deal with this properly when the time arrives."

Jacob appreciated the kind words and understanding, but they didn't take away his feelings of failure. "May I suggest that we do not assume that they are not there or at least nearby? It might be worth having some men go down and search the areas all around the site in case they have already arrived unseen. If they arrived before you posted the men, then they could be on the mountain searching at this moment. They are two very bright and industrious young men, and I would not be surprised at anything they might do."

"I think that is good advice, Jacob. We will begin our own search from the top down and from the bottom up just in case they have already slipped past. I will let you know if we discover anything. Go with God, Jacob," he said, and the line went silent.

"I wish I could be there to help them, but this is now out of my hands and their responsibility. It is time for them to search and protect."

After the call with Jacob, Brother Anteneh realized that they would have to act quickly if they were to locate the Americans and somehow remove them from this area before they themselves were discovered. Within minutes, the word had been spread and small groups of men were dispatched to search every path and every approach to their location. The two men sent to watch the site from above were told to climb down and search outside the area for any sign that the Americans might be there. Within an hour, they discovered the empty Land

Cruiser parked partially hidden about a quarter mile from the site. "They are on the mountain!"

McFadden followed closely behind as Marino walked slowly up the path and away from the spot where they had seen the two men earlier. It only made sense that the path they followed would lead them to some point where they would find evidence of a group of men living, hidden from the rest of the world. The path became wide enough at times for the men to almost walk side by side. But, as they climbed higher, the path narrowed with a drop off to the side that ranged anywhere from 50 to possibly several hundred feet. They slowed their ascent to account for the added danger of a fall. Little did they know that, despite their best efforts to avoid detection, the mountain around them was bubbling with activity. Men moved quickly along familiar paths as they silently began to close in on the trespassers.

McFadden heard the movement before he saw anyone. Above them, he suddenly saw several men carrying rifles beginning to take aim. McFadden couldn't understand what they were yelling, but it was clearly directed at them, and it was not friendly. The first shots missed their mark but caused the two of them to turn and try to move back down the path they'd just come up. They seemed to be putting a little distance between themselves and the men with the guns. The path at this point was only wide enough for one man to move, and Marino was traveling close behind when he suddenly slammed into McFadden, who had come to a stop.

"What are you doing, BB? These guys are trying to kill us. Move!"

"Remember, Tommy? This is the time for that leap of faith we spoke about. We're in the same situation as the last time they chased us. They're forcing us to escape; to leave in order to save our lives. This is the time to make the unexpected response. They want us to escape so instead we let them capture us."

Marino's eyes were wide, and it was clear that he was having a difficult time trying to process this option. "It's against my better judgment, but I'll go along with this. But don't ever ask me to do anything this incredibly stupid again."

Marino was clearly uncertain of this decision. His mind told him to run as fast as he could down the path and back to their vehicle, but McFadden's calm voice threw him into confusion and conflicting emotions — fight or flight. McFadden seemed to read his mind.

"We can do this, Tommy," he said calmly. "They weren't expecting us this time and we've gotten too close. The only way we can hope to find the robe is for them to take us to it." The men descending the path appeared to have slowed down, although there still was the occasional rifle shot. But just like their previous experience, the bandits were apparently bad shots. No bullets hit any of the trees around them and they didn't even hear any bullets passing close by.

Maybe BB was right! With his heart pounding, and his eyes wide in anticipation, Marino settled back and waited to be captured. "You know that, if you're wrong, this isn't going to end well and no one will ever see us again."

They turned to face the men with the guns as they closed the gap between the two groups. Again, the men appeared to slow down as if to give the two Americans one last chance to turn and continue their escape. When Marino and McFadden stopped running, they knew this would be a different encounter. The two men turned and raised their hands above their heads. As the bandits approached, another group appeared from further down the path, unarmed. They were part of the larger search team and were not prepared to actually confront the two trespassers. There was some confusion as the two groups converged on Marino and McFadden and the men spoke among themselves for some time while their guns remained pointed at their captives.

A large man with a heavy black beard and dark eyes, who appeared to be in charge, did most of the talking. Based on the apparent confusion amongst the men, it appeared that they didn't expect the chase would end quite like this. Finally, a decision was made and, as the leader gestured, two men left the group and continued up the path. At the same time, several of the armed men began to herd McFadden and Marino back down the path they'd just climbed.

Although McFadden resigned himself to being pushed along the path by the guards, Marino was having second thoughts. His faith in McFadden's gamble was disappearing with each step. Ahead, he could see that the path narrowed, which meant they would all have to proceed in single file, bandits and captives alike. It was at this point that Marino's instinct for self-preservation took over.

As they came to a bend in the path, Marino spun around and grabbed the rifle of the man directly behind him. "Tommy, no!" was all

McFadden could shout before everything fell apart. Several of the other guards pushed him forward in an attempt to reach Marino. McFadden realized that, despite what he thought might happen, he couldn't let Marino face these men alone. There were shouts and men shoving as they tried to get around McFadden to reach Marino. Several of the men dropped their rifles and grabbed for McFadden's arms to drag him off the path. This was where his 300-pound frame changed the tide of the fight. He had no intention of hurting any of these men, since he still believed they were in no real trouble. Using his size to effectively block the path, he quickly grabbed the outstretched hands and easily maneuvered the men back and forth across the path, bouncing man off man until they resembled a pile of logs strewn across the road. Although a little worse for wear and sporting a few bumps and bruises, none of the men were seriously injured.

Meanwhile, further down the path, three men were trying to subdue Marino but found it difficult. McFadden still believed they were trying to do it without injuring him. The sound of the small battle must have traveled up the path, because several more men with rifles were spotted making their way to the scene. McFadden turned and began to push his way down the path towards Marino, who continued to wrestle with the unarmed guards. Before he could reach him, Marino mustered all his strength and threw two of the men aside. As he broke free from the fight, he stumbled backwards across the narrow path towards the edge and lost his balance. He seemed to hang there for a few seconds, with a look or surprise on his face, as he reached out to grab something that wasn't there. One of the men he had been fighting reached out for Marino's hand, but he was too late. Marino fell backwards off the path and disappeared from view. At that bend in the path, the incline of the mountain fell away and became a sharp drop of about thirty feet.

McFadden heard Marino's yell of surprise as he lost his footing and then heard the sound of his body slamming into the ground below. At this point, all action stopped and the few men with rifles dropped them and made their way with the others towards the spot where Marino had fallen. They ignored McFadden and worked their way to the edge of the path and looked down at the lifeless body. By now, the leader arrived and began to quickly give orders. Men nodded and disappeared in several different directions. McFadden tried to make his way to the edge, but the man grabbed his arm and shook his head. He gestured for McFadden to step back and allow the men to move freely in the confined area.

CHAPTER 36

McFadden moved further down the path so that he was out of their way, yet remain in a position to look down at his friend's motionless body. Marino lay without making a sound. Falling from that height, it seemed only logical that his friend had sustained serious injuries. McFadden cursed himself for allowing Marino to have been placed in this situation. If they had run down the path and tried to escape, Tom most likely would be fine now. Instead, he was hurt and maybe dying from his injuries.

Within a few minutes, two men had made their way down to where Marino lay. They carefully examined him and one man felt for a pulse. After several seconds, he looked up and shouted something to the leader. The man smiled and nodded to McFadden. At least Tommy was alive. How badly injured no one knew at the moment, but at least he had survived the fall. There still was a chance. Men came and went in an organized confusion; up the path and down the path and several more making their way to where Marino lay.

Shortly, two men arrived with a stretcher and worked their way down to join the others huddled around Marino. A large first-aid bag somehow materialized and was lowered to the scene of the fall. No one paid any attention to McFadden now, as he silently watched them work. Shouts and questions and answers echoed as the men with Marino communicated with the men up on the path. Other than to place a blanket over Marino to keep warm, no one moved him. Finally, a small man in a black robe and carrying what looked like a doctor's bag could be seen making his way down the path from above.

When he arrived, the leader apparently explained what had happened and pointed down at Marino. They spoke for several more moments before the little man turned to McFadden, "We will do all we can to help your friend," he said in perfect English. "Please, stand back and be patient. We will have him out of there shortly and into the hands of those who can do their best to save him."

As McFadden watched them gently care for his friend, his mind was drawn back to Colavari's description of the men who had helped him after his crash. *The monastery does exist,* he thought. *And if it does, then the Robe of Christ must be close.* But now forgotten was their adventure of searching for the Robe. If it did exist, then maybe it can really heal and repeat for Tom what it did for his uncle so many years ago.

By now, the little man who had spoken to him had been helped down to where the others huddled around Marino. They stepped back and allowed him to kneel beside the still form. With practiced hands, he carefully examined Marino and ran his fingers over every inch of the young man's body. Watching him work, McFadden wondered whether the man was either a doctor or nurse. He shouted up to the leader and appeared to give him some instructions. The man acknowledged and then barked some orders of his own. The scene was a beehive of activity as men came and went and materials appeared as if by magic.

McFadden watched as the stretcher was lowered down to where waiting hands grabbed it and placed it on flat ground near Marino. The little man gestured for two of the men to kneel beside him. While he supported Marino's head and neck, the other two began to slowly move Marino onto his back. Even unconscious, the pain of being moved was enough to make Marino groan loudly. The two men stopped their movements for several seconds before continuing. It seemed as if hours passed as Marino was gently moved by the trained hands. Finally, he was on his back and a more thorough examination was conducted. Even from where McFadden stood, he could see that Tom had badly broken his right leg and was bleeding heavily from what appeared to be a serious head wound. There was no way to tell the extent of the damage that he must have suffered internally.

After they had stabilized Tom as best they could, several more men came forward and these added hands slowly raised him off the ground as the stretcher slid underneath him. With a steady pace, they lowered Marino onto the stretcher and strapped him securely to it and placed the blanket back over him. The men were silent again as they looked around at the various avenues available back up to the path.

They're never going to be able to get that stretcher back up to this path, McFadden thought to himself. He felt it might be better to just try and move him down to ground level and then take him somewhere for treatment. But then he remembered the Robe. If Marino was to survive, they needed to get him to the Robe.

More men appeared and, after some discussion and gesturing, it was decided what their course of action would be. They began to make their way down the slope, with several men stopping every few feet until they were spread out a few feet apart. The little doctor made one last check of his patient and then stepped back. Four men lifted the stretcher and approached the first group stationed at the base of the slope. The four men lifted the stretcher over their heads and passed the front two handles to the men standing higher on the hill. They then stepped back after passing off the stretcher and moved to the rear. They joined the two rear men and added their strength to keep the stretcher up and level. The two new men in the front raised the stretcher over their heads and passed it up to the next two men positioned above them and moved slowly to the rear and grabbed the back two handles. This maneuver was repeated over and over again as the stretcher slowly made its way up, perfectly horizontal. It didn't appear to move any more than an inch either way.

McFadden was amazed at the strength and concentration of the men as they worked quietly as a team. The stretcher was finally handed off to several men at the top who were assisted as it was laid flat on the path. The entire transport had taken less than ten minutes. The little doctor was almost lifted back up to the path. The men gently guided him up and handed him off to the assembled stretcher bearers still gathered on the slope. Finally, the last of the men began to climb back up to the path. After several minutes, everyone was back and the leader gave instructions, and four new men came forward to take over. They lifted Marino and began a slow walk up the path. The rifles had long since been picked up and several men carried two or three of them over their shoulders, no longer a threat to anyone.

The little doctor approached McFadden. "Dr. McFadden, please follow us up to where Thomas can be better cared for." McFadden was taken aback. "How is it that you know our names?" The little man just smiled and strode quickly up the path.

They carefully carried the stretcher as they made their way quietly up the mountain. In less than a half an hour, they entered what McFadden considered the densest part of the forest he had seen since he and Tom had begun climbing. The men moved surefooted as if they knew every curve and rock. A short time later, as they approached what McFadden considered the crest of the mountain, they arrived at a large outcropping of rocks that completely blocked any way around the mountain. The only choice for anyone coming this way would be to turn around and go back down to look for another path.

They gently laid the stretcher down on the ground. One of the men whistled softly and a wooden ladder suddenly appeared and was lowered from the top of the boulder. The man who had whistled quickly climbed and disappeared once on top. Within a few moments, a large wooden pulley swung out from the rocks above and positioned itself directly over the stretcher. Ropes were lowered until they reached the ground. They formed a sling and the stretcher was placed within the sling, while Tom's body was secured tightly. Another whistle and the sling began to slowly rise. Two ropes were attached to either end of the stretcher and men on the ground held the ropes out and away from the rocks so that it rose easily without swinging. When it reached the top, several pairs of hands appeared over the edge and reached out and swung the pulley and sling in.

The men stood quietly until someone above whistled, at which time they began to climb one after another. They were young, strong men and quickly disappeared up the ladder. When there was only one man left with McFadden, he pointed towards the ladder and smiled. McFadden nodded and began to climb, not knowing what he would find at the top. When he reached the last rung, he was able to step off onto a smooth, flat space on top of the boulder. The pulley used to hoist Marino was being dismantled and the assorted parts were being carried away. An older man dressed in a robe and sandals was there to meet him. He led McFadden along a small path approximately four feet wide and cut into the side of the mountain. Small metal rings had been driven into the mountainside and rope strung through the rings creating a handrail of sorts. McFadden stopped and looked down. There was nothing below them except the open sky and a sheer drop of several hundred feet to the bottom. No other way down or up.

The old man led him further along until the path bent around to the right. As he made the turn, McFadden saw another outcropping of rock, and, beneath that, an opening in the side of the mountain. As he drew nearer, he saw that the opening led into what appeared to be a large cave. The opening was facing the mountain interior so that it was essentially invisible from the air or the ground. *No wonder no one has been able to find them. Without their help there is no way to reach them,* he thought to himself.

He entered the cave and saw that it was even larger than he expected and had what appeared to be tunnels or passageways leading off into the mountain from several different directions. There were about a dozen men of varying age, moving about the area just inside the cave entrance. He looked around but didn't see any sign of Tom.

He touched the old man's arm and asked, "Where is my friend?" The man smiled and led McFadden to a table off to the side and indicated for him to have a seat. He left for a few moments, but quickly returned with some bread, fruit, and water for him. "Thank you," McFadden replied. "But I'd really like to see my friend."

The man spoke for the first time. "Your friend is in good hands. Eat first and then I will take you to him." Even though he wasn't hungry, McFadden sat and picked at the food in front of him and waited. He watched the men as they moved about the area, going about their duties and disappearing into the various tunnels only to reappear a short time later. *How can you argue with people who appear to be so gentle and kind?* He thought to himself.

After what seemed like hours, the old man returned and signaled for him to follow. "I am Brother Anteneh," he said. "I will take you to see Thomas." Brother Anteneh led him into a tunnel off to their right and they walked in silence. McFadden was amazed at the tunnel system. This one was more than six feet high, so he only had to bend slightly as he walked. They passed through areas where several tunnels converged, yet there were no markers or indicators of location or direction. Someone unfamiliar with this network would quickly become lost.

After several minutes, they exited the tunnel and he found himself in an opening facing a hallway with several doors on either side. They walked down the hall and entered the third door on the right. Inside was dark, lit only by two small candles. There were two men in the room. One appeared quite old and the other was surprisingly young. They smiled at him and moved aside, standing near the door. As his eyes became accustomed to the dimly lit room, he saw a small bed against the far wall and realized Tom was lying there. He quickly went to him and immediately saw that he was covered by what looked like an old brown blanket. He was afraid to touch it. *Is this the Robe?* He wondered to himself. He stood staring at Tom and was surprised to see that his friend was breathing softly and seemed to be at rest. The large gash on his forehead had stopped bleeding and looked as if the swelling was already starting to go down.

His curiosity finally overcame his fear, and he slowly reached out and gently lifted the edge of the blanket to look at Tom's broken leg. He stared for a moment before dropping the blanket and unconsciously stepping back. The bone was barely visible through the skin and the leg appeared to have straightened some. The area where it had pierced the skin was red and it, too, had stopped bleeding. His mind was whirling, and he felt his legs go weak beneath him. He was at an intellectual crossroad trying to compare the things he had actually seen happen against those for which there was no logical explanation. He looked for a chair and found one at the foot of the bed and sat.

Brother Anteneh had been watching him as he looked at his friend. He came over and placed a gentle hand on McFadden's shoulder. His touch seemed to calm the big man and he found himself breathing easily again. He reached out slowly and touched the blanket again as he looked up at the old man.

"Is this the Robe of Jesus?" he asked softly. Brother Anteneh did not answer. He merely smiled. "Francis, please come with me", he said. "Thomas needs his sleep and you need some rest. I will take you to your room and then we can talk later."

They left the room and McFadden followed Brother Anteneh down a passageway until they arrived at another door cut into the rock. "Get some rest and I will call for you later, and we can again check on your friend," he said as he opened the door. It was a room very much like the one Marino was in. Brother Anteneh lit two candles that were on the small table in the center of the room. Before he could ask another question, the old man was gone and McFadden was alone.

Despite the excitement of the day, McFadden found the quiet of the room surprisingly relaxing and he laid back on the bed for a few moments. Those few moments turned into hours as he quickly fell asleep. Images of the previous day replayed themselves as he repeatedly saw Tom in slow motion falling from the path.

CHAPTER 37

McFadden didn't stir until Brother Anteneh returned in the morning, softly calling his name. "Good morning, Francis," he said as McFadden opened his eyes. For a few seconds, McFadden seemed confused, as he looked around the room before slowly remembering where he was.

"How long have I been asleep?" he asked as he swung his feet onto the floor and sat up. "You slept through the night, I am happy to say. After what you and Thomas have been through, we were certain you needed the rest."

"How's Tom doing?" he asked the old man. "Is he any better?"

Brother Anteneh smiled and held up his hand. "Don't worry, Thomas is doing very well. I will take you to see him shortly, but right now Brother Samuel would like to see you."

Brother Samuel! It can't be the same Brother Samuel mentioned by the young Ethiopian girl, or the same Brother Samuel that Angelo Colavari wrote about, he thought. Silently, McFadden rose and followed Brother Anteneh out into the hall. They went back into the tunnel and walked in silence, crossing through several junctions and crossroads that led to even more tunnels along the way. After several minutes, they exited into a small opening and a short hallway that led to a lone door at the end

— a large wooden door. There were no other doors in this hallway and it was obvious that this was a private area.

Brother Anteneh knocked softly and a voice inside told him to come in. He opened the door and signaled for McFadden to enter ahead of him. As he stepped into the room, Brother Anteneh softly closed the door behind him. This room, like Tom's, was dimly lit and it took him several moments for his eyes to adjust to the low light before he realized a man sat at a table further back from the door. The room was sparsely furnished with just a desk, a table with several chairs, and a narrow bed in the corner.

The man, much older than Brother Anteneh, rose from the table and approached McFadden. He clearly wasn't Ethiopian. "Francis, I am so glad that you were not hurt along with Thomas," he said in heavily accented English. "It has never been our intention that anyone should be harmed. For generations we have worked carefully to help, never to hurt," he said gently. He offered McFadden a chair at the table and both men sat.

McFadden stared at the older man for several seconds before speaking. "A short time ago, my friend was badly injured and I thought he was going to die. I saw him several hours after the fall and his injuries appear to be healing at an exceptional rate and now it looks like he's going to be just fine. Is it the Robe of Jesus that healed him?"

The old man looked surprised by the question. "It is not the Robe that heals, Francis. It is God's mercy that makes the lame walk, the blind see, and the broken healed."

"But is it the Robe of Jesus?" he softly asked again.

"Yes, Francis. The blanket that covers your friend, is the Robe once worn by Jesus Christ."

The man looked at McFadden and explained, "That is the blanket that has healed so many over such a long time. It was the robe that saved the life of Thomas's uncle, young Angelo Colavari so many years ago. And it has saved countless others over the years that were brought to us for help. We have tried to stay hidden in this mountain for generations, but there are times when mercy cannot stay hidden."

Now that it had finally been confirmed, McFadden wasn't sure what to say. Finally, he asked,

"How do you know our names? No one has even asked who we were."

The old man smiled again. "Francis, we have known about you and Thomas since the day you arrived in Addis Ababa. We have followed your moves as you began your quest to locate Angelo's plane. To be honest, at first, we were not sure what you were really looking for. But over time we realized that Angelo must have left something behind that led you and Thomas to come here. Am I correct?"

For whatever reason, McFadden immediately trusted this man who sat across from him and began to tell him the whole story. He spoke of their meeting with Father Cleary and the Gospel of Henok and what eventually led them to believe that the Robe of Jesus Christ still existed. As he spoke, the other man listened intently to every word and occasionally nodded or smiled. He didn't ask any questions and just let McFadden unburden himself of the secret he and Tom had shared.

When he was finished, the old man spoke as if reliving a time long gone. "We have helped many people over the years, Francis. Most were simple people who eventually came to believe they had just dreamt the experience and had no way to explain how they had been miraculously healed. A few, like Angelo Colavari, remembered quite clearly what happened to them here, and have tried to come back to us. But we live a quiet life of prayer here and no one may join us unless they have been chosen. That is the way it has been for hundreds of years."

McFadden quickly added, "Like the young boys selected from the Muslim and the Christian tribes every 10 years."

Now it was the old man's turn to be surprised. "How do you know so much about how those young boys come to us?"

"Shortly before he died, Angelo sent his nephew, Tom, the diary he had kept for more than 70 years. It started with his crash in 1936 and his rescue by the other brothers. It detailed his trip back to Ethiopia in 1947 and his attempt to locate you. Along the way he became friends with a Muslim man named Josef who apparently told him about the selection process made by the holy men from the mountain every 10 years. He also told him of a little village girl who was badly burned and apparently brought here, where she was healed."

"Of course! Josef's brother Ismael came to us many years ago. It is my understanding that Josef was to join us, but then the war with the Italians changed everything. It was Ismael who brought the young child,

Ayinabeba, to us after she was left to die of her burns." McFadden wondered how this old man could clearly remember so many things from such a long time ago.

Finally, the time seemed right. "May I ask who you are, sir?"

"I am Brother Samuel," the old man said in a kind soft voice.

This can't be the same Brother Samuel, he thought to himself. *If it was the same man, he'd be almost 200 years old. Maybe the Robe was also the fountain of youth for the men living here. Is this the same Brother Samuel who cared for Angelo when his injuries should have surely killed him in 1936, or the badly burned young Ayinabeba in 1927? After all, Ayinabeba and Angelo had both said he was an old man then.*

"When the robe was brought here almost 2000 years ago, it was believed that the best way to protect it was to keep it away from man in a safe place, such as the original cave in this mountain. Here, a group of men would dedicate their lives to ensure that it would survive for all time. So began the tradition of one worthy child from each village to join us and serve the Lord."

"How was it that the man at the car rental agency was so willing to help?" McFadden asked.

"Not all of those who come here stay here. There are some, such as Jacob, who receive their education with us and then go out into the world. With the help of those who have gone before them, our brothers are assisted in establishing businesses or careers that enable them to provide the necessary things, or help, we require to continue our mission of protecting the Robe. Jacob uses his business as a way of keeping track of those who come to the city and why. His friend Tadele assists him, but is not from here. He knows of the holy men in the mountains but knows nothing of our mission. It was he who followed you around the city. But you already know that, since you sent him on a senseless journey out of the city while you and Thomas came here. That was very clever on your part.

"Some of our brothers are in the police and the military and have kept alive the story of the mountain bandits. This has worked very well for years, that is until you and Thomas came," he said with a slight smile. "People would be quite surprised to know how many of our brothers occupy positions of some importance or influence in this country, yet never to abuse their power, only to protect the secret of the Robe."

McFadden suddenly found himself at a crossroad in trying to understand what to believe. Was Brother Samuel merely the ancient leader of this family of religious men, or was there more behind all this secrecy and misdirection? If the Robe could still exist after 2000 years, was it possible that… He was afraid to even think about the possibility. Although confused and more than a little afraid to admit what he felt was the real story, he decided to go with his heart. He chose his words carefully and asked Brother Samuel how long he had lived here in the mountains – although he asked in Hebrew. Without hesitation Brother Samuel responded, "I have been here for many years," – also in Hebrew.

He looked at Brother Samuel as if seeing him for the first time. He felt his throat tighten and his face redden. "This has never really been about the Robe, has it? For more than 2000 years this hasn't only been about protecting the Robe. This has always been about protecting you and the Robe. The man who took final possession of the robe after Christ died.

"Are you Peter? Peter, the rock upon which He would build His church."

The question appeared to take the old man by surprise. His face suddenly looked sad and pained. HIs eyes welled and small tears slowly made their way down his cheeks. McFadden was taken aback by the old man's reaction and thought he had somehow offended him. Brother Samuel smiled at McFadden and shook his head slowly. "You are indeed an exceptional young man, Francis." The old man sat back in his chair and looked at McFadden closely. The statement had clearly affected him. He appeared to age even more after his announcement.

"Be at ease, Francis," Brother Samuel had said. "You are the first outsider to ever get this close to us on your own. I believe you are entitled to an explanation. Would that I were Jesus's closest disciple. But no, I am not that man. Rather, I am one who prays daily and begs forgiveness for my actions. No, Francis, I am not Peter."

"My name is Judas; Judas Iscariot, I am the man who betrayed Jesus."

CHAPTER 38

McFadden didn't know what to say or how to react. He felt a cold shiver run up his spine. *How could this be possible? Could this man sitting across from me really be Judas?* McFadden's mind raced with a million questions, afraid to ask even one.

The man called Brother Samuel continued. "After Jesus was surrendered to the Romans by my hand, I was beside myself with guilt and shame. It was never my intention that Jesus was to suffer. I truly believed that when faced with death He would call upon His heavenly army to strike down the Romans and free His people." As the old man spoke McFadden could hear the anguish in his voice.

"The gospels state that I hanged myself. I will say that I did consider killing myself, but that would have been against Jesus' teachings. The old man seemed to regain some of his strength and his voice appeared stronger. "After some time, I gathered the courage to seek out Peter and the apostles. While most felt that I had betrayed them as well as Jesus, it was Peter who stood by my side and accepted my actions as the will of God and they ultimately forgave me as they knew Jesus would have wanted. At that time, I swore that I would willingly lay down my life in Jesus' name and would do anything to help protect His holy Robe."

"After several years of moving the robe from apostle to apostle, town to town, and city to city in an attempt to keep it out of the hands of the Romans, it was eventually given to me to protect. There were those among us who sought to protect me as well. From that day forward, wherever I traveled I carried the Robe of Jesus with me."

He spoke of how he was finally ushered from Rome by others who recognized the threat he presented to the Romans. It was decided that he must escape to where he wouldn't be found and where he could be better protected. After months in the desert with his small group, they eventually found themselves in Abyssinia, where the teachings of Jesus were already known.

"The Abyssinians in my small group chose this mountain as the hiding place and a small cave as my home. It was believed that I could best be protected if I was kept far from civilization. The cave was small, but, over the next two thousand years, a never-ending procession of young brothers excavated and extended the caves into what you see before you today."

"Sir, may I ask why you are here and not in Rome?" he asked.

"Francis, I am here because He chose me to be here. He has not provided me with guidance for a new direction. What is there in Rome for me? The Robe would become an object of curiosity at best, or worse, a tool to be used for political purposes. The Robe is not something to be worshipped. Its power comes from God, and not any fabric woven by man. I have seen the growth of the church these past two thousand years, and, while there may have been a time when I might have been able to help guide, that time has long passed. The church of today has changed and has become a den of bureaucrats."

"I spend my life here in a way that would not be available to me outside this mountain. My brothers and I pray and worship in our own way, and we help the less fortunate when the situation presents itself. Through us, the Robe is used as a tool to honor Jesus and to heal others as He did during His brief life."

"Is it the Robe that keeps the other brothers healthy and able to survive?" McFadden asked.

"Francis, the Robe is not a fountain of youth. It has never been used to prolong the life of any of our followers. If a brother becomes ill, we nurse him and try to make him comfortable. When it is his time to pass, there is no attempt to prevent nature from taking its course."

He paused before continuing. "Francis, for two thousand years the Robe has been used only to heal those from the outside when we find them. Angelo was one who was dropped at our doorstep. We couldn't let him die of his injuries; injuries that could be traced back to the violence of others."

There was one question burning in his mind, but how to ask it? How is it that Brother Samuel was still alive after two thousand years? The old man seemed to read his mind. "Why do I still live, you wonder? Francis, I ask that same question every morning that I awake and find myself still here among my brothers. I ask Jesus to take me, to let this life end, but He has not heard my prayers." At this, Samuel's voice lowered, speaking softly, "I am to do His work here for however long

Jesus feels I must pay penance for my weakness," he said with conviction.

"Now that you know our story, what will you do with this information? If we were a violent people, your life would be at risk because of what you know. Or we could just keep you and Thomas here against your will so that you wouldn't be able to share what you have learned." Brother Samuel paused. "But we are neither of these. We have never been faced with a situation like this. No one has ever come to our mountain looking specifically for the Robe. You two have been a great challenge to us and caused some long troubling nights. Now that we have spoken, I am no longer concerned for our existence. When Thomas is well, you are both free to leave."

"Tom and I have already talked about what we would do if we did in fact find the Robe. We agreed that, if it existed, knowing that it has been kept hidden and protected for the past two thousand years, we would not be the ones who would betray that secret. We decided that we would continue to talk about this trip as our attempt to locate the site of Angelo Colavari's crash and list this adventure as a failure. We will never mention you, the Robe, or the existence of this location and the brothers who live here for the rest of our lives."

Brother Samuel smiled and nodded. "I believe you, Francis, and have complete faith that both of you will keep what you have found and seen here a secret from the outside world. Once you leave, Francis, you must never return. You know more about us here than any outsider has known in more than 2000 years. Your return would only place us at greater risk of being discovered." McFadden nodded his understanding.

"I can be happy with what I have seen and learned here. We will never betray your trust in us." Brother Samuel called softly, and Brother Anteneh entered from the hall. He had apparently been waiting to be summoned. "When Thomas is well, we will see that you both are led safely back to your vehicle." He stood up and McFadden almost jumped out of his chair in response. "I won't be seeing you again before you leave, but, if you have any questions, Brother Anteneh will be happy to help you."

McFadden didn't know what to say or do and just stood looking down at the old man. Finally, Brother Samuel came around and embraced McFadden, kissing him lightly on the cheek. "God bless you both. We will pray for your safe trip home." The next thing he remembered he was being led back into the hall and following Brother Anteneh down one of the many passages.

There was so much going through his mind at this moment that he followed the old man as if in a daze. After several minutes of twists and turns through the labyrinth of passages, they were again at the door to the room where he had last seen Marino. The door was opened by one of the brothers inside and McFadden and the old monk entered. McFadden was amazed to see Tom awake and alert, and saw the questioning look in his eyes.

"Well, were we right? No one will answer my questions. Am I under the Robe of Jesus Christ? Is it the Robe that's healing me?" McFadden walked to the foot of the bed and looked down at his friend. "We were right. We've found the true Robe; the One Robe."

Marino lay back on his bed, clutching the robe and staring at the ceiling. "It all paid off. It was even worth the fall and the broken bones to finally get here," he said as if talking to himself. "What else did you find out while I was unconscious?"

A thousand thoughts raced through McFadden's mind as he looked at his friend lying under the 'blanket.' The secret of Judas's existence would be difficult for any one man to keep to himself, but likely, impossible for two. He realized that he couldn't risk this information ever getting out, despite his feelings for Tom. Finally, his mind was made. "I actually met Brother Samuel. The same man who had helped the young girl and your uncle all those years ago. He is well beyond one hundred years old, but amazingly alert and aware." He paused while Tom absorbed this new bit of information. "He remembers them both and was glad that Angelo survived the war. I told him we had agreed never to reveal what we found to anyone. He said he trusted our word and we were free to leave whenever you're completely well."

McFadden saw Brother Anteneh standing away from the head of the bed and out of Tom's view. The old monk looked at McFadden, and a small smile appeared as he acknowledged McFadden's decision. Their secret would again be safe. Samuel would be pleased with the outcome. Francis was truly an exceptional young man.

"When can I meet Brother Samuel and thank him for saving me and my uncle?" Tom asked. "I asked him the same question, but he said he was too weak to see either of us before we leave. The few minutes I spent with him really took its toll." McFadden nodded towards the old man with them. "Brother Samuel said that if we had any questions Brother Anteneh would be here to help us." Tom was beginning to show the effects of his injuries and looked to be getting sleepy. "I'll let you rest for a while and I'll come back and see you later." Marino nodded and closed his eyes. He was asleep in seconds.

CHAPTER 39

Once outside the room, Brother Anteneh reached over and squeezed McFadden's arm as acknowledgement of what he had just done. "Please follow me, Francis. I will take you back to your room where you can get some rest. We will continue to watch over Thomas."

He led McFadden back through the intertwining tunnels and passageways and eventually to his room. "Rest here and I will call for you later. Would you like something to eat?" he asked. "No thank you, sir. I'm a little too confused to eat right now. Maybe later." With that, the old man left and McFadden sat on the side of the bed. He finally admitted to himself that he was feeling the effects of this experience and lay back on the narrow, hard mattress, and was again soon fast asleep. Later that day, McFadden's belongings were moved to Tom's room and another bed brought in. While McFadden appreciated them being together, he suspected the change was also made so that their movements could be more closely monitored.

Over the next several days, while Tom rested and slowly regained his strength, McFadden explored the mountain. Once Brother Anteneh realized that their existence was again safe from the outside world, he felt comfortable in answering most of McFadden's questions. With the old man's help and cooperation, McFadden was able to travel throughout the network of caves and tunnels and observe the everyday life of these men who had dedicated their lives to protecting Judas and the Robe. Brother Anteneh explained that some of the young men who came to them did not always stay with them. Many times they were educated and trained for work outside the monastery where they could provide a specific service. With the assistance of those who had gone before them, these young men were assimilated into the secret society whose primary purpose was to protect the existence of the monastery. Some held mid-level positions in the government, while others were in leadership roles in the military. There were those that entered into the business world where they had access to modern technology, such as cellular and satellite phones.

It was one of these local companies that provided the satellite phone used to communicate with Jacob at the Lucky Car Rental agency. The phone was listed on the company's books as being assigned to one of their senior executives — another member of the monastery's secret society. The phone bill was rolled up into the company's monthly expenses. There were several large and successful corporations around the world whose secondary role was to ensure for uninterrupted access to the basic necessities of the brotherhood there in the mountains.

These organizations opened satellite offices in Ethiopia where they were able to contract with local businesses, many operated by their followers, while providing steady employment opportunities for hundreds of men and women across the country. The more he learned about their history, the more McFadden realized that the influence of this secret brotherhood stretched far across this country, and, in all likelihood, in a world outside Ethiopia. That in itself was amazing, but that it did so for 2000 years without ever being betrayed was even more incredible.

Prior to the development of this new technology, communication had been slow and required regular travel between those on the mountain and one or more of their contacts in the city. The more travel and contact with the outside, the greater the risk of discovery. Now, one call from the mountain on the satellite phone started a chain of calls that alerted the key people within minutes. "That is how we first learned of your arrival and your interest in locating Angelo's crash site," Brother Anteneh offered. "Jacob is one of those that were chosen to leave us and work outside. What better way to identify new people entering the city who might somehow present a threat to our society than through a car rental agency? It was his cousin Mohammad, the taxi driver, who brought Thomas to Jacob." That bit of information answered several questions McFadden had regarding their being singled out so quickly.

On one of their tours, several levels below the main living areas, he saw the series of pipes and pumps that provided a constant source of fresh water to the inhabitants. Brother Anteneh explained that a young brother who had been sent into the outside world at the turn of the 20th century had received a scholarship to the University of Berlin, where he had studied engineering. The scholarship had been offered by a successful businessman, himself a member of the secret brotherhood who had been sent out years earlier. Upon graduation, the young man had returned to the mountain where, with the help of those here, designed the building and construction of the intricate plumbing system that drew fresh water from an underground spring. The steady flow of water was also adequate to power a small turbine that provided a minimal source of lighting. Now more than 100 years later, it continued to provide an uninterrupted flow of cool clean water and basic lighting.

Their ventilation system was the ingenious design of yet another of their outside brethren, a Nobel candidate. Utilizing a unique system of his own design, the system was capable of moving clean air through the tunnels and into the living and working areas throughout the mountain. The air was vented through ductwork that utilized the cracks and fissures created during the tunnel expansions over the years. Food and basic supplies were delivered quarterly by one of their members on the outside and delivered by truck to the base of the mountain. They were then carried up by the brothers to an entrance midway up the mountain, almost as inaccessible as the one they had used when they first arrived. It, too, appeared to have been carved out of the rock over hundreds of years, and provided another access point for quick action by their band of "bandits," in the event strangers approach from that direction.

These two areas were well concealed. The one above could only be accessed by the ladder lowered from within. The one on the side was closed off by a large stone just inside the cave entrance that amazingly pivoted and could easily swing into place where it fit perfectly into the opening, presenting itself as a solid wall of stone. McFadden wondered if there was anything that the little community couldn't accomplish.

All of these developments were amazing and McFadden's respect for these men continued to grow each day he was there. As he observed the daily workings of the brothers, his mind began to wander to the more mundane parts of their existence. He knew where they came from and he knew how they lived. But what happened when they died? This was a mountain of stone with no evidence of any type of cemetery. Where did they go?

Brother Anteneh was clearly taken aback by McFadden's question. "You truly are a very unusual young man, Francis!" he said. "Of all the questions you have asked, this is one that I had never expected. You have a truly exceptional mind," he said with a slight smile and a shake of his head. "I had never thought anyone would be interested, but I don't think it will do any harm to share this bit of information. Follow me," he said and led him back into the tunnels. He muttered to himself as they made their way deeper into the mountain. "An amazing mind, an exceptional mind. You would do well here amongst us, Francis."

As they descended deeper into the mountain, Brother Anteneh spoke as if he was conducting a tour for visitors. "When Brother Samuel and the Robe were guided here" he said, "the cave they discovered was lower and located on the far side of the mountain almost at ground level. When they entered that cave, they found several small passageways, almost like small tunnels that nature had created. These initially led a short distance in various directions before coming to rock walls. Over the next several years, these passageways were expanded into a very basic set of rooms and tunnels."

They paused at the junction of two passageways. It was obvious to McFadden that the steep descent was taking its toll on the old man. "Would you like to go back, Brother Anteneh?" McFadden offered. "No, thank you, Francis. Just let me catch my breath for a moment," he answered. "Let's sit on that bench against the wall and I can tell you a little of what it must have been like for them all those years ago."

Brother Anteneh then explained how the first cave that was found had provided the very basic amount of protection for Brother Samuel. But it was quickly realized that Samuel could be easily trapped within, unless there was an additional means for escape. While the cave was being enlarged, others explored every foot of the mountain from all sides looking for yet another place that would provide greater protection.

"After many weeks, another cave was discovered further up," he offered. "It was the discovery of this second cave that revealed just how unusual this mountain was. That cave was much larger and its entrance better concealed." The old man's eyes seemed to light up as he talked about their find. "The inside of that cave revealed another series of small tunnels. It was as if God himself had designed this mountain for their use," he said with excitement. "This whole mountain is carved into sections by a labyrinth of natural and man-made passageways." Anteneh looked at McFadden with bright, alert eyes. "Within a few short years, the natural tunnels were expanded, both from below and above, until they created the basis for what you see before you now. The tunnels climbing higher into the mountain were extended until they reached the uppermost level where you and Thomas entered just a few days ago. Once the upper cave entrance was connected to the one below, the original entrance was collapsed and sealed from the outside. Over the next two thousand years nature has covered that opening so that no one would ever suspect that a cave once existed there."

By now, Brother Anteneh appeared to have regained his strength. He rose from the bench and began leading the way once more. They seemed to travel down, tunnel leading to passageway, passageway leading to yet another tunnel. The air became cooler and Brother Anteneh produced a small flashlight to lead the way. After some time, they came to the end of a passage and faced a large wooden door with an ornate cross meticulously carved in the center. "Francis, we are going back through time," he said as he unlocked the door and proceeded down yet another stairway carved out of the rock. Finally, at the bottom, Anteneh turned a small light switch on the wall and a tunnel appeared before them. "We have arrived at the catacombs of ancient Rome," he said softly.

McFadden looked to his right and left and saw openings carved into the stone wall, three high on each side and each containing a wooden coffin. The coffins were clearly old and man-made, but the cool air must have acted to preserve them evidenced by their remarkably good condition. As his eyes became accustomed to the dimly lit tunnel, he saw that it continued down for some distance before bearing off to the right. "These are the first of our group who came here with Brother Samuel more than 2000 years ago. At that time, little thought was given as to where we would bury those whose time would come. At first, small pieces of ground were found outside where a shallow grave could be dug," he said quietly. "But soon, it was realized that what limited ground was available would be insufficient to handle those who would eventually follow. So, a page was taken from early Christianity, and the catacombs were reintroduced beneath this mountain. Those few buried outside were eventually brought back and placed in one of the early caves while work began down here."

Anteneh paused and allowed McFadden to process what had just been said. "You are standing on ground that was carved from this rock two thousand years ago. Each step will bring you closer to today; thousands of steps past thousands of our brothers. At first, there was just a small tunnel, but, as age and disease claimed our group, it became clear that this project needed to be expanded and continued." He swept his hand across the carved openings and pointed down the tunnel. "Those who left us first have been witness to the thousands who have gone after as the tomb was extended and more room made available. The path begins here, twenty centuries past, and continues forward as we advance into the twenty first century, where we laid to rest our dear brother Andrew just two weeks ago."

McFadden was quiet and just stared from coffin to coffin as he took several steps down the *passageway. This is incredible, he thought. "I am standing next to the remains of men — human artifacts — buried centuries ago. What stories these men could tell.* With a silent prayer, he turned back to Brother Anteneh and nodded his understanding. After a few moments, the door was locked again and the two men began their trip back to the present.

CHAPTER 40

Within a week, Marino was strong enough to get out of bed. Each day, he improved a bit more until his injuries were fully healed. One morning, they awoke to the sound of someone knocking softly on the door to their small room. "Come in," Marino called. The door opened and the small figure of Brother Anteneh entered carrying a tray of food and tea.

Marino smiled at the old man as he took the tray and placed it on the small wooden table against the wall. "The last time someone here brought tea to one of my relatives, they woke up several hours later and miles away," Marino said with a smile. Brother Anteneh nodded and said with a slight chuckle, "Normally, that is exactly what would have happened to you, had Brother Samuel not instructed us to have faith in your word and allow you to leave on your own. When you are ready, several of our brothers will guide you and Francis back to your vehicle and you can begin your journey home."

The following morning, McFadden and Marino were sharing a light breakfast when there was again a knock on the door. Brother Anteneh entered and greeted both men warmly. He had come to look upon the two young men as more than guests and looked forward to their company and never-ending questions. "As much as we have enjoyed your stay with us, it is time for you to go back to your world." He looked at each man in turn. "You must never return," he said solemnly. "Brother Samuel has asked that I tell you how much he respects and appreciates your promise to keep our presence here a secret from the outside world." His voice took on a more somber tone. "The secret of the Robe of Christ must remain within this mountain. Its existence must continue to be protected by the Tekelakayochi until such a time that it is felt the world is prepared to receive it."

McFadden and Marino understood the seriousness of this message, and each man in turn repeated his promise that no one would ever learn of their discovery. As far as anyone was concerned, this journey, while interesting from a tourist's standpoint, had been non-productive. Angelo Colavari's plane had crashed more than 70 years ago and there was no way to ever determine where in the desert it had gone down. There was no plane to find.

Later that morning, Brother Anteneh led the two men through the tunnels for the last time. When they emerged at the large cavern entrance, they were met by the man who had been the leader of the bandits the day Thomas had fallen. He was accompanied by a young man with a wide smile and bright alert eyes. Brother Anteneh introduced them as James and Ezekiel and stated that they would guide them down the mountain and to their vehicle. Brother Anteneh embraced McFadden and Marino prior to their departure. As they walked out of the cave and onto the path, they heard the old man's voice, "Go with God, my sons."

The trip down the mountain went much quicker than expected. Their guides had traveled these paths so often that they knew the shortest and safest routes to the bottom. Because of Tom's injuries their guides moves slowly, and, in a little less than two hours, they were on the ground and a short time later, they were standing by the Land Cruiser. The vehicle had been moved to an area that provided even greater concealment and was undamaged, ready for their journey back to the capital. After loading their packs in the back and removing the branches that had been used to conceal it from any prying eyes, they turned to thank their guides, but the men were gone. Once they had completed their task of guiding the men back to their vehicle there was no need for them to remain. "I didn't even hear them move," Marino said. McFadden looked back the way they had just come, but the forest now hid the men from view.

Although Marino said he had completely recovered, McFadden took the wheel and began the long ride back to the city. There wasn't much conversation during the drive. Both men seemed to be dealing with what they had recently experienced, each trying to decide how this would affect them going forward. For each of them, there were different issues to deal with. They had not only discovered the Robe of Christ and confirmed its existence, but Marino had been the recipient of its healing powers. He had literally lain at death's door and had felt the Robe against his skin as the pain and shock of the fall had slowly disappeared. As miraculous as this had been, there was no one other than BB with whom he could share this experience. The temptation would be great, but his promise to keep silent was an oath he would take to his grave.

McFadden, on the other hand, had an even greater secret to keep, not only from the outside world, but also from his friend and partner in this journey. It was Tom who had included him, and it was Tom who had shared the true nature of their search. He was entitled to know the real secret of the Robe, but to ensure the safety of Brother Samuel's true identity, Tom would have to be left out of this final piece of their journey.

Upon returning to the city, they drove the Land Cruiser back to the Hertz rental agency and paid a rather substantial penalty for having kept the vehicle several days beyond the contract dates. The young clerk behind the desk thought about the call she had received from the Customs Officer more than a week earlier. The two men seemed in good spirits and she wondered whether or not they had received the sad news of the death back in America.

After they left, she called the Customs Office and asked to speak with Lt. Kebede. She wanted to let him know that the two Americans had returned to the city. After being placed on hold for several minutes, she was advised that she must have the wrong name since there was no Lt. Kebede with the Customs Office. After hanging up, she tried to remember the exact conversation of that call. She could have sworn his name was Lt. Kebede. Well, it didn't make any difference now. The Americans were back and could be contacted at the hotel.

The two men took a taxi from the Hertz office back to the Sheraton and found Abraham, their young accomplice in the switching of the vehicles hard at work. He smiled broadly as he opened the passenger door of the taxi. "I tried very hard to keep the car to follow me," he said quickly. "But after many hours he pulled up next to me and saw that I was not you. I hope this did not hinder your plans," he said.

"Abraham, you did exactly as we asked and gave us the extra time we needed to do a little exploring. You were a great help," Marino said as he shook the young man's hand and slipped a hundred-dollar bill into his palm.

Abraham was speechless as he examined the US bill. "If you need me to do anything else for you while you are here, please call me. I will drop everything and be immediately available."

He also explained that, when he returned the Land Rover to the hotel the following day, a man named Tadele had arrived to pick up the vehicle. "He was very nice and showed me the rental papers and said that you would no longer need to rent the car and then drove it away." Marino and McFadden thanked the young boy and assured him that they had accomplished everything they had planned for and would be leaving for the States within the next day or two.

When they checked back into their room, they discovered there was a stack of messages from Aaron Pierce. It appeared that their pilot friend had become quite concerned for their well-being. The following morning would bring one more important stop before they headed back home. They would need to visit Aaron and provide some sort of a story to explain their absence.

Dinner at the hotel that night was a time for small talk as the two men contemplated their adventure and tried to deal with what they'd experienced. Every so often, they would stop their conversation and just look at each other and smile. They couldn't even bring themselves to talk about what they'd each been through.

Early the next morning, they were awakened by the sound of the phone ringing. After several days in the desert and their time on the mountain, the ring of the phone was an ugly intrusion. They'd slept so well those past few days that they had become accustomed to the quiet tranquil life they had shared.

Marino was pretty sure it was Pierce. *No point in avoiding the inevitable,* he thought. As soon as he said hello, he knew he'd been right about the caller. "Where the hell have you two been for the past week?" he barked. "I got pretty concerned when I couldn't find you, or the Rover. I even flew out and tried to spot you guys from the air and swung around the mountains a few times to see if you were still checking out likely crash sites. You boys had me a nervous wreck."

"Thanks for your concern, Aaron, but we're fine. Just got a little wrapped up in the search. We'll be out in a little while to fill you in on the whole trip," Marino offered. "It's nice to know someone was looking out for us. Sorry for any confusion."

"Okay, as long as you two guys are alright. Just get your asses out here and let me know what you found." With that, the phone went dead and Pierce was gone.

McFadden had been listening to one side of the conversation, but could imagine what was being said on the other end. "Well, the time has finally come. What do we tell Aaron?" Marino was quiet for a few moments before answering. "I guess we just try to feed him another line of BS and hope we can sound convincing." McFadden smiled. "I say we just play it by the ear. There was no monastery and no monks to find. We just didn't want to give up so we stayed and explored just about every possible crash site without any luck. There's no reason he shouldn't believe us."

"I'm getting a little concerned. I seem to find lying a little bit easier each time I have to. You don't think I'm becoming pathological, do you?" Marino asked.

After breakfast in their room, McFadden and Marino went out through the front door of the hotel and waited while the doorman signaled the next taxi waiting in line. McFadden looked at the driver leaning against the first cab and immediately recognized their old friend Mohammed. The young man smiled and signaled for the taxi behind him to take the fare. He then turned to the two Americans and smiled and bowed as the other taxi pulled up to the front door. "I guess the word is out that we're okay," said Marino. "Apparently no one is interested in where either of us is going."

CHAPTER 41

After giving the driver their destination, the two men settled back and enjoyed their drive to Pierce's office at the airport for the final time. They had mixed emotions as they made their way through the morning traffic. They both agreed that, without Pierce's help, they would have likely failed in their quest. His experience, knowledge and advice had placed them squarely on the right path. It was because of this and more that made the two men feel a certain degree of reluctance at having to deceive him this one last time.

When the taxi pulled up to Desert Air, they both automatically looked in the hangar. There was Pierce, shirt sleeves rolled up and making some type of adjustment to one of the engines on the Beech King. Pierce saw the taxi pull up and broke into a smile when McFadden and Marino got out.

He put the tools he'd been using back on the work bench next to the plane and they exchanged firm handshakes as he led them into the office. Out of habit, they made their way to the coffee maker and everyone filled a mug. "Well, the prodigal sons have returned! I'm glad to see you boys are still in one piece," he said with a good-natured smile. "I thought the bad guys on the mountain had gotten you," he laughed.

"You're not far from the truth," McFadden answered. "There really are robbers, or bandits, or whatever you want to call them up on those mountains."

Marino picked up the story from there. "We'd already checked out the spots we had identified from the air and were working our way around looking for other potential sites," he said. "Actually, we looked at about a dozen locations over a two-day period without seeing a soul. On day three, all hell broke loose."

They could see that they had the pilot's attention. McFadden shook his head for effect and leaned heavily against the desk. "Yeah, we had just discounted a likely spot, when we heard voices coming from further up on the mountain. Aaron, we're city boys! Neither of us expected to see real guys with real guns coming down towards us, but there they were," Marino added, "I didn't know BB could move that fast, but in a second he was hauling butt towards the Rover with me trailing a close second. There were some gunshots, but I think they were too high up on the slope or there were too many trees in their way for them to take a good shot."

"How many of them were there?" Pierce asked seriously. "We didn't get a close look, but there had to be about six or eight of them. By the time we reached the Rover and fired her up, the gunshots were coming more quickly, so we figured they must have gotten down to ground level," McFadden answered. "We heard bullets passing by as Tom floored the pedal, but, amazingly, we didn't take one hit. Within a few seconds, we were out of range and breathing easier."

"I never really believed those stories about bad guys in the mountains, but I guess they weren't old wives' tales after all," Pierce said. "Well, what happened after that?"

McFadden and Marino were making this up as they went along but they appeared to be enjoying the story and were putting together a pretty imaginative account of their journey. McFadden shook his head, "We drove out into the desert for about ten miles and camped out for a couple of days while we decided our next move. After having searched every potential site we could find, we finally agreed that it was highly unlikely that a monastery and the bandits could share the same area."

"I have no doubt that my uncle was probably cared for by somebody — priests or monks or whomever. I just don't believe it was anywhere near there. If the plane went down out there, then someone else must have found what was left and picked the area clean." McFadden nodded his agreement. "If there was a religious order out there 70 years ago, I think it's safe to assume they are long gone. We didn't see any sign of life on that mountain other than the welcoming committee we ran into."

"Well, guys, you gave it your best shot. I really thought we were on the right path when we found the first plane," Aaron finally admitted. "But I wasn't so sure about a monastery being out there. No one could keep that secret for too long, let alone a couple of hundred years. So, are you calling it quits and heading home?"

Marino spoke for them both. "It's been a great adventure, even if we didn't find anything. We got to see a lot of the country. We made a new friend," he said as he placed his hand on the old pilot's shoulder. "All in all, it's been a very interesting two weeks."

Pierce called for a taxi and, while they waited, they went over all the things they had accomplished and shared a joke or two. "Kid, remember, lay off the sugar when you get back home," Pierce reminded Marino.

The taxi arrived and the three men shook hands and in a few minutes it was over. In the back seat of the taxi, McFadden spoke softly, "I think we handled that pretty well. Even shooting from the hip, the story sounded pretty plausible to me. Aaron seemed to accept our account of what happened out there." Marino wasn't quite so optimistic.

"I'm not so sure. Aaron's a pretty sharp old guy, and I don't think he's quite as gullible as we might want to believe," he questioned. "Regardless, it's done and we're on our way home. Aaron has a story and the "search" is over.

Pierce stood outside the office and watched the taxi as it headed off to the city. *You had quite an adventure, boys,* he thought to himself. *You're lucky to have gotten off that mountain alive. Or were you?* As the taxi disappeared past the row of hangers, Pierce went back to the comfort of his office and took a cold beer from the refrigerator. He sat at his desk and propped his feet on an open drawer. He wondered out loud, "We never did talk about that old beige Toyota, did we?" He took a long drink from the bottle and leaned back in his chair. "Well, maybe someday I'll find out what this whole thing was really about."

Tom and McFadden were quiet during most of the flight back to the states. When they did speak, it was hushed and low, to prevent anyone from hearing what was said, not that anyone would believe them anyway. "Thank goodness we both experienced this," Tom said after several hours of silence. "We've seen and touched the Robe of Jesus Christ. If you hadn't been there, I'd have no one to talk with about this to confirm that it actually happened and that it wasn't just my imagination. This is going to be tough at times not being able to tell people that we made the greatest archeological-religious discovery of all time."

"I know how you feel," McFadden agreed. "But just remember, even though this is a secret we can't share with anyone, we still experienced something very few have in the past 2000 years. Although I had the chance to touch the robe, you were able to experience God's healing power through its contact. No wonder Angelo was drawn back there."

"What do we do now?" Marino asked. "We're used to writing research papers on our experiences in the field and what we discovered or learned. Here we come back from an adventure no one would really believe, and we can't even put the experience down on paper." Then he flashed his familiar broad smile, "But I can live with that."

CHAPTER 42

The second day he was home, McFadden called Father Cleary and told him they had just returned. "I told you we would let you know the whole story, if there was one, when we got back. Is it alright if I come by?" The old priest nearly screamed his response. "Come as soon as you can, Francis. I'll be waiting. Can you give me just a hint?" McFadden told him that the results of the trip really should be discussed in person. The priest said he understood and looked forward to McFadden's arrival.

McFadden drove down the Mass Pike again to Springfield to see Father Cleary just as he had promised. He had agonized over what to tell him and how much. It was clear he couldn't tell him the whole story, but the old man had provided them with invaluable information that put them on the right track. He deserved something in exchange.

Father Cleary had been waiting for McFadden since he had called and opened the door before McFadden had a chance to ring the bell. "Come in, Francis, and have a seat in the living room. I'll get the coffee." The priest was almost running as he left the room and returned in a matter of seconds with two steaming mugs. "Alright, son! I can't wait any longer. Does the robe of Jesus Christ exist, and did you and Tom actually find it?"

Up until that point, McFadden wasn't sure what he would, or should tell the priest. "It's an involved question, Father, but the answer is yes and no. We didn't find the robe, but we learned that it may have existed as recently as the beginning of World War II." Father Cleary seemed to deflate and sink deeper into his chair. He stared at McFadden, anxiously waiting for the rest of the story.

"We learned that there had been a monastery in the mountains north of the capital for several hundred years beginning in the mid-1700s. They were a small group and never had more than ten or twelve brothers throughout its existence. Legend has it that they had the power to heal by wrapping the sick or injured in a blanket, and then nursing him back to health." He waited for Father Cleary to process all of this before proceeding. "They are the ones who probably healed Tom's Uncle Angelo back in 1936. He may have actually touched the robe without ever knowing what it was, or the power behind it."

"World War II came in 1939 and that seems to be the last time anyone saw the monks again. The oral history of the desert said that, by that time there were only three of them left, their monastery had been destroyed by bombing. We searched most of that mountain and never found any sign of there being anything resembling a monastery, or even a building for that matter. The monastery may well have been just a cave in the mountain. Local legend has it that the three brothers were last seen walking into the desert carrying a small stretcher with a bundle secured to it."

"Father, you were right all these years. Your research on the Henok gospel was right on the spot. If you hadn't given us your help we never would have gotten as far as we did." He waited for the priest to say something. Finally, he looked at McFadden with tears in his eyes. "I did do something of value. My research was legitimate, and I may have found the actual robe of Christ, had my work not been censored all those years ago. Francis, you don't know what this means to me. I was actually on the right path all along. Thank you for letting me know."

"Tom and I are happy that we are able to provide information to support the work you did all those years ago. The only thing I ask, is the same thing we asked when we were here before. This can't be shared with anyone else. Tom and I originally thought that this search would have made for a great scientific paper on the quest for a significant religious artifact, but we've decided to let it go and keep it amongst ourselves. Besides, we have no evidence to support our assertions that the robe actually existed, let alone existed 70-some years ago."

Father Cleary immediately agreed. "You can count on my silence. There's no need for me to share my accomplishment with anyone but you and Tom. This is too personal to share with just anybody. This is a discovery that must be kept secret."

When McFadden left, he noticed that Father Cleary seemed more relaxed and maybe more serious than he had been during their first meeting. "I really think this gave him some peace," he told Tom later. "In his mind, this may justify the years he spent on research rather than dealing with a congregation. I think he may have questioned the choices he made earlier in his life and this may have put those doubts to rest."

About a week later, McFadden went to his parents' house for dinner. "Francis, you look like you lost weight while you were away.

Didn't you eat well?" his mother questioned. "No, Mom, actually we had a couple of really exceptional meals at an Ethiopian restaurant just down the street from the hotel. Tom and I made pigs of ourselves on two separate occasions."

His mother wasn't convinced and had made sure that the menu included most of his favorite things: Veal Cutlet Parmesan, spaghetti with clam sauce and several irresistible deserts. For an Irish girl, she was a pretty good Italian cook. She watched as her only child attacked each course with gusto. *He had lost weight,* she said to herself. "Well, I'll fatten him up in no time."

When his mother went back into the kitchen to make some coffee, his father leaned over and whispered as if there was a secret that only they knew. "Alright, your mother's gone! You can tell me what you were really looking for over there," he said as he threw a quick glance at the kitchen door. "You can trust your old man to keep your secret."

McFadden looked at him for a moment and thought maybe he could tell his father the true story. But he knew if he told one person, he would break his promise to Brother Samuel and who knew how long it would be before he told someone else? "I don't know how you figured it out, but you were right, Dad!" he finally said. "But it wasn't gold that Tom's uncle was transporting." He leaned close and almost whispered in his father's ear, "It was diamonds, worth millions of dollars on today's market."

"Diamonds," his father repeated softly while taking another glance at the kitchen door. "I knew you and Tom were looking for something more than just an old plane crash. Well, did you find them?"

"No, we searched for almost a week and eventually found the place where the plane went down after being hit by the Ethiopian gunfire. We figured that the soldiers must have gotten to the crash site after Tom's uncle was pulled from the wreckage. They probably searched through the plane and found the metal strong box with the diamonds and were gone before the Italians could send anyone to retrieve them. "

The senior McFadden leaned back in his chair and sat with a look of satisfaction on his face. "Not bad for an old college professor. You can't lie to your old man, son. I could always tell when you were holding something back." The younger McFadden smiled back. "I knew I'd have to tell you the real story when I got back. But, Dad, do me a favor. Don't tell Mom about this. She'll only get nervous after the fact and preach that I should stay home and avoid anything that could be considered dangerous." Thomas McFadden leaned over and whispered in his son's ear, "You can count on me to keep my mouth shut. Your mother will never hear about your adventure from me," he proudly announced. Just then, Margaret McFadden returned.

"What are you two boys cooking up?" His father looked up. "Just a little bit of guy talk. Men have to have some secrets between themselves," he said confidently. Margaret let it drop but vowed to try and pry the secret from her husband before they went to bed.

As they sat drinking their coffee, Margaret suddenly remembered something she wanted to tell him. "Frankie, a friend of mine in Springfield, called to tell me that Father Cleary passed away in his sleep several days ago. She said she had seen him just the day before and mentioned that he had talked about feeling that his life had been full, and that he had accomplished everything he'd ever hoped for. It was as if he was suddenly at peace with the world," she said. "I'm glad you got to meet him before he died. He really was an exceptional man with a great mind."

"Yes, Tom and I were really happy to have had the chance to spend some time with him. He was very helpful in providing information about early Ethiopia." While his mother brought up another subject, McFadden thought about the old priest and was happy that he had been able to provide him with a resolution to his life's work in his final days. If he didn't know any better, he would have thought Father Cleary had hung on just long enough to confirm that his years of research had indeed been relevant.

Later that night, as they sat in the living room drinking coffee, McFadden filled his parents in on some of the details of their trip. He shared most of the basic issues of how they'd conducted their search for the crash site. How they had met Aaron Pierce and some of the challenges they had experienced. But, overall, they had been successful in finding the remains of the plane and Tom was happy with what they had accomplished.

McFadden was satisfied as well that the trip to Ethiopia had provided the answers to all of Angelo Colavari's questions and that the issue could finally be put to rest. It had been a miracle that had saved the young Colavari, although he would never know of the 2000-year-old secret that had brought him back from an almost certain death.

For Marino, the adventure had an additional effect. While not a very religious man, he started going to mass on Sundays and had even gone to confession after many years. He often thought of his injuries and how he had been healed. At times, the urge to share that information with others was almost too much to control, but he'd given his word. He and McFadden had found the most significant piece of religious history known to man, and had sworn to never betray its existence. He knew they never would.

Almost 7000 miles away, Brother Anteneh knocked softly on the door and entered, carrying a light breakfast for Brother Samuel. For almost 70 years, he had cared for his old friend and looked forward to this private time they shared each morning. Samuel was still in bed. He was usually up and reading by this time. He called gently but the older man didn't respond. He approached the bed and saw that Samuel was on his back and did not appear to have moved all night. He touched the old man's arm and slowly he opened his eyes. Brother Samuel seemed confused for a moment, and then a look of resignation claimed his face.

He was still on the mountain and again faced yet another day with his brothers. Jesus was not yet ready to call him home.

ACKNOWLEDGEMENTS

I would like to thank everyone who helped me navigate the long road to creating and finishing this book. To my fiancé, Marylou, and my sister Peggy, thank you for all your support and encouragement. To Carol Noyes and Judi Turner, my excellent beta-readers, whose thoughts and suggestions proved invaluable. To Andrew Warren who provided critical information on the "how to" of self-publishing. To Colton Allen, editing/proofreading master for turning a manuscript into a book.

And special thanks to USA Today Best Selling Author, Ernest Dempsey, who unselfishly helped a first time author reach his goal.